GABRIELLE FILTEAU-CHIB... environmental activist. In th... family and home in Mont... moved into a wooden cabir... region. Based on true events, ... being adapted for the big screen.

DAVID HOMEL is a literary translator and an author. He has twice won the Governor General's Literary Award for Translation.

"A gripping thriller and an ode to nature's preservation"
CORINNE RENOU-NATIVEL, *Croix*

"With infectious energy, Gabrielle Filteau-Chiba [...] defends her territory: that of nature and wildlife, threatened by man's greed, and that of women, where predators forever lie in wait"
VÉRONIQUE CASSARIN-GRAND, *L'Obs*

"A breath-taking story [...] a great adventure novel that sows the seeds of revolt, which no collar could ever restrain"
LAËTITIA FAVRO, *Livres Hebdo*

"A thrilling dive into the harsh winter of the Haut-Pays de Kamouraska, where nightmares and wonders live side by side"
COPÉLIA MAINARDI, *Marianne*

"In the heart of the forest, a woman finds the solitude she feared and hoped for [...] an exciting and disturbing novel by a new Québec author"
MARINE LANDROT, *Télérama*

Gabrielle Filteau-Chiba

FERAL

Translated from the French by
David Homel

MOUNTAIN LEOPARD PRESS
WELBECK · LONDON & SYDNEY

Originally published in French as
Sauvagines in 2019
by Éditions XYZ

First published in the English language in 2024 by
Mountain Leopard Press
an imprint of
Welbeck Publishing Group
London and Sydney

9 8 7 6 5 4 3 2 1

A CIP catalogue record for this book is available from the British Library

ISBN (PB) 978-1-80069-902-1
ISBN (eBook) 978-1-914495-59-5

This book is a work of fiction. Names, places, events and incidents are either
the products of the author's imagination or are used fictitiously

Designed and typeset in Sabon by Libanus Press Ltd, Marlborough
Printed and bound in Great Britain by
Clays Ltd, Elcograf S.p.A.

MIX
Paper from
responsible sources
FSC® C104740
FSC
www.fsc.org

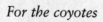

For the coyotes

They were responsible for the world. It was their duty. Nature, harsh and generous, commanded them to be rigorous in their practices and live according to the code of wise hunters.

Serge Bouchard and Marie-Christine Lévesque,
Le peuple rieur – Hommage à mes amis innus

Feral: untamed, undomesticated; hence, wild, savage.

PART ONE

Peace and Quiet

I

Coyote's Brown Eyes

JUNE 25

The chains bang against the kennel partitions, preventing escape. The unmelodious howl of hundreds of animals lets the boss know I am arriving. They have sniffed me out on the wind. They bark with excitement now that I am closer and have sunk into mud up to my ankles on the all-terrain vehicle trail that leads to their jail. I search out the cage of the last litter, the one I have travelled all this way for.

I was not looking for a husky with eyes the colour of Lake Louise. Instead I was after a mixed-breed female with brown eyes like mine. In my family and at the kennel, blue-eyed children have special status. My brothers and sisters whispered that I was the product of sin. My father suspected that a marital quarrel led my mother to tumble for the postman or some other man better endowed. All my life, the colour of my eyes reminded him that I might be the fruit of his wife's betrayal, a woman who descended from Eve. Under our roof, jealousy and bad faith were more powerful than reason. But the fact is genes sometimes leap a generation or two.

Here, as in every sled dog operation, the most expensive puppies have eyes of different colours. The animal that attracts my attention is a brown-eyed female with a mouse-grey coat. She is not eating. She shivers on a bed of straw while the others stretch and roll onto their backs. The man in the cage says she has a slight heart murmur and will not have much of a career as an athlete, which is what is expected of her. A skinny dog that cannot spend her life pulling French tourists looking for an authentic northern experience will never earn her daily meat, and will be put down with the others that have grown too old to be useful. Mismatched eyes might have saved her, but one night her mother, out on an expedition, fell for a coyote, so everyone expects her offspring will be hard to train. In other words, the bastard is doomed, too useless and ordinary for anyone to adopt.

"She's the one I want."

No hesitation. I pet the unfaithful mother who lets me take her daughter without a growl. Calmly, she watches us go down the path. Maybe she recognises the scent of compassion. With the bundle of fur under my arm, I go back to my truck, remembering the day I escaped my own family nightmare. The dog prison fades in my rear-view mirror, and I drive with a smile. The puppy has dozed off, its nose on my wrist. My fingers on the gearshift have gone numb, but no matter. I have found my right-hand dog, a new arrow in my Wildlife Protection Officer's quiver.

From one shore of the Saint Lawrence to the other, then from Rivière-du-Loup to the Crown lands, we eat up the road to our refuge under the sugar maple trees. By the time the hunting season starts, the trees will be involved in intense competition to see who can turn the reddest. An abandoned sugar shack in this outlaw land is where I hid my trailer. The Winnebago was seized on a pot plantation a couple of years ago. I bought it with a week's pay and had it towed as far as the transporter dared to drive it into the woods.

The road is rough, and the forest swallows us up. I head towards the Three Lakes hunting camp and take my secret turn-off. On this road, there are more moose prints than tyre tracks, and the low branches of the spruce close up behind us. A few more turns and we will be at our sheet-metal hideout in the shade.

A woollen blanket awaits you, nicely folded, at the foot of my mattress. I promise you will never wear a chain. I'll take you everywhere I go, and show you everything I know about the forest. One day, maybe, you'll be able to get along without me.

Darkness settles. The owls celebrate the hour of the predators. Soon the stove will take the humidity out of the air and I will see to the mosquitoes.

My weakling puppy, unfit for pulling a sled, slips between my knees. I think of a name for her as she hides her curious face beneath the fur of her tail. She whimpers in her sleep, dreaming, perhaps, of the prey that got away.

And to think that the mushers back at the kennel wanted to put you down. You will never see your mother again. My dear orphan, we will look out for one another. Side by side, we will be better equipped to take on the bullies who hunt only for the pleasure of dominating and destroying. I'll start by petting you with all the tenderness in my body,

I will bury my nose in your fur that smells of wet straw, the pallet where you were born. It may be difficult to tame the wildness that runs in your blood. But even if you stay rough-mannered, you will protect me, I hope, from the poacher crackpots who have put too many of my colleagues six feet under. Lady Luck will smile on me from the passenger seat with her white fangs, and the men who want to intimidate me will back off. Despite all our gadgets, my service weapon and years of experience, the guys who set snares are always better armed.

The poachers aren't the only ones trying to live off me. I decided to cut short my solitude a few days ago when I discovered fresh claw marks on the trunk of the apple tree, not far from the shack. The culprit climbed to the top of the tree where a cage of suet for woodpeckers danced in the breeze. The impolite animal gorged itself on the seeds that had fallen to the ground, then moved on to my strawberry patch. I remembered the gardeners' unwritten rule. Three times more plants than they hope to get fruit from. A third to keep, a third that will never flower, and the rest for unexpected visitors.

Human or animal. Expected or unwanted. Friendly or famished.

The distance between the lacerations on the wood showed that it was an adult bear. Now that it has been by to reconnoitre, it will be back to turn my supplies into its breakfast. The lengths of sheet metal that serve as walls will not keep it out.

I cook rice with lamb on the fire and set out the meaty

results, the colour of mud, next to the puppy. Her darting eyes evaluate the danger, then she laps up every last drop.

You won't stay skinny. I'll put some meat on your bones.

Too many people call their dogs Jiffy or Jappy or Luna. I am fresh out of ideas for short names that sound good when shouted in the woods, that you can call at the top of your lungs without irritating your throat. A vowel at the end that will carry like an echo. Yoko, or Kahlo? The letter "k" is fashionable these days.

Until I can find something better, she will be Coyote. My dog already has her style. She takes up position in front of me on the path to the woodpile as if to tell me she will be supervising the heating of our trailer. Then she trips over my rain boots and falls onto her side. Looks up at me, mischievous, her belly inviting. It is as soft as mallow leaves. Astonishing how much joy an animal can bring someone who has so few friends in her life, who disowned her family and suspects her parents left the hospital with the wrong baby. I paged through dusty albums and family trees. Maybe there is an explanation somewhere. Meanwhile, I keep the proof in a pocket, next to my heart.

In the yellowed photograph, a slip of a woman stands very straight next to her barrel of a husband. Almond eyes, braided hair, moccasins on her feet. He is dressed like a trapper, pipe in hand, walrus moustache, high forehead. He squats down next to her as her eyes jump out from the picture, pleading *Save me, somebody*. Even in that position, my great-grandfather is as tall as she is, and his hairy paw wraps tightly around his young wife's waist as if the prey he has just brought down might somehow still escape him. My brown eyes must come from her. And from her, too, my insatiable desire to learn everything about the First Nations. If I could bring together the transcribed words, the tales of the bush and the poems of the taiga, I might grow closer to my roots and join her, my Mi'kmaq ancestress with the Christian name invented for her wedding night.

To leave family and society and live in a trailer parked deep in the public forest might seem strange. But that is the key to my mental equilibrium: to live as close as possible to the animals that I have sworn to protect. And as far as possible from my family who were never curious to know who our great-grandmother was, the woman with piercing brown coyote eyes.

Back at the truck for the last trip for supplies before nightfall, I put the photograph back on top of the sun visor, where it rides with me most times. I run my index finger over the careful handwriting on the back.

Hervé Robichaud
and his wife Marie-Ange
1903

You don't look like a Marie-Ange, and you know you're not in heaven. Petrified is more like it, backbone ramrod-straight like the barrel towering over you. I spare a thought for your wedding night, curled up upon yourself. I imagine your real name that speaks of the beauty of the land, not of submission beneath white sheets and wedding dresses.

I wish someone had told me your story. Maybe I would have felt more at home among your descendants if I had known your lullabies, recipes and lost illusions. The suburban bungalow that smelled like baloney and mothballs stifled me. Mealtime prayers, bedtime prayers, the fear of strangers, darkness and the animals outside – the endless litanies of xenophobic blame threw me into a rage. I had to get away from those people before I turned into them. I needed a full-time forest, mountain slopes with no borders, where all are equal before the elements, the cold, the rain and the wind. The woods tutor you in humility, believe me. A sanctuary of beauty forgotten by people who live in cotton wool. A temple of open arms and lowered guard.

There where the Appalachians are born, the back country of Kamouraska, the luxury of open space is defended with pagan rituals. Facing down the carnivores, walking the trails morning and evening, pissing in strategic spots along the way. Finding edible plants, tracking invisible fauna, setting down landmarks in my great living space, and retracing my steps to the abandoned sugar shack, the trailer, my mattress.

I chose to live on this unorganised territory, but try to explain that to a bunch of guys without the game they came for because the habitat has disappeared. Or to a bear that just had its acres of raspberries chopped to pieces under the Hydro-Québec power lines before it could tuck into its summer banquet.

Thanks to Coyote, I am armed with a nose that can sniff out anyone intending to get too close to the trailer. When she gets older and bigger, I will let her out of the truck when

I approach fishermen with their creels that are too full, and hunters hiding a suspicious number of ungulate hooves under their tarp, and Sunday hikers who might be tempted to take advantage of a woman alone in the wilderness to satisfy their needs.

Because where we are, no-one can hear me scream.

I leave my long black braid hanging free down my back. Sometimes I wonder if I shouldn't just cut it off, and give up my artifice to be safer in this land of men burning with alcohol and the desire to kill. I might be better at my job, which is to regulate the slaughter. Everything is as good as gold here, and cash is king. Pay for your licence and be done with it, you can take your seven lynx a year from the woods. Soon the quotas will be a thing of the past according to my sources in the Ministry.

Somebody wake me up from this bad dream.

No, here no-one can hear my cry of rage. Except my dog whose fur stands on end. Frightened by the sound, she asks me with her brown coyote eyes, *What's come over you, old lady?*

2

Water off a Duck's Back

SEPTEMBER 26

Gunshots. I wake up in a fury.

At my feet, Coyote watches for my next move. I wonder if at the kennel where she began life the dogs understood the link between a gunshot and one of them not returning from the woods with the boss. If the sound of bullets echoed the Grim Reaper's footsteps, the way it does for me.

A gunshot at dawn a week before bow-and-arrow hunting season opens is the work of a cheater finishing off his prey. I do not believe that some hunter is target shooting at four in the morning. I swear I'll catch you, poachers.

The trailer is carpeted with dirt-stained jeans, dank socks and pine needles. The windows are fogged up, but the morning light is strong enough to make the dust motes sparkle. The coffeemaker gurgles on my propane ring, and snow geese cackle high above. I go out and sit on my porch steps made of embossed metal, wrapped in my wool blanket in the colours of the Hudson's Bay Company. Respectfully, I wait for the flight of the courageous migrators to pass above my head before taking my first sip.

"Greetings, ladies."

Coyote does not show the same reverence. She disappears

immediately, but I know where she has rushed off to thanks to the chipmunks protesting *chip chip chip*, high in the branches. I move towards the old maples and spot her jumping, as if she had a chance of catching the little rodents twenty feet above her head. I appreciate her optimism. A dog needs a good helping of it to stay steady in this forest of jokers.

I harvest what Nature offers me. With my knee or my heel, I snap off the branches broken by the wind. My lodgings are so compact I can heat the place with dead-wood. The cords I gather in the underbrush are taller than I am. I feel more secure with a hefty supply of firewood than with a well-filled bank account.

The falling leaves learn the choreography of letting go. On the horizon, beyond the sugar shack, stand spruce all of the same vintage, as far as the eye can see. Clones. Future two-by-fours that will be hammered into a new porch to replace the planks eaten away by carpenter ants, since they have no other wood to gnaw on.

The film "Forest Alert" made a big impression on me. It was the first documentary and the last movie we saw in high school. That year, my French teacher dazzled me with singer Richard Desjardins' lyrics, then burned images of mass deforestation into my awareness. Desjardins inspired my first resolution, which was to buy pens with green ink to remind me that someone had to stand up for the trees that were still standing. I had the wild idea that the pen was mightier than the sword, and that the former could teach others care and vigilance for our northern forests. Lately,

I have started buying red pens to represent the blood of animals killed by poachers. But the colour of my reports will not change a thing. I am just about the only Wildlife Protection Officer in my unit who believes that the woods are not an all-you-can-eat buffet.

Where will they hide, the spring deer that come to nibble on the tree bark? What despairing sight will the snow geese see when they fly above our massacred forests on their way back from the north? I can't help it. When I drive past a clear-cut zone, my eyes leave the road, I feel sucked into the emptiness. A moose or a lorry could be coming right at me, I wouldn't see it. I can't I just can't I can't look straight ahead when, to one side, dead trees ooze sap in silence, their bodies piled up along the ditch, stained with orange paint.

I tidy up my trailer, put on my least dirty pair of jeans, throw the rest in a heap, lace up my steel-toed boots, take my cap from the dashboard, slip my braid into my jacket, blow my nose, then finish off the coffee that cooled down as I thought about everything that eludes me, the ones who get away.

"Come on, Coyote, let's go hunt poachers."

It is raining poachers. And we're a long way from water off a duck's back.

I reach up to free the dead leaves from the patched gutters of the sugar shack that helps camouflage my house on wheels. My water tastes like rust, but it is free and no doubt very rich in iron. Coyote prefers to drink from the puddles on the way to the truck. She prances from one mud hole to the next, drinks from each one, and gives me tender looks as she wags her tail. This is a better place for her than the picket she would have been chained to among the pack of sled dogs, all howling their heads off that it's their turn to pull vacationing foreigners down the snowmobile trails. Or suffering the awkward thrusts of blue-eyed males to produce litters of high-priced puppies.

In this life, if you have blue eyes, you're ahead of the game. Even in a dog's life, the ugly ducklings understand that truth.

"Come on, princess!"

Coyote jumps into the truck. I will spend a long morning on the road wondering why so few of us are supposed to cover such an enormous area. Our presence seems purely symbolic. Maybe the whole point is for trappers to kill the predators, and hunters to take a lot of small game, and fishermen to pay for their licences. Then once everything is dead, the forestry companies can take over. They will call the disaster "semi-intensive cutting with ecological integration of indigenous productive species". Or – why not? – "deforestation centred on the targeted conservation of vulnerable populations". The Biodome lynx in Montreal will enjoy more visits than ever, since it will be one of the last in Quebec.

When I talk like that at the office, they tell me I'm pessimistic. But I'm not. I know what's happening on the ground. And I won't let my years of experience make me blasé.

On my lunch break, I park near the Manie River and give the dog some playtime as I examine the banks with my binoculars. Her orange safety vest is too big for her. She climbs onto a fallen trunk, goes to the water and drinks thirstily. I whistle. She lifts her eyes and watches.

That's right, stay where I can see you. Tire yourself out.

Coyote springs, nose and front feet together, and catches a gopher under the dead leaves. I eat my salad with no appetite. She barks with delight at a yellow jacket lulled to sleep by the cold among the last autumn flowers. Then sets out after a chipmunk that won't last long. My granola bar is as dry as death. Coyote finds a grey partridge nest and wolfs down the eggs, looks up at me with a spark of wild instinct in her eyes, then chews on grass to purge herself. I laugh when I think that her instinct earned her a more nutritious lunch than mine.

I am going to feed this amber flame. She will be my child growing wings to fly. If something happens to me, I know she will survive in this no man's land. A mouthful of cheddar and I get going again. Coyote climbs onto the seat and dozes off immediately. She opens her eyes when we hit a deep rut or take a sharp turn. A look exchanged, confidence restored and she goes back to sleep. Maybe one day an exemption will let me take an intensive training course with her. Though we would have to hide the fact from the canine squad that one of her parents could be a coyote. So far, I have seen only German shepherds, Labradors and retrievers at work. But isn't a German shepherd an Alsatian wolf dog?

You might stand a chance after all, my half-husky, half-coyote from Charlevoix.

A new logging road is under construction to the east. Detour past Otter Lake. I drive slowly, open the window wide and lean out, to better sense the presence of something moving among the trees. Trailer tyres dumped in the ditch. I stop to pick them up, keeping my eyes on the entrance to a lot where someone has nailed a fresh "Danger: Hunters at Work" sign. No vehicles. At the end of the paths where crab apples have been set out for deer, I know there are boarded-up cabins and A.T.V. sheds weakened by last winter's record snowfall. The sun sinks, setting the tops of the tall spruce on fire and promising orange-hued twilight soon. Time to head home. I scribble a few notes in my log. Another day of racking up the kilometres without much in the way of victories. Except that of making a living.

We are lost in the geography and I like it that way. In the Kamouraska back country I taste the immensity of silence. Peace and quiet. The setting is magnificent and my solitude sweetened by the distant songs of animals. When the blues get the better of me, I go to see my old friend Lionel in his cabin on the banks of the Rivière-aux-Perles. He tells me what it was like to be a Wildlife Protection Officer thirty years back. The biggest trophies, the most savage hunters, the guys who moved on.

Back at the trailer, Coyote is agitated, and it is clear we've had company. Fresh adult bear tracks lead to my compost bin. More tracks in the mud cross the maple grove. The animal even investigated the raised rainwater tank I use for my cold showers. Attracted, perhaps, by my citronella soap.

*

I hear branches snapping behind me. The sound moves off to my left.

We must have surprised you as you were casing the place, Mr Bear. You are studying me from a distance, I suppose, wondering what kind of creature I am.

"Come on, Coyote."

I open the trailer door just enough. She heads for her blanket and I start a fire. Luckily, I have two big logs left over. For kindling, I cut up my oldest pair of jeans, then use my holey socks and the envelopes from my mail. The recipe works. The stove ticks with the heat. Perfect. I can stay behind my four walls with my dog all night, my rifle close at hand between the mattress on the floor and the wall in case I have to reach for it in the middle of the night. My service weapon, a Glock 9 mm, is stowed in its holster as back-up. A woman is always better off if she's prepared.

I think of my great-grandmother again and the measures they took back then to protect the camps and wigwams from bears. My walls are sheet metal and not birch bark, pine branches and skins and sheets sewn together, but I have seen a hunter's trailer gutted by a famished bear. And the documentary where a woman on her own above the Arctic Circle splashed hydrochloric acid around her building to irritate the grizzlies' sense of smell. For now, I'll lock the door and make sure my weapons are loaded.

There is only one person I can count on: myself. There is no-one else to call.

The last time I saw my family was at Christmas. I refused to say grace. I didn't want to pretend any more. My Gaspé grandmother was not there to make fun of the ceremony on the sly. As a child, when no-one was watching, I would play with the small immaculate figures of the Nativity scene under the tree. I hid the Virgin Mary beneath the fake snow made of felt and sparkles because at dinner my father said that all women were the same. Sullied by original sin, demi-virgins – he winked at my mother – and shameless hussies. I did not know which category I belonged to, nor the Virgin Mary either, who, the way I saw it, must have been the perfect mother, beautiful and loving despite the burden of maternity, unlike mine who blamed us for ruining her body and sapping her strength. When she saw my reaction, my grandmother whispered not to worry about the statuette and her miracle child. No woman should feel shame when she is carrying life. I miss my grandma. At the last Christmas dinner, the first one without her, once the prayer was done, everyone crossed themselves. They all thanked the Lord for the meal but not the woman who cooked it. They praised the Holy Father but said no words of remembrance for my grandmother. I was boiling inside.

"If god exists, she's a liberated woman, free and fertile. You can take it from me."

My brothers and sisters stared at me like I was a witch, blasphemy incarnate. In the silence that followed, picking at my food, I wondered what Mother Nature might actually look like. Artemis, maybe, the Greek goddess of the hunt, or the Sumerian Inanna. Winged, with talons, taming wild beasts and protecting deer, widows and orphans.

This evening I am praying to the goddesses and the great

spirits that might be listening, imploring them to keep the predators from my trailer. I will set aside some apples for them next fall, and place offerings on their pathways to show I am a good neighbour. And I will stop at nothing to catch the men who trap and shoot them.

"Remember, guys, we're on the same side."

It is time to open a brick and while away the hours of insomnia. I pull out a dog-eared novel from between the sofa cushions. Before losing myself in a parallel universe, I peek out of the window to make sure nothing is prowling around.

When the character John Irving invented in *Last Night in Twisted River* explains that he has been careful ever since the unfortunate incident in the logging camp, and that he always keeps an iron frying pan above his bed, I look around for mine. There it is, on my pile of wilderness guides. Everything is close at hand in my tiny trailer. Whether it is a bear's nose or some crazyman's skull, the thing's weight will make up for the lack of precision.

You know your loneliness is getting bad when you say goodnight to your sleeping dog and smile at your frying pan.

3

The Queen's Jubilee

SEPTEMBER 27

I dream that the trailer door has been ripped to shreds by a bear. Its claws have cut through the aluminium like a knife through butter. I am surrounded by a stink that can come only from a bear that has been sweating since birth in its only suit of clothes, licking the fermented juices of garbage cans and eating skunk scat.

Despite the wisdom of my forty years, I still have nightmares about monsters under the bed.

The smell is just Coyote, though it has filled the room. She is dying to go outside and relieve herself. Her scratching at the door is an alarm clock that wakes me up long before dawn. I open the door for her, put on my slippers, take a look outside – all is well – and get the wood stove going, then head back to bed for another half-hour as I watch the sunrise lay swathes of colour on the sky. The orange hues of autumn give way to frozen pinks. Winter is coming. The geese have flown south. The bears are looking for food. And I have the day off.

I kick myself out of bed, then get up and air the trailer. Step outside and stretch my arms in the cool mist. Water a bed of lichen, then wipe myself on caribou moss. Feel completely in my element. Time for a glacial shower in beach sandals under the spout. I don't take my time, I rub myself hard to get the cold off my skin. Conditioner is never an option. Once I have rinsed off and am ready to put on my clothes, I stride over to the line. My wardrobe fits nicely on a single rope between two trees where my everyday sweaters and jeans are taking in the fresh air. When I am out of clothespins, it is washday. My clothes are soft and dull, the colours pale. A palette of pastels, beige, pink and brown like grains of sand under the microscope. Beauty doesn't shout its name. The timeless tint of seashells. Today I do not feel like hiding under modest woollens. Wearing a towel as a turban, I walk back to the trailer, stepping on bear tracks. Luckily there are no fresh ones this morning. Inside, I choose from the clean clothes in the suitcase that holds my uniforms. It is my birthday and I want to look good even if I am unlikely to meet a soul. I will not wear a baseball cap, I'll let my hair flow free, and put on a T-shirt and jeans that are a little less worn, and go for a pair of striped lamb's wool socks. I brush my teeth and spit in the direction of the forest, then evaluate the results in the rear-view mirror.

"You're getting old," the long white hair shining on my head tells me. That hair wasn't there yesterday.

I pull it out.

"Ten more where that one came from."

I warm my fingers on my coffee cup and watch my dog digging up something. I have a surprise in store for her. The annual pilgrimage to the American border to see an old friend on this make-believe sick day that rounds out the weekend. Two full days for the round trip at a leisurely pace. That should be enough.

I remember the long hikes I used to go on with an old classmate. We would head for the forest every time we could. The guy was crazy about fishing, and he made his own flies from raccoon fur. Getting through the school week was an exercise in survival for him. He never finished. One day he threw a garage sale and sold off everything and bought what he needed to take on the Appalachian Trail with his Siberian husky. Three months' walking with his house on his back. When he took a day off by a stream, his dog would amuse herself by fishing with her paws in the shallow water. Proudly, she would carry the fish in her mouth to her master, who rewarded her with dried meat. The treat had to be better than the fish if he wanted her to bring it to him. As the time passed, a heartfelt petting session was enough to keep the barter system going. An occasional trout grilled over the coals was a better dish than the dried food that long-haul hikers carry. He might be the right person for an opinion about the bear prowling around my trailer. As I recall, he had two bear encounters. The first time, his dog chased the animal away. She returned a few hours later, missing her bag. The bear must have ripped it off her. It had a few days' worth of kibble and the last full water bottle. I would love to hear his laughter over the phone, telling me not to worry. But he doesn't have a number any more. Hubert is one of those guys who smoked so much of the chemical marijuana the bikers were selling that he lost touch with reality. A strange fantasy took over his life. The government was spying on him to manipulate his mind and tax his wallet. He burned his mail if he didn't recognise the handwriting on the envelope, or, worse, if it was printed. No person of sound mind should be getting mail from robots. Maybe he ended up like Thoreau, behind bars for refusing to pay his taxes. In his case, it would be for the parking tickets whose accumulated interest had skyrocketed. That Hubie! Are you squatting in your tent somewhere, making yourself a bowl of oatmeal sweetened with a spoonful of honey in warm water?

Inspired by my reverie, I slip a chocolate bar into my pack.

I go through my library to see which survival guide will accompany my wanderings. You, faithful friend. By the campfire, you will describe the possible scenarios of me being eaten alive. But not tonight. I won't let a bear spoil my birthday.

I drive along 287 towards East Lake. I slow down when the asphalt disappears in a cloud of yellow dust. There must be a van pulling a load of wood ahead. I pull over and turn on the radio. Yesterday, three men went missing on a fishing trip in the sector. No news. The families are worried. The provincial police are asking the owners of hunting camps to take a look and see whether the men in their sixties holed up somewhere on the Crown lands. I think of my bear, and of the lost men. Even if it is my birthday and my colleagues think I am unreachable, I abandon my plan and turn onto the logging roads I know like the back of my hand.

Sorry, Tall Pine, old friend. I'll come see you another time.

After a fruitless exploration of the woods, I come to the firing range at the end of the afternoon. The place is empty. Only the Queen on her jubilee poster washed out by the sun, stapled to a square bale of hay. I take out my service weapon and bullets and aim for Her Majesty. I think of my country that is not a real country, slaving away in Confederation, then remember the three men lost in the woods. If they went fishing, they must not have weapons. When they get hungry enough, will they eat their jar of worms, or find chanterelles and trust the *Rubus pubescens*, the dwarf raspberries?

My gun makes a metallic click. The bullets rattle in my pocket, and the target dares me.

Pow!
　　　Pow!
　　　　　Pow!

Three imaginary holes in your crown that turned us into drawers of water, factory hands working for a pittance, mumbling French into our beards, crushed by the fear of extinction that made us resentful and spiteful towards each other. As if our survival were threatened by difference. As if we did not deserve to govern ourselves. Your Highness, I am delighted to squat on your "Crown" lands, but allow me humbly to inform you that the real queen of the bush is me. It's my birthday, and I'm giving myself a gift.

Pow!

Pow!

Pow!

I go and inspect the target. Coyote stays put. Strange. I stare at Elizabeth II and think for a second or two. Then Coyote starts barking. Her eyes zero in on a spot at the edge of the woods, a few metres above the ground. She doesn't blink. Her pupils are dilated. She holds her breath. She looks quickly my way, then goes back to staring at the same spot, insistently, right *there*, as if she wanted to point her finger. She has spotted something.

At the tip of my boot, I notice the fresh road apple where flies are laying their eggs. Shit, indeed. Bear scat. I back off and go quiet. I look up. Nothing moving. The wind must be giving me away. I breathe in. I have my weapon, and the bullets are in the back pocket of my jeans.

No time to lose.

I reload carefully, backing away. As I pull the bullets out of my very tight pocket, I see something moving in the leaves. I can't believe my eyes.

Three black bear cubs are hanging high in a larch tree, looking down and whimpering. My neck muscles tense. Coyote is barking her head off. The alarm is sounding. Time to get out of here. My right hand is sweaty and it's hard to grip the bullets. Note to self: you're something else, Ms Wildlife Protection Officer with no ammo in her gun when the bears come calling.

Whoa, Bear. Whoa, Bear.

The first words that come to mind. Memories of a

33

campfire conversation where a tree-planter was telling us that English-speaking hunters have been going after bears for four centuries in Canada, so it stands to reason that the animals have learned a little of their language. He had more experience in the woods than I did. At the time I hadn't even begun my training.

But I did have my opinion.

"You're nuts, man. Bears don't speak English."

Right now, though, I have nothing else to hold on to. I say *Whoa, Bear* and don't look the cubs in the eye, and retreat quietly.

The idea is stupid. If bears had heard one human language enough to understand something of it, it would be a native language, not a colonial one. Sadly, I don't know how to say "bear" in any First Nations tongue.

The mother is somewhere close by.

I can't call on my great-grandmother because I don't know her real name. Marie-Ange Robichaud, if you hear me, protect me. My own mother paid no attention. Every morning when I tried to talk to her, her eyes never left the newspaper. Right now, I wouldn't mind retreating into a man-bites-dog story.

The bear cubs are unhappy. They climb higher. I execute my retreat. I am losing my cool. Coyote goes on yapping, and that isn't helping my cause. Or maybe it is.

"Where are you, Mama Bear?"

The cubs go on calling for their mother and I curse the fact that even if I wanted to do the same, there is no mobile network in back country Kamouraska. Not for me, and not for the three lost men who must be out of batteries and hope.

That's it, almost to safety. My heart is about to explode, my mind is jumping every which way, and I can't find the handle. The spiciest curses burst from my mouth as I jump into the truck and lock the door. With her lowered ears, Coyote seems more afraid of my anger than the fury of the mother bear that is now crossing the shooting range diagonally in our direction. I fire up the engine and lean on the horn. The bear stops in her tracks, looks at us and rears up on her hind legs. Is a windshield bearproof? She studies us through the fog of her myopia, then sprints off towards her young.

I spend twilight wandering over logging roads in search of the three men and the silver pick-up described on the radio. They must have gone to ground somewhere. All the rescue services have been mobilised. Ordinary citizens, the provincial police helicopter, sniffer dogs, patrol vehicles, even tree-planters are crisscrossing the forest. Day two, and no sign of them. There is still hope as long as they haven't met up with as many bears as I did.

The wind stirs. The night will be chilly.

I head for my friend Lionel's cabin on the Rivière-aux-Perles road. A little comfort won't do any harm. Four solid walls either. After all, it's my birthday.

As usual, the door is unlocked. I find familiar objects at the centre of the table. The basket of camping dishes on the wooden box, the blankets hanging out of the reach of mice, a few cans of soup, and everything necessary to light the place. Lionel expected me to stop by before he returned to go hunting.

I share my soup with Coyote. Then I clean up a little – mice are messy. By the light of candle stubs, two oil lamps and a headlamp with failing batteries, I read my guide. Study the pages that tell the tale of those who died and those who were lucky when they came across sharp-clawed she-bears that can devour hikers or let them live. The conclusion? Playing dead, face down, is a good way to protect your viscera, but if you do play dead and the bear decides to tear you to pieces anyway, get up and run for your life. My survival guide doesn't tell me what to do with the pieces, or how to hang on to your organs as you go.

Tomorrow I am going to sew a bear-bell on Coyote's collar.

Once I am wrapped up naked in my mummy sleeping bag, I devour my birthday girl chocolate bar and look out of the cabin window for the first stars. The silence is lovely, broken only by the clicking of the stove and the sighs of my dog dreaming of chipmunks. Even if I missed my annual hike and my rendezvous with Tall Pine, I feel like a queen in the prime of life. My hair is clean, I spent the day in the woods with my dog, sidestepped three or four bears, travelled the roads on a mission, and found shelter at a friend's place. Now I will take my pleasure by myself as I contemplate the stellar jewels below Orion's belt, my mouth full of melted chocolate.

4

Bloodhound

SEPTEMBER 28

The day starts off right, even if Coyote does not answer my call. I let her out early this morning and went back to bed. I enjoyed the luxury of sleeping in as she explored her new territory around the cabin. But she did not return for her kibble. Maybe she is in heat for the first time. If I were her, I would go hunting for a wolf.

You can go for a romp in the woods, puppy, as long as you come back with a bellyful of future soldiers.

I slip back into my sleeping bag and lay my book flat, then sprinkle a little pot on the cover for my Saturday morning joint. The coffee-cannabis combo is excellent when it's your day off and you're in a cabin at the far edge of the world, in Saint-Bruno-de-Kamouraska, the last village before the endless public forests that lead up to the mountains of Maine. My dear friend Lionel's rustic house is on the concession road where everything ends and everything begins, as the people in Natashquan say about Route 138, which runs between civilisation and Labrador. Like the benevolent owners of other remote shelters, Lionel never locks his door when he is away. His place is my second base camp. Since he is old enough to be my father, I decided to adopt him. We treasure each other with the filial love of people who have lost their families. Retired game warden, respectful hunter, earnest ecologist, he is a grumbling mentor, a rare example of someone I love to talk to.

On the porch lies a heap of feathers, Coyote's doing. Mist hangs over the grass yellowed by autumn. I squint to bring the distant fruit of the mountain ash into focus, and the elegant branches of the reddening bunchberry, and, who knows, the horizon from which big bears might be watching me.

My she-wolf's cry cuts through the forest that has begun to wake up. Birds take wing. There is rustling in the bushes, but Coyote doesn't show herself.

"Come back, puppy!"

The hours go by. I turn the pages and worry gnaws at me. I eat lunch alone, light my morning joint again, and throw a log on the fire. Yoga on the sunny front porch. A surprise Indian summer day teasing us with its fading pleasure.

The little bell on the table reminds me that my dog has no experience in the woods. I will not leave this place without Coyote. The three lost men will have to wait.

I lace up my boots. As I walk into the forest, I think of how I messed up yesterday at the shooting range. We barely made it to safety. Female black bears sometimes leave their young at the foot of trees. The babies can climb to safety in case of danger while their mother goes foraging in peace. Stumbling on them seldom ends well. Alerted by their cries, the mother will attack in self-defence. Luckily for me, she was far enough away to give me time to retreat.

I hear barking on the wind.

It's her. Not the bear, my dog. The leaves dampen her call. My hair stands on end and I move faster. My dog needs me. She is somewhere in the white spruce, up ahead. I run blindly towards the wavering sound of her distress. *Ahooo*, a call I have never heard. She must be injured. The minutes tick by. Her cry grows weaker. I sprint down the path. Her low whimpering torments me. I run, guided by her voice. Don't give up. Keep crying, puppy. I can't find you unless I can hear you.

The sun is low and I still haven't found her. But I am getting closer. I call upon my lucky star, Marie-Ange. I imagine her polishing a pearl rosary with her prayers. Protect my journey into darkness. Shield me from bears so I can find my best friend. Make sure my dog won't bring me face to face with the most feared mammal in the land.

I trip over something. A pile of deer hooves. Sawed off on a bed of bones. All around, in the bushes, too many traps to count. On the right, a heap of dirty bottles that must have contained the urine of females and other liquids for luring. A coyote-poaching site judging by the bait, the diameter of the snares, and the paw prints of recent victims. I only hope there are no leg-hold traps at my feet. They are illegal, but that's never stopped anyone. I have confiscated my share of them.

"Coyote?"

She responds feebly. When I call, she barks. But her voice is compressed, as if every breath takes all her energy and empties her lungs. She must be suffocating.

I ease myself into the ditch by the Rivière-aux-Perles bridge and head into the underbrush again, fooled by the echo. There are traps everywhere. A cow skull. Tufts of fur. Darkness joins the carnage and adds to my distress. The spruce trees are dense. Their branches scratch at my face. There, a break, just ahead, where four-legged creatures can pass. The smell of rotting flesh. A calf's chest cavity. Hanging in a tree by my head, a cage where a marten is struggling and growling. If not a marten, then something else small and fierce. I respect animal life, but I won't set it free for fear of it leaping at my face, with its instinct for vengeance. I hear it spitting at me in a rage.

Coyote's painful cries. I am not far now. My lamp shows me a bloody heap on the ground. My stomach turns. At my feet lie the remains of an animal, recently skinned. My whole body begs *No!* Then a sigh of relief. The thing is dead, but it is not my dog that was butchered. My headlamp shows me the way through sharp branches. I step over giant bones, the femurs of a moose.

Suddenly, reflecting the light, two golden circles in the darkness. Warm relief flows through me and my heart pounds. What is this creature looking at me with insistent round eyes, ten feet away? An animal staring, unmoving.

Yip!

The slightest little sound. But it's her! I recognise that hiccup of a note that Coyote makes when she is in a joyful mood. But she can't move. She is tangled in twisted cables. I try to separate the two snares that are choking her, I manage to loosen the collar and tear my knuckles on the braided wire. One down. The second is attached to two tree branches that I snap with my boot, putting all my hatred into the act.

Once she is freed, Coyote slips through my fingers and I lose sight of her. Everything is dark. My lamp gives out. I shake it, it comes back, then dies again. I am not out of the woods yet. I paid such close attention to the sound of her suffering that I lost my way. My headlamp batteries are dead. My hands are bleeding. I am lost.

lost lost lost lost lost lost lost lost lost lost lost lost

And surrounded by traps and carcasses to lure animals. Dead calves. The smell is sickening.

"Fucking bastards!"

The scene of horror is the work of a poacher. Predators everywhere.

"Concentrate, Raphaëlle."

lost lost lost lost lost lost lost lost lost lost lost lost

"Get your bearings."

The buzz of fear drowns out everything else. Get a hold of yourself. You turned forty yesterday, you don't have kids or a girlfriend, and you have never known love. One day you'd like to build a solar-powered log house, and canoe down endless salmon rivers that never lose their beauty, and see Anticosti, the Salluit fjord, the Métabetchouan river and – why stop there? – Scandinavia. Think of all the beautiful things awaiting you and get your bearings. The stars, the bark, the moss, the way the trees lean, the echoes of running water. Yes. I hear the road in the distance and the Rivière-aux-Perles close by. The sound of a vehicle bouncing over the hump before the bridge, the sleeping policeman that gets bigger every year with the spring runoff. One day it will carry away the bridge with its force. I listen to the murmuring water.

"Breathe in, Raphaëlle, find your inner peace, then find the way back."

I move towards the bridge and the river, calling my dog's name. She can't be far. A few metres away, I hear her lapping up water. That's it, now I remember the ditch and the stream I jumped over before stumbling into this trap. One by one, I retrace my boot prints in the mud and come upon Coyote, disfigured, but wagging her tail when she looks up between two gulps of water. She moves towards me. She wants to be petted. I fall to my knees and sob. Her nose is twisted, her neck striated with dried blood, her face terribly swollen. She is practically unrecognisable. Painful to see.

I hate the poachers who can do whatever they want. I have never seen so many carcasses and so much bait at different stages of decomposition. The trapping season hasn't even started, yet there are heaps of fresh meat and the snares are brand new.

I push aside the branches to make my way through the trees and get back on the road. Coyote moves ahead, walking slowly, her head low, bent at a painful angle, her tongue out. Even wounded, she is my guide. I can't see more than a foot in front of me, and my headlamp is useless.

Finally, my boots scrape against the steep path that leads to Lionel's cabin. Coyote sits down. She needs a break. Then she falls onto her side, exhausted. I lift her gently and take her in my arms. I don't even feel her weight.

The worst is behind us. Let's go home. It's pitch-black out here, and I need to bandage our wounds.

*

I dip my scarf in boiling water and wash the dried blood from Coyote's neck. She relaxed once I breathed a puff of smoke from my joint into her nose. Marijuana makes wounded dogs sleep, my hiker friend told me. Thank you, Hubert. Your remedy worked. As she sleeps, I lift her jaws, find the places where her fur is torn, pull off thistles and debris from her lacerations.

Fighting with a mechanism she didn't understand, which tightened with each attempt she made to free herself, Coyote tore her neck, ears and muzzle. Her fur is warm and humid. No more dried blood. Just cleaned wounds that I cover with honey and thyme. My toast will go without tomorrow. The mixture will disinfect her cuts, and she will lick herself, as dogs do, without getting sick.

I set her on the sofa in a nest of blankets. She is too tired to move. I wonder whether she will make it through the night. My unquiet mind keeps me awake.

I retrace the path I took. I am sure that in broad daylight I can find the site where the poacher set up shop. No way I'll miss it. I need to do some house cleaning. Lionel must have a pair of bolt cutters. I will neutralise the snares and pick up the trash.

As for you, poacher, I'll set a mantrap when the time comes.

I am furious that people go on shamelessly trapping animals for their fur. They hunt them down when they are already fighting the destruction of their habitat. Carcasses and garbage lie in the woods like an open-air dump, and four hundred years after we arrived here, we still haven't understood that this land is not a colony whose resources can endlessly be exploited.

Tomorrow, if Coyote is alive, I will go into town. Our blankets are covered in blood, and the place where people wash their dirty laundry is where all the village gossip gets aired. At the motel laundromat, I will have a chat with the hunting widows, and as my stuff is drying, I will cross the street and visit the outfitter's shop. By comparing anecdotes, I might be able to put a name to my search.

You don't know it yet, but I will hunt you down. Any good hunting dog can become a bloodhound with the right training. This dog will sniff out the prey from far away, and rescue the venison before it perishes. It will recover the game, wounded or dead, in the thickets. That is how I will hunt you, poacherman. Like a bloodhound, I won't leave your trail.

5

We Are Watching You

The Admiral Motel on Admiral Street is so rundown it ought to be demolished. Until that happens, welfare cases, hunting widows and roadside whores fill its rooms.

The door to room 127 is always wide open. For four quarters, I have the pleasure of contemplating my blood-stained blankets getting beaten by the agitator as the neighbours, sitting in their plastic Adirondack chairs bought at the Korvette discount outlet, watch me from behind the blind spots of their Dollarama sunglasses, arms crossed. They are probably wondering if I killed someone. I wish. My monthly trip to wash my clothes in the village is my one weird contact with civilisation.

The hunting widows are not loquacious this morning. Once my blankets are dry and folded in my truck, I cross the parking lot and go into the outfitters. The tinkling bell announces my entrance. I nod to the clerk, who knows who I am.

"You look like a real woman without your uniform, Miss Robichaud."

The small talk quickly leads to the reason for my visit. Yes, the clerk is aware that someone is trapping coyotes in the back country. No, he will not tell me who it is. The person he will not name has probably been his best buddy since kindergarten. We make a stab at conversation as we walk past the rows of flies, traps and boots. I head for the display of devices that imitate animal calls to lure the big ones with the richest pelts.

"Sorry, ma'am, but it's confidential. I can't tell you."

"Listen, you know as well as I do that confidentiality is for shrinks and lawyers, not stores that sell hunting and fishing gear. I'm sure you know the person I'm looking for. He's an expert. And I need a pro to solve my problem."

I run my hands over the spools of snare wire. It's as shiny as the kind used on the traps near Lionel's cabin.

"You've got too many coyotes around your place, ma'am?"

"More like bears, lately."

"I can see why! I wouldn't mind prowling around your place either."

I take a step back. I feel the urgent need to get away from this man who reminds me of so many others. The feeling of being a piece of meat in their eyes.

"I'll leave you my card in case you change your mind."

"Raphaëlle Robichaud, Wildlife Protection Officer . . . Now I know your first name."

"My number is at the bottom. Don't hesitate to call."

I glance up at the camera overlooking the cash register and smile but say nothing, in case the clerk gets scared and decides to erase the recording. I leave the store empty-handed. A woman in a housecoat on the other side of the street waves and comes over, holding something rectangular in her hand.

"You forgot this next to the dryer! You wouldn't want to lose such a nice little notebook! Your drawings are so pretty. Excuse me if I took a peek. I was looking for a name inside. You left in such a hurry with your basket, but then I saw you on the other side of the road."

There is nothing subtle about her wink.

I take the object that doesn't belong to me, and pretend to be relieved to have it back. I clutch it to my heart and thank the lady. Part of me hopes she slipped a scrap of paper inside, a name, a clue, anything. I asked a lot of questions at the motel, and this lady seemed to listen more attentively than the others.

"Be careful," she adds, leaning closer. "If I were you, I wouldn't ask those guys at the outfitters too many questions."

She turns on her heel and walks away.

A torn off piece of paper is sticking out of the notebook. A scrap of newspaper with a phone number scribbled in haste. I put the notebook on the truck dashboard.

Coyote is waiting for me on the seat, busily licking her wounds. She is in a pitiful state, but she will survive. I take the main road to the Cross Concession, listening to the radio. Still no sign of the three lost fishermen. I am about to turn onto the hunting camp road, but then I change my mind.

U-turn.

I go back to Lionel's to clean up, then stop at my trailer to pick up provisions for the weekend. I will explore the A.T.V. trails near Crown Lake. The three men who

47

disappeared went fishing, so they can't be far from lakes with fish in them, though they might have split up, each walking in a separate direction to look for help.

I follow the Rivière-aux-Perles and keep an eye on the entrances to the woodlots. There must be a lot of small abandoned cabins out here. No garbage cans on the road, nothing but tall grass. If people are living there, they don't go out much. I stay on the road until just before the bridge, then park behind Lionel's cabin to think things over. An old Québec Solidaire election poster with the slogan "Standing up for our Forests" leans against the building. I rummage through the glove compartment and pull out a Sharpie, then pet Coyote before locking her in the truck, the window opened just enough. I head for the crime scene to send the poacher a message.

To the guy trapping coyotes here,
the season hasn't begun yet.
Our dog almost died in your snares.
Stay away.
We are watching you.

I do not sign my name and I use the plural. This is not my property, and I cannot legally keep a trapper from practising his art if I don't own the land. But Lionel would never have given permission. I do not sign "S.O.S. Poaching", which is my department. Better leave it to the guy's imagination. All he has to do is call, and he will find out that I am responsible for operations in our Fur-bearing Animal Management Unit, or F.A.M.U. 77 for those on the inside. A man on such close terms with death should not know that the Wildlife Protection Officer investigating him is a woman who lives alone in a trailer with no mobile network. And that her dog is in such bad shape she would not attack him. And worse, that sometimes she keeps her bullets in her sweaty paw instead of her charger.

What struck me most during my time at the Duchesnay Forestry School were the memorial plaques in the hallway. They honoured the officers who died in the line of duty. Not just died. They were murdered for doing their jobs.

Game officers Médéric Côté and Ernest St-Pierre shot on *chemin de la Petite-Belgique, Saint-Louis-de-Blandford, 1972.*

Agent Alain Chouinard, while participating in an action against poachers, shot with a rifle by an individual hunting white-tailed deer at night in the Lower Saint Lawrence, 1985.

Agent Luc Guindon, struck with an arrow and fatally wounded. The moose hunter was poaching at night near Sainte-Agathe, 1989.

49

Agents Fernand Vachon and Nicolas Rochette along with their pilot Yves Giguère perished when their plane crashed during a night-time anti-poaching operation in the Beauce region, 2005.[1]

There was no record as to whether the poachers who attacked these men were caught. When it comes to these crimes, impunity is the rule. Like pirates on the high seas, politicians in their offshore tax shelters, and dealers of white powder in the logging camps.

My role, among other things, is to protect the northern forests from fur thieves who trap with no respect for Nature. They are not hermits taking animals for subsistence deep in the woods, nor First Nations people transmitting the rituals of their age-old knowledge. These guys are in it for the money to the detriment of our ecosystems.

On the job or off, protecting the forest is my vocation.

Sad to say, coyotes are not respected here, even by my colleagues who are supposed to protect fauna of every kind. Depredation rules around the hunting camps. Men play God and receive the appreciation of those who turn a profit from the industry. More game for the hunters, more money in the outfitters' cash register. As for the furs, since the price is extremely low, there is no trouble finding buyers. In the cities, people line up to buy a lynx or coyote collar to complete their brave explorer look. A furry pompon on a cap made in China. What is poached in Canada is shipped overseas, then sent back as an accessory on a thousand-dollar coat. Of that money, if he is lucky, the trapper gets fifty dollars. For trapping to pay off, pelts have to be pulled from the forest by the dozens.

There, my work is done. I cut the snares and hung my warning in a visible place. I even emptied what was left of my detergent bottle on the ground. I don't feel too guilty. The stuff is biodegradable.

This guy obviously knows what he is doing. His snares are expertly placed. I found a couple dozen. I will keep them as evidence for the forensic lab.

I drive until the asphalt ends between spruce as straight as soldiers. Back to my lair, the beige trailer with mauve stripes. We are lucky. Coyote is doing better already. The swelling on her face is subsiding. I hang my blankets, still slightly damp, on the line. My clothes dance in the wind as flights of wild geese pass overhead. I catch a whiff of Parfums de Provence soap powder. If I can smell it, the coyotes will, too, and know where my dog got caught. Animals are smarter than people think.

I start a fire, and soon I am hypnotised by the wavering flames. I imagine a demon's shape in the coals. Game and predators have been moving through these woods for millennia, past the same spots. Pheromones. Water. A healthy distance from humans and noisy roads. Trappers know their comings and goings like the back of their hand. The man in my sights is a connoisseur of the Saint-Bruno woods where he sets his traps. He is patient, diligent, assiduous. He checks his traps every day to harvest his fur-bearing loot. He will read my sign very soon.

How will you react, poacher, when you see my act of

sabotage? Legally, I had no right. "No-one may knowingly hinder a person unless he is the owner of the land. The sharing of territory by users must take place in a spirit of harmonious cohabitation." You will probably decide that an ordinary citizen did it. Someone who happened to pass by, perhaps a frustrated vegetarian.

I open the notebook that the woman in the housecoat gave me. I will call her when I have a signal. She probably heard me asking about trappers in the area. She must have some info.

I memorise the number in case I lose the paper.

The notebook has me curious. Inside the little volume, drawings everywhere, not a free inch of space. The letters are round, feminine, careful, sketches of flowers, leaves, animal shapes in the margins, page after page. On the leather cover, a drawing filled with a disturbing energy, letters carved with a blade. I run my finger over them, then open to page one.

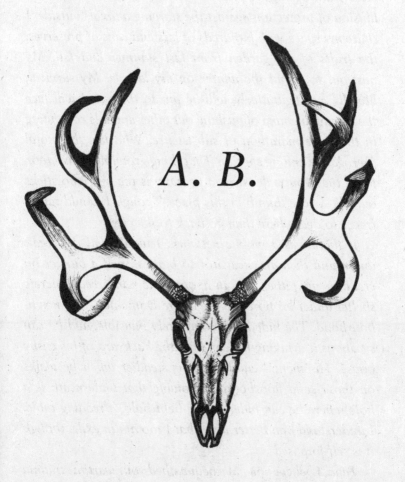

A. B.

Cabin fever
Winter #2   December 15

Here I am again, the prisoner of four walls that offer the illusion of protection against the starving animals outside. I share my space with hundreds of jars and cans of preserves, the fruits of my garden from last summer and fall. My mission: to spend the winter on my laurels. My survival, literally and figuratively, will be put to the test. I will face the ethical dilemma of pushing out other animals competing in the same marathon of subsistence. Who has the moral prerogative among species? That thing growling at my door, for I, the Montrealer turned peasant, is the one who sticks out like a sore thumb in this place. Though I would rather freeze to death here than go back to the city.

If there was a mobile network, I would call the credit union and then an excavator to build myself a bunker on credit as my father did, an apocalyptic reinforced concrete shelter under his porch in the Notre-Dame-de-Grâce neighbourhood. The hideout is completely invisible, and he can sit above it drinking his coffee in the backyard of his cushy house. His mental equilibrium is steadier when he walks on those solid floorboards, knowing that underneath is a hole where he can hide, a bare light bulb, a reading table. I understand him better now that I too am in exile, though it is self-imposed.

Papa, I believe you have bequeathed your wartime trauma to me. I dream of an armoured vault deep in the woods, filled with provisions and books. Pronounced the way you do in German, it sounds better. Boon-ker.

Boon-ker. That safe place where my heart can stop pounding when my imagination starts playing tricks on me. Am I going mad or is this the right decision?

You will tell me not to wait to start digging. A person can't be too prepared for war, and don't forget to install a drain in case of flooding and several sump pumps to keep the concrete good and dry. Put your favourite chair nearest the largest load-bearing wall, and whatever else, don't trust anyone. Bar the door twice. Survival situations bring out the worst behaviour.

"There is no lock that will keep your closest friend from coming in and stealing your last bullets and your last supper. Don't trust anyone."

Yes, Papa, I always bar the cabin door twice before going to bed.

"Remember, Anouk, our family lost everything in World War II. Everything material can disappear. Don't forget. They even threw the piano out of the window, meine kleine Maus. But no matter, you will retain what is essential: languages, ideas and the words you have memorised. Learn everything you can. Make it an obsession. What you bury in your head cannot be taken from you."

Dear Papa, I wait for the end of the world and draw the curtains to keep from looking out. Avoiding all visual contact with the characters that will destroy my equilibrium. The enchantment of the forest — sorry, Gabrielle Roy — has become a wood of sorrow and disenchantment. But there are things more frightening than wild beasts. There are the humans.

One day, perhaps, when you get too old for your Montreal boon-ker, you will come and join me here, Papa, in my cabin. You have never been. I am not even sure you understand that I live by a small river and not the great Saint Lawrence, because in German both the large and small varieties are called Fluss. *You must picture me living a perilous life on the banks of our national treasure, the plaything of the tides and the rising waters of climate change. No, Papa, my river grumbles, but it will never flood me out.*

Time goes by slowly here. I count the days. How long has it been since the last time I left the forest? I will break my own record. Turning feral is the challenge and I will meet it.

The cabin is a mouse trap, a dank library, a refuge for me, half-Canadian and half-German. The only time I feel at home is when I am on a plane between the two continents. Comforted by the prospect of returning from a trip and finally seeing my house again, but when I do, I am ready to leave. Only the cabin calms my nomad self and its restless wandering. Only here do I find silence and manage to set aside my anguish, or at least put it down on paper. I have time to concentrate on what I want to learn. I escape into the lacy poetry of northern mosses and picture a virgin horizon far from here. I travel with novels, I study botanical treatises, I sketch the treasures I find as I walk through my territory.

And since I still have time before the next war, and because it's too late to build my boon-ker, I ready myself for winter. Outside, the enemy is preparing his yearly siege.

There is refuge in the universe of a magnifying glass hovering over lichen, in the lexicon of the infinitely small.

Peace is a matter of moss. I picture myself on a bed of bearberry. When my long hair, red like peat moss burned by the sun, mingles with the sphagnum, I will let my soul fly free. A chorus of birds will sing at my bedside.

I regret only one thing. I have not saved much from my cabin fever. Always vigilant, I confront the winters, but with no real goal. At least I gained a sense of peace. I succeeded in surviving a respectable amount of time and breathing my last far from Notre-Dame-de-Grâce. Don't take it the wrong way, Papa. Good night. I promise I won't forget to double-bar the door and slather myself with pine resin. My throat is killing me. I am heading for a big-time cold. I shouldn't have gone to the bar in search of hands less calloused than mine. Three pints in vain. The barmaid willing to talk to outsiders must have been carrying a virus. But I would rather die alone of a violent case of the flu than hang around Emergency in Notre-Dame-de-Fatima for thirty hours. Tomorrow I will write my will in the absence of witnesses.

Joint in hand, I spend the evening in the company of this lady hermit, studying her private drawings, reading the secret dreams of a woman who has cast a spell on me. She says she lives by a river. Anouk B. She forgot her diary in the laundry room at the motel, which means her cabin is not far away. That is, if she still lives there, if the woman who gave me the notebook didn't find it months earlier, if Anouk survived that winter . . .

I need to return her diary, if only to beg forgiveness for my prying.

As I read the pages by the light of my headlamp with its fresh batteries, I breathe an occasional puff of smoke on my snoring dog's wounded muzzle.

My fingers lacerated by the traps show no signs of infection. Anouk B. reminds me that neither do I have a last will and testament. I don't want to end up in a cardboard box stowed beneath a row of identical stones decorated with discoloured bouquets of plastic flowers, in a mortuary plot by a highway. Scatter me at L'Anse-Pleureuse, where I can be united with the seashells of my childhood.

It will all work out, you'll see. In any case, I have no possessions.

O.K., one last page, chosen at random, then lights out.

Montreal, I am leaving you.

My parents thought we were living in a prestige neighbourhood in a city of possibilities. I grew up among bourgeois bohemians. I spent my teenage years in the crowds in the underground, climbing the social ladder, playing my cards right. I went to work in a noisy office that promised advancement, but I got sick of the nine to five, everyone with their styled hair gnawing at their fingernails as they tapped away on their phones on crowded buses, waiting to get out of town for the weekend. I went to museums on Wednesdays, when the rest of society was fastened to their computers, to rest my eyes on some colour, but a parade of spectacled art-lovers was there to do the same. No escape. Even climbing Mount Royal meant joining a parade, everyone with a foldout stroller and a dog on a leash with matching collar, or jogging along with white earphones and the latest sexy devices. I never understood servility in dress. Nor wanted to elicit men's desire for my body before they knew my soul. I never bought into the ideal of uniform, perfected forms of beauty. I just don't fit in.

For peace and quiet, I had to buy a cabin in deepest Quebec, a place that cannot be geolocated. I turned into a back country hermit.

Even there, incredibly, there is no peace. Inspectors show up, arguing that my rainwater collector which is set higher than the sink constitutes a water pressure supply system, which necessarily means a standard septic installation. I hate the word "standard". I don't want to be a standard person.

Why is it that all around people have the right to spread two inches of liquid shit on the ground, then dig ditches to drain the faecal fluids from their megafarms into the river? Whereas I'm not allowed to take a piss in the snow. You won't find a single trace, Mr Inspector. I dig holes with a shovel. That keeps me in shape, it marks my territory and it

59

decomposes. "Be careful, Mme Baumstark, if you refuse to obey the law, the town can take legal action against you." Good Lord, a hermitess can't even have her own outhouse! It is a thousand times more logical than doing your duty in drinking water and wasting electricity making the pump work ten times a day to flush your product into a hole excavated by a backhoe. In other words, it is forbidden to shit on your own land, even if you are the only human being for miles around, to avoid the "contamination of neighbouring wells". What about the "fertiliser" from those thousands of pigs, is that better? "Don't act like you don't know the difference, Frau Baumstark." The inspector must be getting a kickback from the construction Mafia, forcing taxpayers to install Cadillac septic tanks while the millionaire agrobusiness guys can go on polluting arable land and what's left of the rivers. I feel like shitting on his car. But I stop myself. I hear Papa whispering, "Low profile, low profile."

Then the Jehovah's Witnesses got into the act. I pasted on a smile when they handed me their propaganda. What a rag! Witnesses in the middle of the forest. The only thing I could think of was: Hell is Other People. After their visit, I considered building a fence like the kind they have on deer farms, solid mesh, fourteen feet high, posts dug deep into the ground, totally impassable.

Leave me alone, inspectors, pedlars, messengers of the Apocalypse. I have been living alone for two years in a back country cabin. That must mean I don't want to see anyone. AND THAT MEANS YOU.

*

I close the notebook, determined to read the whole thing. My *alter ego* lives in these pages. I slip Anouk's diary under my pillow. Check my gun jammed into the space between the wall and my bed. My brain is turning like a hamster on a wheel. Alright now, Raphaëlle, don't head out on another of your impossible quests. You need to be in good shape tomorrow. A brand-new week. The three men who disappeared need help, and a concerted effort must be made to find them.

6

Open Season

Pale pink dawn. The trembling aspen are turning yellow. Rifle shots and A.T.V. engines pull me from sleep.

"Jesus, some people are quick out of the blocks when it comes to poaching!"

I put on clean socks and a T-shirt that doesn't smell too bad, then my uniform furred with dog hair. Head for the hills, moose. Bow-and-arrow season officially begins this morning. Where's my belt? The guys hiding in the trees with their bows must be swearing a blue streak when they hear the gunshots that will frighten the animals into climbing higher into the Appalachians, all the way to the snow line.

My clothes dance in the wind. Nothing finer than a clothesline holding the patched essentials of a life without artifice. Woollen sweaters, underwear that has seen better days, washed-out pants, and socks that don't match. Is it my blood or the sheet metal roof that makes my underwear smell like rust? The softness and warmth of cloth – that's what matters. Nothing like my rough, stiff, black uniform.

One of my uniform shirts was ripped from the line, and it took off flying into the woods. There it is, at the foot of a tree. The wind was strong last night. I hold a clothes peg between my teeth and shake the wrinkles out of my shirt, then inspect the ground for fresh bear tracks. To my complete stupefaction, I discover large boot prints that give me a case of the shakes.

Someone came walking by here over the weekend . . . O.K., calm down, maybe it was just a curious hiker admiring the autumn colours.

Behind the trailer, I find more tracks, and put my foot in one of them to compare the size. I note the form of the soles, shaped like a four-leaf clover. The person went around the back of my camp. One of the three lost fishermen?

Coyote is convalescing on the trailer's welcome mat. She is getting better fast. I eat a crust of bread, rinse my throat with yesterday's cold coffee, and bite into an apple. One by one, I analyse the footprints of this new prowler with feet bigger than the hind paws of the bear that was reconnoitring here last week. A colossus who wears size twelve at least.

Dear bears, forgive us our fur trade. Let me live long enough to attack the poachers and protect the hunting rights on Crown lands. It might take generations to undo the fear that makes you avoid us, and the unhealthy pleasure men find in shooting you at point-blank range.

In the coming days, the roads from the city to the back country will become a funeral procession. Hunters will throw away empty packs of cigarettes, empty cans of American beer, cheese curds, and bags full of viscera from the game they have killed. The garbage I clean up will reveal other, older layers. The proof that plastic takes centuries to decompose, and that most hunters do not make the connection between the quality of the habitat and the survival of a species. The irony! They pollute the territory of the very animals they want to put on their grill. They disguise themselves in the colours of the forest to profane the land and everything on it. Then they call themselves woodsmen.

Maybe we could make a difference if we sensitised people. The optimist in me thinks so. But deep down I don't think so. We won't change our ways until we have destroyed everything.

I finish breakfast over a few more pages of Anouk's diary. She has an appetite for men and women both. Paradoxically, her need for affection is combined with a disgust for human beings. I read her memories of an unnamed lover who migrates from page to page, between sketches of belugas with crosses for eyes, and a still life entitled "Chickadee with Broken Neck". A secret garden of shadow and light.

I close the notebook and open the door for Coyote.

My eyes fall upon an object leaning against my window. Did the thing come out of nowhere, or did I not notice it until now?

A braided metal cable, stained with fur and dried blood. A snare. The spring is rusty and jammed against the cable, which is new. It has been twisted over twice before being folded sideways. A signature technique. Exactly like the snare that almost killed Coyote.

Someone put the thing against my window as I slept soundly last night. Yesterday, the sun was low when I returned – could I have walked past the trailer without seeing the snare? The boot prints of the man with big feet are fresh. Could he have followed me on foot? The poacher is one step ahead of me. Someone must have told him where the local protection officer is squatting, the one with the long black braid who won't give up. I bend down and inspect the tyre tracks. My vehicle only. The poacher came on foot.

He could have spotted me near Lionel's cabin, sabotaging his traps. Or someone in the village could have told him I had been by his trap line. The guy from the outfitters, the one the woman in the housecoat warned me about. Or someone from the laundromat who thought I was asking too many questions.

I am up against a real strategist. He must know the woods if he parked far enough away that I wouldn't hear him, and took the trouble to walk here. The worst hypothesis: this is not the first time he has come prowling around, just the first time I've realised it. And only because he wanted me to know. He left tracks and ripped a shirt off the line.

He is challenging me on my own territory. He knows where I live. He could be hanging around right now. I look at my underwear on the line, take an inventory of the boot prints in my yard, and examine the line of spruce. Maybe he has been watching me for a while.

As I trace his footsteps backwards, I notice sap flowing down a trunk deformed by a dark mass that looks like a chaga mushroom. But chagas grow only on yellow birch. I walk over to the spruce tree with its trace of sticky sap. I see why it is there. A trail camera, screwed into the trunk.

65

The lens is pointing towards the sugar shack. No, towards the rainwater tank, exactly where I have my shower. I take down the camera and pull out the memory card and put it in my pocket. Return the camera to its position, though I feel like stamping on it with all my might. Judging by the texture of the sap and the length of its trace, the wound on the tree dates back. The spying is nothing new.

Suddenly I am ashamed, like the first time I bled. At summer camp, in the middle of a canoe trip, I had my period. Maybe it was the effort of portaging, or the cold water that came up to my thighs at times, or the moon, I don't know. All I remember is the gasp of fear that arose from ignorance. My mother, full of grace and Christian prudery, never explained how a girl becomes a woman. The camp councillor came to my rescue. Behind the blue tarps around the dug latrine, she showed me how to stick the wings to my underwear. My face was crimson with embarrassment. I hid the stain on my pants by tying a sweater around my waist, even though the evening was cool.

My blood is pounding. I feel it in my ears and cheeks, red with anger. If the trapper wants to poach, that's one thing. But for him to come onto my land and spy on me naked, that's another. I feel dirty. My camp has been violated.

Somewhere deep in the glove compartment of my service vehicle is a can of pepper spray. A present from an old girlfriend, a gift from our last night before I went off into the forest. I remember the gift card.

To protect you from the big bad wolves.
Be careful, Raphaëlle,
my fearless love.

Our last night, with too much wine, ended badly. A fight tore us apart instead of it ending in sweet love.

I was always running away. She hemmed me in. I liked to sleep on my side of the bed, and she wanted to wrap herself around me. I was wild, she civilised. I forgot her birthday, and she knew how many months we had been together. I was indifferent to material things; she loaded me down with gifts. I liked to make love outside, and she was afraid of bugs.

In other words, it could never have worked out.

But thanks for the pepper spray, Sophie. Again, you were right. My peace and quiet are gone.

PART TWO

Happy Hunting Grounds

7

Insubordination

OCTOBER I

Tuesday morning, sitting among the ferns, sipping coffee. I have to push myself to get going. There are the registrations of yesterday's hunting results to compile, but where are my tally sheets? Coyote is waiting for me in the truck. My lunch is made. I am the one holding things up, dragging my feet. I have had enough. I hardly slept at all. My forehead and temples and eye sockets are buzzing with tension. I couldn't stop thinking about the prowler. I tossed and turned, hot flashes and cold sweats. Maybe I'm coming down with something. I don't have anyone I can talk to. After my second coffee, I wonder if I am becoming paranoid. I am utterly disgusted by the trap on my window ledge and the man who probably has pictures from the trail camera, some back country poacher who collects coyote pelts like hockey cards and trades them for almost nothing. Maybe he is jerking off right now to photographs of my summer showers, sessions of self-enjoyment and towelling down, naked under the sun. How could I have so far lowered my guard?

I remember my past failures every time I tried to come down on a poacher. And even if I emerged from court victorious, I always felt that the meagre fines and the judge's homily were all for show. No-one really cares what happens here. An occasional slap on the wrist is not going to change anything. Flimsy laws like ours will never protect the fauna.

My coffee cup is vibrating to the motor's hum. To each her stimulant. I begin my daily ritual with apprehension, my belly brimming over with bitter coffee. I cast an imploring glance at the sepia photograph of Marie-Ange peeking over the sun visor.

I picture the goddess Artemis accompanied by her golden deer, bow in hand, watching over the Cervidae that will die like flies today, tomorrow and the weeks to come. But not for ever and ever, amen, if I have anything to say about it.

Fall is the season of pursuit, the hunt. I am the arbiter who will expose those who cheat. I haven't liked my job for a while, and I am going beyond the limits of my juris-diction. My sense of duty pushes me into hanging on for another season, though I have no more taste for it.

The forest is dense. Men use the cover to kill more than the limit. A game of cat and mouse. When they meet me on the road, I keep my eyes open. Just because there is only one buck in their truck doesn't mean there aren't two more dead ones waiting in the woods. Hunters lie like rugs. Some are better at it than others. I try to keep my inner peace. The way you protect a candle flame against a delin-quent wind, using the palm of your hand, even if it burns.

I used to think that my work at the Ministry had some

value beyond the hours noted on my payslip. I travelled through the infinite forests and parks as if I were on a mission. Deepening my knowledge. I am a Wildlife Protection Officer, but I don't protect the hunted species. I am a government pawn on a chessboard that is too big for me. The title sounds noble on paper. Sometimes I feel like a parking meter whose job is to make sure the hunting industry keeps the village businesses alive. I smile politely at people who parade drunkenly on A.T.V.s, hauling bloody trophies with the spark of the victor's pride in their eyes as they emerge alive from the woods.

They got their kill. And they had their fun. They want to start all over, a cold Bud in their hand. The slim hunter-outfitter of the old days has become a pot-bellied collector. My thoughts of the stereotypical obese hunter in camouflage overalls and fluorescent orange cap are interrupted by the regional news on the radio.

The government has decided to abolish trapping quotas – I turn up the volume – *for two types of lynx in Quebec. It will now be permitted to take more animals over a longer period of time. In a press release, the Ministry of Forests, Fauna and Parks stated that there are sufficient numbers of this feline species to go ahead with the decision.*

"Sufficient numbers, shit! They don't even have a count of the animals!"

Beginning this fall, the trapping season will run from October to March. Trappers in Quebec will be allowed to capture lynx without having to respect quotas, and that includes bobcats.

I'll be damned. My Ministry sources were telling the truth. The death sentence for lynx in Quebec has just been signed.

What am I, a scarecrow? What am I doing here? Who is going to be next – polar bears? Easy to rationalise. Since the ice floes are melting, we're better off shooting all of them before they head south, looking for us. We'll go on pretending that the climate crisis is an ecological drama for teenagers.

*

Sitting on the hood, I watch pickups pass with moose tied on top. I don't react. I don't even stop them to check their licences. I'm too discouraged. I nod and wave. Go on your way. The guys at the wheel, beer in hand, wave back. They're in a good mood.

They move on to the next level. "Hey, there, pretty thing! Need a pick-me-up?"

With steel in my eye, I let them know they'd better keep going.

I climb into the truck and bump up the volume on the newscast. The three men are still missing. Coyote is sleeping in the triangle of shadow cast by the door. I make an executive decision to abandon my post. There are endless roads not on any map. "Without monuments", the surveyors call them. That is where I will spend the afternoon, searching, wandering.

I take to the road, meditating on my uncertain origins

and the hole I am living in. On the seat of my truck, my hard-to-close lunchbox, full of snacks I can eat with one hand as I drive along roads I rename according to what I see there. Motherless Calf Curve. Cow without Calf Dead End. Flattened Fox Track. Hunted Prey Concession, where I found an animal that had died of exhaustion. Which one breaks my heart the most? There's no telling.

I'm thinking of the lynx's future. I refuse to accept that I'm naive and deluded because I don't agree that Nature is an all-you-can-eat buffet. But that's not what the lobbies think, and they rule.

The last rays of the sun begin slipping through the trees. For a few more hours they will go on lurking, the hunters in their blinds and the moose among the boughs, and the three men somewhere in the woods.

This is bow-and-arrow season, but I hear gunshots everywhere. I'm supposed to track down, single-handedly, the cheaters who park near manure heaps on farms and fire point blank at coyotes digging up gophers, animals as desperate as the gnus dying of thirst that come to drink at rivers where alligators lie in wait. Their desperation is so great they risk their lives to live another day.

Cross-sections of sequoias as old as our era, giant elephant tusks, moose antlers, thick furs ladies love to receive – these trophies display our desire to possess and to profit.

What do we become if we lose our sensitivity to banal cruelty? Animals ourselves, heartless and mindless.

As a Wildlife Protection Officer, I live with my Orwellian

title as I go on protecting the hunting and trapping industry, allowing killers with no sense of proportion to run free and empty out our forests. As if fur-bearing predators have no place in the food chain. I am not in the mood for compromise.

An A.T.V. pulling a trailer emerges from the woods with moose hooves sticking out. At first glance, it looks like there are two animals in there. And only one hunter at the wheel. I block his path and step down from the truck. I'll play cop and see if he has his licence. Hoping that a trio of accomplices will appear. And that my day will not end in a cat and mouse game with a hunter who knows full well that he needs two licences per animal, and not two animals with one licence.

"Good evening, sir! Raphaëlle Robichaud, Wildlife Protection. Can I see your licence?"

"What do you know, she's fresh out of school! I'm a lucky man."

"I would laugh if it wasn't the thousandth time I've heard that. I even thought of shaving my head to spare myself the jokes of dirty old men who can't control themselves."

"Sorry. It was a compliment. I . . . I figured I was lucky to be stopped by such a pretty woman. Don't take it the wrong way."

"You were lucky today. A female and her calf."

"Yeah, we're happy. We'll have meat for the whole winter. My brothers will be here soon. We all have our licences."

"I hope so for your sake. We'll wait for them. Park over there and cut the motor, please."

I note down the butchery, the moose lying in the trailer. A final glance at rigor mortis. One will not have to live without the other, and that is some consolation. My duty stops there. I will keep my pain for myself. But my sense of insubordination will not let me go.

The sky is low with clouds. Drizzle keeps me inside the truck. Coyote licks her paws while I finish my paperwork, unfold my topographical map, and study the less accessible zones of the Fur-bearing Animal Management Unit. I need to catch up on lost sleep, and wake up early to explore new roads in search of the lost men. The regional bureau has issued its directive. Every time there is a lull in the action, comb the back country and find them alive. I make an enormous detour through the sector, stopping at the office at the end of my shift. I pass swamps full of stunted spruce and return to my trailer as night falls. I ask my colleague to check licences tomorrow while I patrol the backroads and answer emergency calls. She is new in the area, and less at ease on public lands than I am. She likes human contact, so she is quick to agree.

I think back to when I was hired. At the time there were five of us. We were a real team. Today, only three remain, with one heading for retirement, which means that the new one and I will have to cover a territory with seven trapping zones, nearly three hundred and eighty square kilometres.

My headlights pick out the woodpile.

I see with horror that my door has been forced. There is fresh mud on the steps. The rug has been kicked off to one side. Coyote starts barking.

With my hand on my gun, I knock down what is left of the door and storm into the trailer.

8

By the Scruff of the Neck

OCTOBER 2

I couldn't sleep. I spent all night looking at it. Wondering what to do. Hold it in my arms? Take it with me? Abandon it here?

The coyote pelt that was placed on my bed is flaming red, like a fairy tale fox. It smells of musk and peat moss. Soft, spotted fur. A beautiful animal that died for nothing. I reach out my hand and touch it, stroke it, console it. Immerse myself in its odour of sweat and fear. Around the eyes it isn't completely dry. Along the length of its spine the fur stands straight up, the way my dog's does when she assumes the defensive position. The legs are nearly black. One of them is shorter than the other. Poor animal. I pick it up by the scruff of the neck and put it back on my bed gently, as if to ask forgiveness, through the deference of my actions, for what was done to it.

I tidy up the trailer. Put my bag by the door. Nothing to it, my whole life fits into a seventy-litre backpack. It can hold a fixed volume of well-packed items, and there is a weight limit to respect if I want to be able to manoeuvre comfortably. The essentials. Gun, bullets, dried fruit, a little flask of liquor for wounds to the body and the soul, dog food, leash, a bowl, canteens of drinking water, headlamp and batteries, lighters, pepper spray in the inside pocket of my jacket, knife in my right boot, essential oil of wintergreen, cannabis. I take a deep breath. Slip Anouk's diary into the pocket of my backpack. *Zip* – let's go.

I leave my trailer behind. My throat is constricted and keeps me from breathing deeply enough to fill my lungs. My bitterness turns against me. It is burning me from the inside, the vulnerability of being a woman, the shame of having to flee a predator, the frustration of being checkmated by an outlaw. I am a very sore loser.

My dog sniffs at the dead animal's skin. I could have left last night, but I couldn't make the move. I decide to take the pelt with me. Maybe the lab can figure out something about the technique and link it to other animals that were caught. Accepting the gift binds me to the poacher. But its beauty is so striking that I want to honour it. Undo the damage. Shame shame shame.

The early morning light is vague. A little grey, a little heavy, burdened by the sadness of leaving my well-organised home. Like the great horned owl that pillages nests, the poacher has made me leave mine.

Now I have two coyotes. One is very much alive and has my back. My first child. The other did not have mixed blood or a life to look forward to, but it wore a flaming orange coat. They share the back seat of the truck. Coyote is curled up on the skin, sleeping peacefully. Maybe the scent reminds her of her mother. The truck is filled with a particular smell that is not unpleasant. It reminds me of the dogsled kennel. A scent of forest and sweat, black spruce and fear.

Better get away. The poacher is crazy enough not to stop where he did.

The key is in the ignition. The trap sitting on my bags on the passenger seat torments me. I feel about as safe as a piece of meat in an arena full of wild beasts, even with my hunting rifle, my Glock, the knife in my boot and my old girlfriend's pepper spray.

The sun is coming up. I have an appointment at the Deschênes Campground I can't miss.

Relax. You're not expected until nine o'clock.

I have time to go by the forensics lab. I have twenty traps whose spring mechanism is exactly like the one left on my window ledge. The blood and fur on it can be analysed. My colleagues will be able to tell what kind of animal suffered and died in that trap. And I have the pelt that can reveal plenty of information about the poacher's cutting and tanning methods. An unknown telephone number, the data from the memory card, a break-in to report.

But something, a little voice inside, cautions me to keep quiet about my investigation. Running my big mouth in the village was my first mistake.

Relax, Raphaëlle, maybe he doesn't have bad intentions.

Of course he does, girl! He spied on you and broke down your door. And he hung a coyote trap on the side of your trailer!

First things first: move to a safe place. The lab can wait. Then go to work as if everything is normal. I go and piss in the bushes. Coyote joins me and urinates on top of my puddle. I pull up my pants fast. My hands are trembling.

The symbolism of the killing object and the gift of the pelt have me freaking out. My speculations are like poison. What if it was more than just a warning or a head game? He wants me to know that he is hunting me down. The stand of maples is on his trapline. I have been in his sights for a while. I pissed him off by destroying his traps. He must have seen my truck with the Ministry's identification. He probably knows who I am. He could have called the number on the truck and made a fake request for information. And the nude photos he has . . . He could humiliate me in front of my colleagues, and make me more vulnerable than I already am as a woman in a man's job. The trap is there to destabilise me. I'm on his territory, and he is running the show. He the hunter, I the prey.

You're smarter than me. I didn't see it coming. Strange how you're always one step ahead. Which makes me think you've been watching me for a while.

"Alright, Coyote, let's get the hell out of here."

I have a heavy foot today. The yellow lines on the asphalt flying by at top speed are the key to my peace of mind. As long as I am driving, and they are flashing past with the sun high in the sky, I don't have to decide. I need to talk to someone who will get me out of the vicious cycle of my thoughts. I hit the brakes and consider my situation. I have to stop this escalation.

I fill my tank in the village and go along the main street to rue Deschênes. I am thirty minutes early with a disgusting gas station coffee on the dashboard. The radio gets on my nerves. No news, apparently, of the three lost fishermen. Not even their vehicle, the object of all that blind searching, has been found. There is no hope for them. I park in the shade, open the windows a little, and pet Coyote. She knows the ritual, and curls up on the passenger seat. From the outside, all that's visible is her two pointy little ears. I smile. The first sip of coffee burns my tongue, and the stuff runs down my fingers and stains my uniform. When I set my thermos on the hood, my hands are still trembling.

"Madame Robichaud! Happy to see you."

The Saint-Bruno librarian, a frail little woman in a long grey raincoat, offers me her hand. My eyes fall on the heavy ring on her finger. An ostentatious rock for a woman with so little coquetry. She motions me to follow, but even from here I can see the logjam that threatens the street and the cottages. Rivière-du-Loup is as high as during its spring flood stage. Its waves lap at the lawns, and its waters are brown from the gardens it has invaded, dangerously close to the houses. The beaver family has returned.

"Do you see that?"

Madame Foisy points to the heap of trunks of deciduous trees, home to the beaver lodges. The river has left its bed on the north side. Buildings are flooded, and the basement entrances have water halfway up the doors.

"It had better not freeze like that."

"No. It had better not."

"Are you on your own, Madame Foisy? Do you have anyone to help you?"

"My husband died this summer, and I have to sell the place. I have no choice. It's hard enough as it is with the bank and the insurance because we're in a flood zone. Everyone who was interested changed their minds. I can't have an open house with water this high."

"My condolences, Madame Foisy. Your husband was a good man. A hard worker."

"That he was. He would have known what to do about the beavers."

"It looks pretty bad. We're not going to waste any more time. Have you heard the forecast?"

"Rain, wall to wall. The basement is already taking on water. Same goes for the neighbours. I've got their keys. The town has known about it for two weeks."

"Sorry, I would have come sooner had I known. But don't worry, we're going to take action. Normally you need a special permit from the Ministry to capture wild animals and dismantle their dam – except in the case of an emergency. And with seven cottages here and maybe others upstream that could be flooded in the next few days . . ."

"Drive the road that runs along the river. You'll see, it's gone over its banks up there, too."

"And the weather isn't on our side. Madame Foisy, I'm going to bring in a professional trapper, Gilles. I know him, but I forget his last name. He's a member of the Federation, he'll probably do the job. But we can't do anything as long as the animals are in their lodges. I'll need you to put in writing that you're asking permission to dismantle the dam, since we're on private property. That's still your land, over there, across from their biggest lodge?"

"Yes. We have four acres west of the last cottage."

"Good. Wait for the trapper and show him the dam. I'll go along the river to see if there are any others. We don't want to cause a domino effect."

"You don't need to do that, Madame Robichaud. My son was here on the weekend and he went down the river in a kayak. This is the only one. The town knew all about it. Didn't they say anything to you?"

"No. I'll go right over to their offices. We'll need to get the machinery ready. A shame no-one told me about it earlier. Technically, yesterday was the deadline for not inter-fering with spawning grounds, but now there's no choice. We'll have to open up a breach with a power shovel. In the meantime, do you have sump pumps?"

"They're all running full time."

"Good. Wait for the trapper and the town officials. I'm going to put pressure on them to make things happen faster."

The sky is growing dark with rain clouds.

"Thanks, thanks for coming."

"Always a pleasure to see you."

"Likewise. And talk to your friends. Maybe there's a Wildlife Protection Officer looking for a cottage with water off the front porch."

She laughs, without pleasure, then walks me to my truck. My coffee has gone cold and is scarcely drinkable.

If the town had reacted faster, we might have been able to scare away the poor beavers. Now Gilles has no choice.

He will have to use traps that kill. The lack of communication will cost lives. At least the hides will go to the taxidermist's in Saint-Aubert and the meat will be eaten.

At the town hall, I suspect the officials were secretly hoping that the poor people from the campground would be flooded out once and for all. That they would lose their spots and have their tiny cottages demolished to make way for a new vacation site for rich taxpayers. The town could claim the land as far as the floodline.

I go to their offices and throw my weight around. I shake up the assembly of gossipers who were going on about how Mrs Something's car was seen in front of Mr So-and-So's place. They drag their feet, but finally they get moving. I run through the points on my to-do list: the trapper who will capture the animals that will be sacrificed, the equipment that will have to be rinsed so hydrocarbons won't get into the water. Then I will have to follow up on everything with one of my colleagues with a landline so I can write my report. The town bigwigs give me hostile looks. I ignore the secretary-treasurer, who is pulling her hair out over the costs incurred by dismantling the dam. I don't bother to comment on her new desk made of black-cherry melamine that fills the room, nor the two giant screens, the thermopump that regulates her climate, the stylish art on the walls and the beige stucco finish that complements her makeup. I do what I have to do, no small talk. I'm angry at having to participate in the death of animals, which could have been avoided if people had been more efficient. It wasn't the beavers' fault. They set up house in the wrong place.

"Thanks. Have a good day. Here's my colleague's card. She's in Wildlife Protection, and she'll be your contact person for this job."

The metal door slams behind me, and I jump. Outside, thunder rolls. A storm is brewing. I put Coyote on a leash and take her for a walk in the village. She needs the exercise since I don't let her run free in the forest. My uniform attracts attention. Three men in rocking chairs on the porch of the veterans' home call out greetings. Coyote sniffs every post and wants to go faster. I feel like people are watching my every move. What village do you live in, poacher?

The rain on the road is hypnotic, and I drive the remaining kilometres to Lionel's place without a thought in my head. The mental timeout does me good. Then I recognise a vehicle driving past, a Jeep with enormous wheels made to take on the roughest logging roads. My hamster starts spinning twice as fast.

You come to my place on foot, from behind. There is an entrance not far from where you hide your vehicle to go poaching near the hunting camp, and you also have an invisible parking spot near Lionel's cabin, on the banks of the Rivière-aux-Perles. If you came prowling around my place at least twice when I was away, that means you were watching me. You chose your times to set up the trail camera, hang the trap at my window and put the fur on my bed. And pick up the memory card while you were at it. You must have been pissed off not to recover the one sitting in my pocket. Everything was going so well until I sabotaged your setup.

You struck back to frighten me with the trap and the fresh skin on my bed. It must have special value in your eyes, am I right? It really is exceptional. I never saw a coyote that red. Why did you give it to me? A peace offering? Or the hand of a pervert softening up his prey, getting an eyeful, salivating, patient, before sinking his teeth into its neck?

A horn blares behind me. I was at the stop sign, lost in my thoughts. My heart rate goes back to normal when I reach the paved highway that leads left towards civilisation. And right, into a spiderweb of logging roads that wander, trackless, all the way to the American border.

I am caught in a vortex, a Bermuda triangle in the forest, driving in circles. I don't know where to go. Straight to Lionel's cabin, to the office to hand in my report, or to the lab to show them the evidence? The sun is beginning to go down. I call my colleague and confirm tomorrow's tasks, then ask her to schedule me a tetanus booster in Rivière-du-Loup. My hands are healing nicely, but I don't want to take a chance. Truth is, I am stalling for time. There is no budget for an investigation and the resources needed to produce well-documented evidence. I have to play my cards right. My two sleepless nights aren't helping. I can't make up my mind. I think about Lionel, and what he would do in this situation. He always said his cabin is never locked, don't hesitate to use it. My hands are clammy on the wheel. My head says it's a good plan, but the poacher traps near his place. I could run into him. Coyote might get caught in his traps. Maybe I should sleep in a motel in town.

Listen, Raphaëlle, you're armed to the teeth, you're

driving a government truck and you have a radio. What's the worst thing that can happen to you – an unfriendly confrontation?

I don't know. I have a bad feeling. My instinct tells me something isn't right in that guy's mind. Or is my imagination twisting everything around?

Alright, I'll go and sleep in Lionel's cabin. He should be showing up for the moose hunt in the next few days; the rain won't change that. At least there's a solid door I can lock from the inside, not like my trailer. The poacher had no trouble forcing his way in. I come to the T-junction, turn onto the concession road along Rivière-aux-Perles, reach the bridge, then take the drive up to the cabin, trying to see if a vehicle is there. In front of me, tyre tracks have dug two long trenches in the mud.

A few metres ahead, a rusty black pick-up that smells like death. A hunter's truck. An old four-wheel drive made for the woods. I memorise the licence plate, then get out. I am going to confront my predator.

"Anybody there?"

No answer. I leave the door open in case Coyote wants to join. I get out and walk, though I'm not sure where I'm going. Coyote hops down, catches up to me and follows on my heels. I wander to the back of the lot, then retrace my steps. Suddenly I'm cold. My wet hair sticks to my forehead and rain streams down my cheeks. My lovely autumn, gone from flamboyant to lugubrious. A bad turn. I go over to the vehicle.

The paint on the hood is a constellation of tiny impacts

from thousands of stones. A necklace of wolf teeth hangs from the rear-view mirror. I look around, then listen for footsteps. In the back of the pick-up, four-foot-long logs, a chainsaw, a gas can. Coyote sniffs the tyres. Lifts her leg and marks her territory. Our territory. I can't help but smile.

The seconds seem like hours.

I stare in through the driver's side window to see what is lying on the seat. Old gloves, sandwich wrappings, a little plastic case that must contain fishhooks, the usual stuff. Then my eyes fall on what I least expected. On the passenger side, a pile of well-folded clothes. My clothes! My wash that was hanging on the clothesline this morning at dawn, and that I abandoned in my hurry to get the hell out of there. On top of the pile, a pair of powder-blue underwear edged with ragged lace and, at the crucial place, unmistakable, a bloodstain. My blood.

He sniffed out my blood.

That bastard, he stole my clothes, my underwear. I hesitate, my hand on the door. I want them back but it's locked. I punch the window glass and the pain is immediate. I choke back a curse.

I have to stop myself from smashing the window with a rock. I won't let him leave with my clothes, especially not my underwear.

Coyote barks. Someone grabs me by the scruff of the neck.

9

The Cat Is out of the Bag

OCTOBER 2

"Don't you ever scare me like that again, Lionel! Oh, Papa Wolf, I'm so happy it's you."

"Me, too, girl!"

I hold my old friend in my arms. The tension in my neck vanishes. I bury my head in the crook of his shoulder. His wool sweater and his Santa Claus beard are scratchy. He smells of wet tobacco and smoked bacon.

Side by side, like father and daughter returning home, we go towards the cabin with its old shingled roof besieged by moss and pine needles.

Hiding by the scene of the crime is a good strategy, and so obvious that people dismiss it straight off. I decide that the cabin just might be the place to lie low. The reaction expected of me is that of a frightened prey taking to her heels. Instead, I will hunker down in the predator's shadow and go unseen. With two Cerberuses, not one.

We walk into the cabin that smells like smoke and mouse droppings. I will clean this place from top to bottom in exchange for my friend's hospitality. I have earned my asylum. The threat is real. Three or four black bears and one perverted trapper later, I have obtained refugee status.

Coyote immediately takes over the worn rug with its washed-out pattern, the same one she slept on during our clandestine stay on my birthday, less than a week ago. An eternity. The cream-coloured curtains are drawn and the windowsills lined with dead flies and fine dust. Part of me wants to push the heavier pieces of furniture against the front door and cower here, as quiet as a floorboard, as tense and ready as a bow. On my spot on the sofa, I will be more discreet than the rodents in the walls.

Happily, with Lionel here, my worst scenarios fade.

"I wanted to get back in time for your birthday, Raphaëlle, but I had problems with the pick-up. Damned piece of scrap! Can't trust it for two cents. I shouldn't have bought it, but my Toyota gave out on me, and I needed wheels to go hunting."

"You couldn't have shown up at a better time."

"You just about jumped out of your skin!"

"I didn't recognise your new truck. I thought it belonged to a badass poacher."

"You've got bags under your eyes."

"I just turned forty. Not getting any younger."

Lionel chuckles. His soft Sea Wolf eyes see the distress I cannot yet describe. He knows how a few clouds on the horizon can quickly give way to catastrophe. He has faced many storms in his time. He is a level-headed man who can anticipate danger on sea and on land; he has taught me everything about the woods in the time I've been here. We've spent hours walking the public lands to the major landmarks. The lookouts, the rock faces, Tall Pine. His bushy eyebrows curl up and touch his cap when the air is humid. Solid Lionel, a man who enjoys life generously. Everything you could want from a father. A woodsman who won't back down from a fight. He knows the age of trees and can identify a bird from its song. He comforts the little girl in me just by being here. Anyone who wants to hurt me would have to get past him first.

"I figured you'd be at your camp, but all your stuff was gone, except your clothes on the line. That seemed strange, especially when I saw your trailer door was kicked in. And since they said it was going to pour today, I gathered up everything that shouldn't get wet. Like you – you're soaked. I'll get you your things. I folded up everything, it's in my truck. Get some dry clothes on, then you can tell me what's up."

I feel such relief. Standing in his single large room, I peel off my wet things. Lionel closes the door and keeps his eyes on the floor as he hands me my dry clothes. Then he picks up what is lying at my feet and hangs them by the stove. Soon a fire is going with cardboard as kindling.

"You know, my girl, you can tell me everything. I've seen it all before."

"I know."

"What's happening? You don't look right."

"Something crazy. I don't know where to start."

I hang my wet socks on the pegs for mittens and crouch down next to the stove. I wipe the rain from my face with my shirttail.

"Anything to do with the three guys who disappeared?"

93

"No. I don't think so."

"Have they been found? Any news from the office?"

"We've been looking everywhere. I spent the weekend going over the concession roads in the back country, back and forth, in case I missed tracks running into a ditch or something. I drove every possible track around the hunting camp, then East Lake, up to the U.S. border."

"It doesn't look good for them. A week in the woods, and heavy rains on the way."

I drop onto the sofa. Coyote lies at my feet. I untie my braid and wrap it around the top of my head. One day I'm going to cut it off, once and for all.

"Tell me what happened, Raphaëlle. The whole thing."

"I flushed out a hard case, Lionel. And he's not just going after animals. One nasty poacher. He left me a hide. He's been watching me."

"He's the one who broke into your trailer?"

"Yes, and he's poaching around here, by your cabin. Things have gotten personal. This morning, my hands were shaking. I hear a noise and I jump, I feel like I'm being watched. I don't know how I'm going to go to work tomorrow. I'm trying to keep from smoking too much pot. Normally I only smoke on weekends, but now I just need to let go. I don't know if I'm being paranoid or if this really is trouble. I can't expect any help from the office."

My friend listens to my misadventures and says nothing. His gentle eyes urge me to spare no details, and go over every piece of evidence out loud. The shape of the crampons from the boot prints. The workings of the spring mechanism on the trap. The model of the trail camera. The phone number scribbled on the scrap of paper. The diary.

"Doesn't mean anything to me."

"What about Anouk B.?"

"Don't know the name. Go get the hide from your truck. I want to see his method, how he cut it. And lay out the big map of the regional park on the table. It's on top of the cupboard with the preserves."

With a pencil, I make a black dot for the trailer and the place where Coyote got caught.

"I think like you do. Your poacher is on foot. To get to the maples and the sugar shack, he must have parked in a woodlot to the north, right there, or else . . ."

"Or else what?"

"No, we're going at it from the wrong angle, Raphaëlle. The area is too vast. He must be in good shape, walking four or five kilometres an hour."

"There are dozens of access points on the logging roads."

"One thing's for sure. He's trapping by the maples and around here."

"That would explain why I've seen so many animals the last few weeks. I crossed paths with a bear and three cubs, and then I saw lynx tracks and raccoon scat."

"His traps must be everywhere. Let's make our lives simpler. We'll give him a code name. Any ideas?"

"Gargamel."

My Sea Wolf likes the nickname. From now on, I am under curfew until Gargamel has been neutralised and can do no further damage. Lionel loves investigations. His job took up so much space in his life that he lost his family. Being a game warden, back in the day and today as well, is a vocation. You don't stop wanting to protect animals just because your shift is over. You don't stop being concerned about them because your pension is in your bank account and you have hung your uniform in the closet. The vocation lives on in us and makes us who we are.

Lionel goes out to have a look at the spot where Coyote nearly met her death. I am angry at myself. I forgot something: the cage. The days went by, and I was so emotionally invested that I neglected the details. When I went back to pick up what I could and cut the snares, my eyes were on the ground. I didn't hear the animal. Maybe it was dead by then. A marten. Or a fisher. It wasn't big, but it had been in a nasty enough mood to spit at me.

The cabin is warm now. I heat up some pork and beans in a little pot. Stir it as I stare out the window. Lionel comes back with a plastic bag. He drops it on the front step before taking off his boots in silence.

"Your sign is gone. And I didn't find any other traps. But good God, there are bones everywhere. A regular cemetery."

He hands me a pink collar. A medal and a tiny bell hang from it.

"What's this?"

"Read it."

"Kitty Galipeau."

"The address is on the back."

Lionel goes back outside and pulls the cat out of the bag. He shows it to me through the window. *Rigor mortis*, its tongue out. A nice tortoiseshell colour. He puts it back in its plastic shroud.

"I feel bad, Lionel. It's my fault. The cat was alive when I found Coyote that night."

"It won't be the first time we've found pets in traps."

"I can't take it any more. I've got a crazy person after me, the lynx quota just got abolished, people are shooting everywhere in bow-and-arrow season, the three guys who disappeared must be dying somewhere as we speak, and now a dead cat. Coyote could have ended up like that."

"Your dog will be alright. Huskies are tough. She's not even whimpering."

"I know, I know."

"What's your plan, Raphaëlle?"

"What do you mean, my plan?"

"When it comes to that crazy bastard Gargamel, you and me are going to catch him. I have an idea who he might be. I was still working, you know, when that young woman disappeared in 2013. In my whole career, I never saw a case so badly bungled. Like someone on the inside decided to slow down the procedures. We ended up with two teams. One that worked on the alleged poaching in the area, and the other from the provincial police that investigated the missing person. But the left hand didn't talk to the right. When the dust settled, no charges were laid. But we suspected who did it. Gossip, rumours. The same name kept coming up when the beer loosened people's tongues in the bar. We searched for a while at the office, but the poaching equipment we seized was sealed, part of the exhibits.

And we were told loud and clear to let the real police do their work."

"The young woman was never found?"

"Why do you think I walk in the woods so much, Raphaëlle? Sure, I like fresh air and all. I'm still looking for her."

"No body, no murder. But why did you quit if the investigation meant so much to you? You could have told me about it. I could have searched and reopened the file."

"My old colleagues weren't necessarily my friends. Some of them are still working. I didn't want to ruin the atmosphere for you. The office made it clear: I had exceeded my duties. They told me in no uncertain terms to trust the provincial police and get back to my job. But on my own time, I would go by the Scout camp and walk the woodlots. We must have missed something, we needed just one solid element of proof and they'd let us reopen the investigation. You have to understand, Raphaëlle, that back in 2013 there were all kinds of shifty people on the team who didn't want the truth to get out."

"I understand. Which is where this funny feeling comes from. You think there's a link between the woman who disappeared in 2013 and the traps and the poacher spying on me?"

"There are two young women, and a lot of coyotes. When you talk about coyote trapping around here, the same name keeps coming up. I'll tell you the whole story. But first, let's change your bandages and take the cat back to its rightful owner."

"Lionel, tell me something. Do you like checking hunting licences?"

"Is that a joke? It's like asking a cop if he likes stopping speeders. It's a punishment, sitting cooped up in your truck and waiting, watching people come out of the woods, loaded down with game."

"Same with me. I'm taking shifts at the welcome centre next week. My hands need time to heal. Officially, I can drive, but holding a pencil is too painful."

Lionel takes a red case down from the wall. I have never seen such a well-equipped first aid kit. He has had his share of injuries in his life and it shows. A career in the bush, pursuing people off the beaten track. I unwind my bandages. The cuts are healing nicely. A few layers of gauze and I'm ready to go.

"We'll take your truck, Raphaëlle. My pick-up isn't up to it."

"Come on, Coyote."

We head for Mill Road. A trim little house with a manicured lawn and pink petunias in window boxes. The door opens before I can knock. The lady must have been watching from behind the blinds. She stares nervously at the truck where Lionel waits.

"Good day. Madame Galipeau?"

"That's me," she says, her eyes on the box under my arm.

"Raphaëlle Robichaud, Wildlife Protection."

I don't have to explain. She takes the box and holds it to her breast. Lionel and I placed the cat inside next to its collar, nestled on a length of jute. She opens her eyes wide when she recognises me. We came across each other at a village meeting the time she denounced some kids who had chased a moose on their snowmobile until the animal dropped dead of exhaustion. I remember her car afterwards, covered with eggs and toilet paper.

"Madame Robichaud, I can finally stop looking for her."

She thanks me from the heart, tears in her eyes, as if I had saved her cat by climbing the tree behind her house and bringing it back to her, safe and sound.

"Do you know who might have done this? Who's trapping in the area?"

Silence.

"It's too close to people's houses. The trappers' code of ethics states they have the responsibility to keep a safe distance to avoid the accidental capture of domestic animals. I wouldn't want other families to lose their pets. I nearly lost my dog last week."

"Nearly? He survived?"

"Yes. She."

"You're lucky. Listen, we all know who traps around here. But we don't want to make waves. Everyone knows everyone else, you understand. The truth will eventually come out."

The woman lowers her voice, though no-one could possibly hear us. Including Lionel, sitting nearby in my truck. She runs her eyes along the skirt of the forest. I think of the boot prints by my trailer. Imagine the poacher in his jacket with stained sleeves, his head hidden under his hood. I watched too many horror films growing up. I'm ruined for life. It is better to picture him as a cartoon Gargamel. He is less real that way.

"You're afraid of this trapper, aren't you?"

She avoids the question.

"Thank you for taking the time to bring back my precious Kitty. I'm going to bury her in the yard beneath the lilac. Have a good day."

The woman in her pink Phentex slippers retreats a step, hand on the doorknob. The conversation is over. I smile out of courtesy and head back towards Lionel, disappointed.

As I am going down the first step, she whispers a man's name.

His name.

Your name.

10

My Lone Wolf

OCTOBER 3

The mountain is a promise. If I reach it I will be saved. No looking back. The beast is not far behind. I am barefoot, but I don't feel the pain of frostbite, just an immense weight, as if with every step I have to lift enormous snowshoes that sink deep into the unforgiving, powdery snow. I watch myself from above, running like prey, hoping the Appalachians will offer salvation. I am wearing a long white coat and the coyote's red fur on my shoulders. I can make out the shadow pursuing me, but from above, as if my eyes were an eagle in the sky. The white snow is blinding. I watch myself bog down, leap forward, accelerate, exhausted. That is what the predator is counting on. I run in endless pursuit, and I will not give up. I am not young, but I am running for my life. I don't know why I want to reach the summit so badly. Even if I escape the shadow, the cold will not spare me. The black beast uses my imprints in the snow to move forward quickly, it feels no fatigue, it knows that with its endurance it will soon catch me. My lungs are exploding, my throat is pierced by arrows of ice. The creature is only a few strides behind. I hear its rattle, or is it my own? I imagine its cry, or the eagle's cry. I stumble and succumb, my red face in the snow, my throat on fire and my mittens covered with frozen crystals that do not melt. The cold fills my pores, turns me to stone. I lift my torso, afraid my chest cavity will break apart. It is the end, I am spitting blood, my breath whistling like the wind. The beast is on me, there, close by, sniffing me, lying on my back. Parting my coat. Its fangs in my neck, grabbing my wrists and pinning me down. Pain spreading, the heat intense: it is stripping me of my skin.

Bang!

I leap from the bed, gasping for breath.

An evening grosbeak has broken its neck against the window glass. I look out at the misty edge of the forest. The flock of birds as yellow as birch leaves veers upwards. In the darkness, among the trunks of the cedars, an illusion tricks me. Someone is there, standing, watching. The remains of my nightmare.

Coyote rubs her flank against my calf. I open the door for her and she grabs the bird from the ground. She will find a spot further on to dissect the victim. The figure I thought I saw has faded into nothingness.

Lionel is snoring in his rocking chair by the woodstove. My wool Hudson's Bay blanket is tucked under his chin. I have never understood how people can sleep sitting up with their arms crossed over their chests. I accepted the sofa bed and deprived my old friend of the sleep he needs. As if he's heard my thoughts, he opens one eye, shifts his weight and returns to the arms of Morpheus. I put on my socks and creep out onto the porch without waking my host. Since

I was yanked from sleep at dawn by an evening grosbeak and a nightmare, I might as well wash off my anxieties. I am not going to let Coyote run free, not with traps all around. I drag myself to the pump and lift the arm. It squeaks in protest, but in no time my pail is full. I rub myself with a half-frozen washcloth. My skin turns red, prickles and shivers. The water wakes me up faster than a thermos of coffee. The bite of the cold is persistent, like the memory of my bad dream. The sun prepares its timid arrival. As I dress hurriedly and do battle with my clothes, my nightmare returns. The black beast. I make a quick braid, push a hat over my wet hair, and go to the truck. The north-east wind runs through me like a flight of harpoons. I call my dog. She does not come at first. Fear takes over again. I open the door; she was in my blind spot the whole time. To my relief, she jumps onto the seat.

As I drive, I feel the memory card digging into my thigh. I can't wait to sit down at my office computer and begin my investigation in earnest. With my colleagues out in the field, I will use the privacy for the more delicate parts of my research. I think of the pieces of the puzzle I described to Lionel, and get the feeling he is holding something back. He has a bone to pick as well, and is not ready to tell me everything.

In my defence, Your Honour, I must beg your pardon. I did everything backwards. I destroyed the integrity of my evidence, I transported it from one place to the next, from the trailer to the cabin, the cabin to my truck, I threw everything in a cardboard box on the back seat covered with dog hair. I will have nothing worthwhile to take to the forensics lab. But part of me is relieved I had the smarts to keep everything to myself, without getting my colleagues involved. The mole Lionel mentioned could still be among us.

*

Yesterday, on the road back to the cabin, Lionel and I listened to the radio. The vehicle that belongs to the three missing men was discovered near East Lake. The fate of those men weighs heavily on Lionel. They are the same age as he is. Getting bogged down on a muddy track could happen to anyone, starting with me. With no mobile network in the back country and no-one within walking distance, their only hope would be to find shelter in a hunting camp with food and water. But not everyone leaves their doors unlocked for the neighbours. They would be more likely to come up against individualism, materialism, double-locked doors, surveillance cameras and barricaded windows – that is my experience.

I concentrate on driving. But in my mind, I repeat the name the woman whispered to me. It is a kind of mantra. When I park and cut the engine, the radio goes silent. I can't help it, I have to talk about it.

"Lionel, Madame Galipeau mentioned a name."

"Shh, don't say anything. I'll help you, you can count on me. But for now, keep the name to yourself. We'll call him Gargamel, like in the Smurfs. I don't want us to influence each other. We'll compare our results when the time comes. Are you going to the office tomorrow?"

"You bet."

"Good. Do your research, but on a computer that no-one else uses. Don't leave evidence. And if you can, print me up a photograph of the dirty creep who set up the trail camera."

*

I never drove the road between Saint-Bruno and La Pocatière so fast, nor walked through the office door so early. The place is quiet. I fill two coffee cups to the brim and sit down in my cubicle. I slip the S.D. card into my personal laptop that I keep here, since I can't recharge it in my trailer with no electricity. I cross my fingers and hope it will work, that the technology will recognise a kindred spirit. The machine could decide to act unfriendly and declare its incompatibility. Not this time. A window opens. *Click, click, click.* The files are downloaded.

The horror appears.

It is like staring at a clear cut, the forest devastated, the earth vulnerable. Pictures of me, naked.

I choose the series dated September 27 and scan the pictures of my last shower, the morning I turned forty. It is like travelling back in time. Seeing myself naked on film casts me into the past, to the high school party that ended badly in a basement bathroom. I had drunk too much, smoked too much, maybe somebody slipped me some G.H.B., I will never know. I was the last party girl with a horde of horny teenage boys making fun of me. Instead of wiping up my vomit, holding back my soiled hair, they amused themselves by pulling up my sweater. *Come on, Raphaëlle, show us what you got.* Every move made them bolder. *Do it, man, she passed out, I want to see her tits.* There were steps, someone coming down the stairs. My best girlfriend found me, got the boys out of the room, sobered me up. Good thing I earned my diploma before digital cameras and social media came along. Would I have finished my studies if they had put the pictures of me they had taken that night on the net?

I scroll back, fighting the urge to delete the whole thing. I look at pictures of me washing. I am absent in one series, the morning the mother bear was patrolling the path. She sniffs around but does no damage. To think I was afraid of her! Another file, an earlier date. A doe and her fawn move through the maple grove, eating fallen apples. Thirty or so photographs of them enjoying a leisurely family meal. The next file dates back a week and a half. Eureka! A man in army boots, hood on his head. He steps away from the camera. That's it. You just replaced the memory card, you shameless pervert. The first picture of the bunch. Your bearded face stares into the camera. You must be adjusting it to make sure the lens is positioned right. I look into your deep green eyes.

Eyes like that I won't forget.

Loud conversation announces my colleagues' arrival. They are talking about the missing men, whether or not they've been found. Hurriedly I print a colour copy of the last image, fold it in four, and bury it in my uniform pocket. I close all the windows on my desktop, eject the memory card and slip it into my wallet.

I dial the number written in pencil on the scrap of torn paper. No answer, no answering machine. You have to give informers time. Then I get an idea.

I go online and type in *Sexy Quebec woman hunter*. I am rewarded with a picture of a chick in rain boots, corduroy pants and a forest-green hat kneeling next to a freshly killed male deer with impressive antlers. *Voilà*, my new profile picture. For the background, I use the covered bridge in Saint-Onésime-d'Ixworth. A few passes over the keyboard and my fake Facebook account is a done deal. I add some pseudo-friends, I like some pages – Three Lakes Outfitters, Husqvarna, L.S.L. Singles, Harley-Davidson – and publish some sunsets on the Saint Lawrence, toes in the sand and cute chihuahuas to complete my local identity.

Then I type in the suspect's name that the lady in the Phentex slippers whispered to me.

Marco Grondin.

I hear my colleagues' conversation.

"One of them was found!"

"Yeah, too late. And it looks bad for the other two."

Before I click on Marco Grondin's profile picture – I'm sure it's him – I take a deep breath. Keep it all inside. The big man with the green eyes stares back at me. Handsome like all heartbreakers. Like the serial killers behind bars whom no-one ever suspected. You, Marco, masturbating to photographs of me taking a shower with Mother Nature. You, Marco, poaching coyotes out of season and trapping people's pets because, out of sheer laziness, you set your snares along roads in residential districts. You broke into my trailer, rummaged through my things, then laid your best trophy on my bed. Have you developed a fascination for your prey? Did you want to violate another part of my privacy? Are you going to accept my friend request?

Yes, says the little red flag at the top of my screen. That didn't take long.

I print your profile photograph: you showing off with the stiff body of the red coyote like a stole around your shoulders.

11

Rough Thelia

OCTOBER 3

My headlights illuminate the edge of the woods. There were too many people at the office and too many things rattling around in my head. I decided to go back to Lionel's cabin with my laptop riding on the passenger's seat. You never know.

A note on the table tells me he is at the garage for his pick-up, and that he intends to spend the night at his camp by the river. He needs time to think. I put down the thick file unearthed from the dusty cabinet at the office – the file labelled "Marco Grondin". As a cover page, I place the printed photograph face down on the folder. The picture from the memory card, his eyes in full view.

I lock the cabin door from the inside, feed Coyote and roll myself a fat one. My mission: get the poacher's profile out of my mind. The stiff dead coyote, flaming red like the blazing colours of fall, draped around the victorious trapper's shoulders.

You're as proud as a peacock. Your friends posted their comments. *One less damned coyote on this earth. We should kill them all, they're vermin. Good catch, Marco, you going to make a cap out of it?*

The photograph is two weeks old. Before that one, you were standing – yes, standing – on a bear carcass. And then there is that post in the middle of summer, where you are selling fifty coonskin caps. One of your friends chimes in: *Did you kill them all yourself?*

I feel like vomiting. Find a memory hole in my brain, cannabis. I have seen so many corpses I have begun thinking of my own deathbed. Just make sure it's not a coyote hide, or a snowy mountain with a black beast peeling off my skin. I escape on the wings of smoke and the diary of a woman unknown, her poetry, her lists of northern moss and fantasy drawings. All that to forget the lone wolf on my trail. The soothing effect of C.B.D. makes itself felt. My jaw relaxes. I travel through the pages of the diary, making it mine, staring at the drawings of lichen and leaves in the margins. I reread the passages that bring me peace, and avoid imagining myself murdered in the line of duty.

On a bed of bearberry, when my long hair, red like peat moss burned by the sun, mingles with the sphagnum, I will let my soul fly free.

I turn the page and discover what Anouk Baumstark will bequeath, and to whom. Her cabin and her little section of forest, in trust to Protec-Terre. Her car, to the battered women's shelter in Saint-Pascal. She wants her ashes to be scattered to the four winds where the taiga begins, anywhere so long as there are no people or buildings around.

I really should write a will. So few possessions, yet so precious. Starting with Coyote; she could stay with Lionel.

The next pages are addressed to her father, and the Universe. Suddenly I feel very alone. I wonder who I would write to, apart from Lionel. I face the paradox of who I am, and my failure with Sophie.

Maybe some part of me was afraid to get involved and be revealed completely. I needed a secret garden where no-one could come in. I needed distance. Love on a leash is dependency. It's not that I don't want love, but I want it to be simple, like the call of the geese that follow the seasons with no questions asked.

I see myself without disguise. I clung to my secret garden even when I was part of a couple, and now I am disturbed by a stranger's voyeurism. But I am no better: here I am, fascinated by Anouk B.'s life. I disgust myself. I finish this last page, then shut the notebook, promising to put it aside. In any case, there is no relation between this hermit and my investigation. The diary was just the house-coat woman's excuse for approaching me. Which means I have no reason not to try to give the notebook back to its owner.

And then there is this rough sweetness in her words that does me so much good.

Why does the nomenclature of lichen make me think of the nicknames of whores from the far north? Maybe because the quilled botanists who named the lichens of Labrador praised the beauty of the vegetation as if they were making love to a woman with their tongues. Perhaps everything in Nature is ruled by sexual energy, from birth to copulation, conception to the final ecstasy, the whole procession orchestrated by the pineal gland. Maybe we can't escape the feminine condition and the dichotomy of gender. Trophy or captive, tease or easy virtue – whatever else, I am in a dead end because I prefer to make lists of northern mosses alone in my cabin than go out to the bar in the hope of meeting a warm body. One-night stands are not my style, even if I haven't fucked for a year. Not since Riopelle, that strange bird who fell from the nest, a rare bird who took flight too soon. At least my lunar cycle was right on time. Not that I don't want to fuck like an animal, but I'm afraid of what comes afterwards. Physical contact, yes, but the human kind, no, I don't want it. I am better off in isolation, studying my moss and not giving in to the desire to smell and bite and consume another body. Maybe it is instinct returning, because winter is coming and as the storms rage, I know that misanthropy will weigh upon me like snow on the roof. But I will not go to the bar hoping that a man or a woman will follow me back to this mouse-ridden hole, and hoping as well that after making love, he or she will understand that I don't want company for the rest of the night. I am better off being the companion only of poets and immersing myself in the sweetness of lichen names that take the place of caresses. Only that doesn't work. Everywhere, between the lines, there is this silky bed, moist and fiery, that inspires choreographies in me and moaning between the sheets.

Snow rock moss
Sprig moss
Curly beard moss
Rusty ragged moss
Recurved brotherella
Brown shield moss
Mountain thatch moss
False beard moss
Nut moss
Arctic hook moss
Round-stemmed entodon moss
Fan moss
Olney's grimmia
Narrow-leaved wetland plume moss
Polar brook moss
Ringless spoon moss
Millimetre moss
Small mouse-tail moss
Starlike bristle moss
Long-leaved fork moss
Hair silk moss
Awl-leaved pygmy moss
Common nodding moss
Thickpoint bloom moss
Elegant peat moss
Rough thelia
Crisped pincushion moss
Hoary rock moss
Ontario rose moss
Two-ranked moss
Rough Thelia[2]

Easy Pickings

OCTOBER 4

As I slalom down the dizzying main road that offers a magnificent view of the vast fields of genetically modified corn and soya in tight rows next to the manure sprayer, my mobile picks up the first bar of coverage. I park. I use my trip down to the village to call the housecoat lady. No answer, like before.

I am thinking of trying the evasive informer's number a second time when my telephone starts vibrating. The office is ordering me to proceed immediately to Kamouraska, Respite Road. The dispatcher's tone makes it clear that my being A.W.O.L. yesterday was duly noted, and that I had better make up for it by being a good soldier from now on. I start the truck and think of Lionel. By now he must be back home, and will have unfolded the photograph of the green-eyed poacher. I made sure not to leave him the one where the man is smiling like a bloodthirsty conqueror with the red coyote around his shoulders. I hope Lionel will be there when I return. And ready to say what must be said.

There is only one subject on the local radio station, and that is the misadventures of the three men who went missing

September 26. They did bog down on a muddy logging road at the end of the afternoon that day. They could not free the van from the mess, and spent the first night in the vehicle. The next day they began their long march, the sole survivor said, that saw them push deeper into the back country of the regional park, towards the American border, misled by an A.T.V. track that seemed to be heading somewhere. In the end, they decided to separate, hoping to increase their chances of finding help, a strategy that resulted in the tragic end of two of the three friends. The first was found dead in a bed in a hunting camp on Crown lands. A heart attack, according to the authorities, though they were waiting for the autopsy report. The second man's body was lying some twenty kilometres further on. Dead of dehydration, or so it appeared. The third man had some knowledge of outdoor survival techniques. He headed north, came across a stream and some wild berries. The search party located him on the American side of East Lake. The elected officials of the region all agreed on the reason for the tragedy. The complete lack of mobile phone coverage was intolerable. Two men perished and a third nearly died, yet they were all carrying telephones.

I turn off the radio and cut the engine. An endless freight train is passing on the grade crossing. I slip Marco Grondin's picture under the sun visor and take out the portrait of my great-grandmother. She looks back at me, her eyes full of animal fear. *Save me, somebody*. Like Coyote's brown eyes when she was caught in the trap. Then I read something new in this picture I have gazed at so often. Marie-Ange, her stiff posture, the appeal in her eyes, the position of her hands. Hands clasped, but not submissive. They are hands ready to grab a weapon. The determination not to be crushed by brute destiny.

What can we do to stop you, Marco? Your file tells the story of twenty years of infractions, supposedly accidental captures, exceeded quotas, frightened landowners who refuse to testify or even sign a written statement.

We would have to have a weighty file and experts to coach the witnesses before we could drag Marco Grondin before a judge who would order his toys to be seized, and let him stew in the juices of some nasty fines. That will never happen; the punishments are never more than symbolic. Nothing for the son of prosperous farmers.

A few slapped wrists over the years were not enough to keep you from getting back in the business. I will not rest as long as you are out there, prowling the back country. The injustice is too great. How many coyotes have you taken, even when the season isn't officially open? And who buys your furs? Foreign companies that sell them to rich city-dwellers who stroll with their coats open and their decorative hoods thrown back on their shoulders?

It's simply not cold enough in southern Quebec to wear furs made to protect a person from the biting Arctic winds. Red or black goose-down jackets with fur collars are all the rage. The explorer look just to cross the Champlain Bridge by car. Adornment for people who cannot spell or locate a single northern village on a map.

The cars of this endless freight train fly by at top speed.

Dozens of black tanks of heavy crude oil from Alberta, carrying the messages of graffiti artists. Followed by containers of every possible colour loaded with stuff imported from somewhere else. Maybe even a cargo of luxury coats with a new twist – lynx collars.

The fur trade is inseparable from the colonial history of this land. I am horrified by slippers trimmed with rabbit fur, or a majestic fox stripped for, at most, two hundred dollars, or the fact that a beaver hide is worth less than an hour's work at minimum wage. I was enraged when I read that more than a thousand coyotes were trapped in just one year in the lower Saint Lawrence region. Year after year. To that number, you have to add the ones that were poached and did not show up on any register.

Wow, a thousand, I tell myself as consolation. That means they're reproducing like pros!

I wonder where the thousands of bodies lie. I picture autumn leaves falling on skinned animals and hiding the crime scenes I could not find before the snow fell, wiping away the evidence. I know Mother Nature will not let those bodies go to waste. They will feed the humus and the hungry scavengers.

Nothing is lost, nothing is created, everything is transformed.[3]

The rusty containers rattle by to the sound of warning bells.

Instead of the Canadian Forces planes being used to support the Americans, they should be flying over our air space and counting the survivors. At least make an inventory before lifting the quotas on our northern beauties! How many Arctic foxes are left? At what parallel does clear-cutting actually stop? Why is it more important for a warplane to speed over the Atlantic than for our government to bring electricity to the First Nations reserves once and for all? Here's one for the authorities: how many F-18s would you have to sell off to eliminate hunger in this country?

Maybe if I went to bed with the right civil servant, I could get access to an infrared camera and cover my management unit digitally.

Give me the tools and I'll give you results, Boss Man. I will find the secret setups of poachers who have grown fat with impunity. No more returning dogs and cats with their collars to heartbroken families.

Crimes against animals often attract no attention. I have no-one apart from Lionel to tell how I feel. One of my colleagues once advised me to send my C.V. to a veterinarian clinic if I really wanted to take care of animals so badly.

Get with the reality, Mme Wildlife Protection Officer. You're a powerless pawn on the happy hunting grounds.

I was wrong to think that my role would be "to maintain the fragile equilibrium between humans, fauna and its habitats: to protect, educate, prevent". That was the Ministry's motto, though now it sounds more like the sophist rhetoric of *Brave New World*, served up with a *1984* sauce.

In the rear-view mirror, I can see that my eyes are ringed with dark circles. A volcano of emotions. Frustration: I am not serving Nature well enough. Anger: I have stopped belonging to the human tribe. I am afraid of losing control, bursting out in violent eruption, a lava flow that would tip these weapons over and set them on fire.

I cannot believe how long this train is. The proof of conspicuous consumption. I had better calm down. I take inventory of the objects around me and draw a deep breath.

My eyes fall upon Anouk's diary on the dashboard. By the time I give it back to its owner, I will have read every page. My unhealthy curiosity has turned to growing admiration. I have started imagining what she looks like. The train has me stuck here. I will read a final page.

When there are men around, you should know what to expect.

I am thirteen years old. A cold January, minus 20. I am starting to fool around with boys. My parents go to the cottage every weekend and leave me home alone. I am so hard to get along with that they would rather let me grow up too fast than tighten the parental controls and have me run away. They understand that much. I am underage, but with my mascara, steel-toed boots and black coat suitable for the funeral parlour, I look almost like an adult when I hit the corner store to buy the cheapest bottle of white wine and two chocolate bars. I pay for these luxuries with my babysitting and bathroom-cleaning money. The boys take care of the rest.

Four of us in a parked car. The motor is running to keep the heater and the radio working, but we aren't going any-where. I alternate swigs of wine with bites of chocolate. The cheap stuff goes down better that way. I know that by the time I finish the bottle, I will be good and numb, lulled by the siren song of Pink Floyd's backup singers.

"The Great Gig in the Sky" will be my farewell.

I don't remember the name of the driver who was rolling a joint under the yellowish dome light.

Then, surprise. Flashing lights are all around us. Panic in the car.

A guy in back I've started sleeping with tells me, "Anouk, give me the bottle. You've got nothing to worry about, you're underage, you'll be alright. Just look pretty and keep your mouth shut."

I hand my bag to the cop so he can search it. I'm not the one with something to worry about. One of my friends gets handcuffed in the slush. My favourite part of the tune accompanies our arrest. Then the piano falls silent. I open my coat to the cop's hands. By the time he is finished, he will know the curves of my body better than my premature boyfriend. The cop runs his hands over my intimate places, over and over again, to my distress.

"Alright," he tells me. "Spread your legs and put your hands on the hood."

No, not that. He forces me. His orders. I am not wearing mittens. I press my bare hands against the icy metal. The cop's fingers slip between my buttocks and examine my pelvic region. I close my eyes as tight as I can. The song sears the memory of fat fingers searching for the swelling of my lips, cursing the thickness of my jeans and his lack of time, since he needs to touch every part.

Have your fun, you pig. Just let me go when it's over.

My friends get arrested for possession, obstruction of justice, public mischief. The cops are so patient with me that my hands freeze to the car. Maybe their searching petrified me. I turned into a statue and they forgot all about me as they filled in their paperwork.

I was naive. I thought men my father's age would act like parents with me. The next day I had my first piano recital. I suspect my interpretation of Beethoven's second concerto was perfectly pathetic. It turned out to be the coldest possible interpretation, an ode to frostbite and the abuse of power.

Not until years later, when the ice gives way under my weight as I fill my kettles at the river, do I understand that my anxiety attack that night was entirely or partly the result of hypothermia.

In the ambulance, they scream at me to make me admit I do drugs. I can't stop shivering and hiccupping. Hyperventilating. Everything feminine and fragile in me is hurting.

"What did you take?"

"Dark chocolate and white wine."

"Don't joke with us," the vulgar ambulance attendant yells.

"I don't do drugs yet," I tell her. "I'm waiting to be of age."

"And a big mouth on top of it. Why are you shaking like that? Why are your pupils dilated?"

"Because I can't feel my hands. Because I'm afraid of you."

My only mistake was to sit in the front seat of a car where someone was rolling a joint. The cop who searched me to his heart's content threatens to call my parents.

"Go ahead. They don't care if I drink wine with my friends."

"You're not allowed to drink at your age. Especially not in a car."

"It was cold out. We just wanted to listen to music and stay warm."

The pain in my frostbitten hands increases with every beat of my pulse. The fear that I'll have to have my fingers amputated and never draw again. They keep yelling at me to tell them what I took.

"You let me freeze with my coat open and my hands on the hood!"

No expressions of regret. The fat-fingered cop offers to drive me home. I don't want him watching me go up the steps to my empty house with the Pink Floyd song in my head, and his hands lifting my tits to see if I am hiding something illicit.

My friends get taken to the cop station. I walk home, drunk and sullied.

I sit in the shower with my clothes on and let the hot water flow over me until the tank is empty. My hands are as red as lobsters. My soaked clothing hangs heavy. I get undressed and rub my skin with cold water to remove all trace of the rummaging fingers of authority. My history teacher at school. My karate coach. And plenty of men later, when I think about it.

Note to self: don't trust men. And trust cops even less.

The woman from the ambulance told my parents everything. They did not bawl me out. Instead, they advised me to extend my wariness to every human being I would meet for as long as I lived.

The next weekend, they went up to the cottage and I went back to the store to buy a bottle of wine and two chocolate bars.

13

The Big, Bad Great Horned Owl

OCTOBER 4

Once the train hauling bitumen and other horrors moves on, I drive past a patrol car and think of Anouk slumped in the shower, feeling dirty, one of the events in her life that made her want to live alone. I am going where I was told to go, towards Kamouraska, its topography sculpted by the ice age. Even if it is for work, I like coming here, travelling back in time with the houses and their mansard roofs, porches decorated by colourful gingerbread, breathing in salt and algae from the river, and the yeast of morning ovens. Crossing the village, I feel calmer, and picture myself fifty or a hundred years in the past. I imagine women knitting by the woodstove behind closed doors, setting their work aside for a quick pick-me-up to warm their insides, men reading a folktale out loud, shutters beaten by the wind, children giving life to their toys . . . the childhood I wish I'd had. The houses are built solid in Kamouraska, log constructions, their bright colours somehow fitting perfectly into the landscape. The handsome white one, the little blue one at the corner, the big brown construction by the wharf. Nothing in common with the prefabricated modern castles and architectural horrors displaying their bad taste. When you think it can't get worse, you reach the pork mega-factory a few roads further on. Installations made of wine-red plastic, fake fieldstone and sparkling black asphalt shingles. The municipalities welcome the great palaces of disposable animals with open arms in return for the juicy property taxes.

On Respite Road, I consider the position of the recalcitrant farmers who live by the Saint Lawrence. They refuse to respect the few metres of vegetation that is supposed to be left along the streams to filter out, in some small measure, the poisons from their fields. The river will swallow it all.

I park in front of the white cedar shake house. Remember, Raphaëlle, you are not here to remake the world, but to help a young woman in need. I examine the treetops for the nocturnal bird that apparently attacked her yesterday, which is the reason I was called here.

Good morning, Master Owl, perched at the top of your tree. Tell me, are you terrorising the neighbourhood? Count on me not to apply my office's protocol. By light of day, you must be in your nest. I am not sure of your intentions, though you must have had your reasons for attacking a woman of small stature at nightfall. Ah, now you are taking wing. Even from here, I can see your little tufts that look like cat's ears. Sorry to have bothered you.

I am not going to fire into the air to frighten the bird, or disturb it into abandoning its nest. Air-tight protocols are fine for the office, but every encounter with an animal is unique. Nothing is simple, guys. Using the violence of your service weapon is the last resort.

I once read the work of a journalist who described how

animal behaviour adapts. He took the case of elephants. In the Democratic Republic of the Congo, they learned to avoid ivory hunters and move closer to game wardens. In the Shaba Natural Reserve in Kenya, the pachyderms emigrated towards protected areas and did not cross their lines, despite the absence of borders. There was no visual indication of where the reserve began. Yet the elephants felt they were safe there; they knew they would not be shot at. They had the intelligence and sensitivity to discern the difference between humans, the enemies and the allies, and move into spaces where they would survive. So don't ask me to pull out my gun and frighten the fauna for every little problem. If I meet up with them when I am in a vulnerable situation, I hope the animals will anticipate my good intentions, and how I have always opposed those who would ruin the reputation of my species.

Bang bang, he shot me down . . .[4]

Lionel took Coyote into the woods with him, and I miss her already. She has made a place in my heart, especially since I thought I might lose her. I swallow the rest of my cold coffee, salute the picture of Marie-Ange on the sun visor, and slip on my officer's decorum.

A teenage girl opens the door. She is wearing a lime-green dirt bike helmet and clutching a paddle to her chest as if her life depended on it. Her bangs are plastered to her forehead. I put out my hand. She puts down the paddle.

"Raphaëlle Robichaud, Wildlife Protection Officer."

"Daphnée Santerre. Glad to meet you. Thanks for coming so quickly."

I shake her hand. It is clammy. She must have had a sleepless night, too. Nervously, she describes the bird that attacked her several hours ago.

She takes off her helmet and places it by the paddle next to the front door. On the kitchen table, a first aid kit is open and its contents spread about.

"You came at just the right time. I need help changing my bandage. You can see what an angry owl can do to a person. The wound isn't deep, but it hurts like hell."

Luckily, yesterday evening she was wearing a jean jacket on top of a thick polar fleece. Both items are torn at the shoulder and stained with blood. They, too, were left in the front hallway. As I help her apply ointment to the nasty cuts on her forehead, we begin talking like a couple of old friends.

"Were you able to see the bird that did this to you?"

"Yes. It was an enormous dark-brown owl with little ears and a high-pitched voice like fingernails on a chalkboard, only louder. Like a freight train putting on its brakes."

"A great horned owl."

"I've never been so scared in my life! I thought it had torn my shoulder off!"

The injured girl lets her emotions flow. It was dark out. When she reached the cabin that her family usually uses only in summer, Daphnée brought in her things, using her car headlights to see her way in. Her arms were loaded down, and she hurried towards the door. That's when she got hit in the shoulder the first time. She dropped the cooler on her foot. The sudden pain in her toes. Frightened, she ran towards the porch. In total silence, no sound of wings or feathers, the owl returned from behind and swooped down on her again, its wings extended, attacking her with its talons a second time.

I open my logbook to take notes as the girl tells me the story of the assault, not stopping for breath.

"I was feeling for the doorknob in the dark and telling myself how stupid it was that I couldn't find it because it's my family's cabin and I've been coming here forever, but I couldn't find the door or my keys to get in even though I'd put them in my pocket. I started searching my jacket pockets and then my pants, not in this one not in that one, but they had to be somewhere and then I thought maybe I'd dropped them at the same time as the cooler but I was too afraid to leave the porch and that's when it came back and attacked me again. Its beak was wide open and I was scared it would tear off another piece of me or put out my eyes. I felt my jacket tear and then a burning feeling and the blood flowing into my bra. I curled up in a ball in front of the door to protect myself and started crying and then I felt my keys stabbing me through my jacket. I managed to get into the cabin, but it didn't go away. It wanted to attack me again I saw it outside and heard it screaming. It hurt my ears, it kept banging into the window like it knew it could break the glass and come into the living room and finish me off. I never imagined an animal would throw itself against a window to come and kill someone . . ."

She pulls her clothing away from her shoulder and takes off the bandage she managed to paste on with one hand. It is not possible to see how serious the wound is. The entire area is covered in dried blood.

"Daphnée . . ."

"Why? Why me? What did I do to deserve this?"

"Daphnée, take a deep breath. On the count of three, I'm going to disinfect the wound. Ready? One, two, three. That's good. Breathe out now, I'm going to apply the gauze."

"Ouch!"

"It's almost over. The wound is clean. It doesn't look infected."

I push the sterile gauze against her skinny shoulder. Her whole body is trembling. She is hyperventilating. I look at the damage; luckily she was wearing two layers. Owl talons are like razorblades.

"You should take a bath with sea salt or a little fir oil. You need to calm down, and the water will help cleanse the smaller wounds. But keep your shoulder dry, out of the water."

"I understand. Thanks. You sound like my mother, I like that."

"Do you want me to call her?"

"No. No need. She's right here."

Daphnée points to her heart.

"Sorry."

"This would have never happened to her. She had a way with animals, like a green thumb, she fed the birds, even the raccoons. They loved her at first sight, and they would come right up to her. She spent her last days wrapped in a blanket on the porch watching the blue jays eat from their feeders. They would hop up to her chair like they knew she couldn't come to them. All she wanted was to watch them with the tenderness she had left. That summer we built a million bird houses and stuck them on every post. When Mama died, we stopped putting seeds in the feeders."

"You should start filling them again. The birds will come back. It's true, feeding them can interrupt their migration patterns, but feeders are part of the cooperation between our species. Think about it. Seagulls take advantage of ploughed fields, robins perch in our fruit trees, herons find food in our ponds, small seed-eaters do very well around our silos, birds of prey take care of road kill and the remains hunters leave behind, and seabirds follow boats. With all the tree-cutting and drought, I think feeding them is the right thing to do."

"But the owl was trying to feed on me. Why do you think it was doing that?"

"It could be rat poison. It creates dementia in large birds of prey."

"I don't get it."

I hesitate. Will she accept my explanation? She doesn't seem very friendly towards the Strigidae. At the same time, here is an opportunity to get her to reconsider her place in the food chain.

"Owls that live around farms eat a lot of small rodents. And the mice and rats in barns, over their lifetime, eat a lot of microdoses of poison. Not enough to kill them right away, but the toxic materials are stored in their tissues, and the predators that feed on them are poisoned in turn.

Biologists have studied the issue. They've noticed changes in the behaviour of birds of prey exposed to accumulations of poison. They become more aggressive and unpredictable. Or they die before their time. But before they do, they go out of control, probably because their nervous systems have been interfered with."

Daphnée looks unimpressed. I ask her to point out the path she took so I can have a look around. Maybe with my binoculars, I will be able to spot feathers, leftover bones, droppings or the signs of a nest at the top of the tree.

In the wet grass, the girl's footsteps are even until half-way between the car and the porch. The cooler was left open on the ground. Long running strides mark the progress of her flight.

Daphnée taps on the window and points to the tree where, she believes, the bird lives. She opens the door a crack.

"Before you came, I put on my helmet and got the paddle. I was going to set out some fondue meat at the foot of the tree. I thought we could trap the bird in a cage."

Great horned owls are nocturnal, I explain to her, and animals are not so easily tricked.

If I call the office, my colleagues will suggest chopping down the tree to force the horned owl to fly off to another spot. Daphnée does not know what to think, poor girl. I am a Wildlife Protection Officer, and I will have to find a solution. But I don't have one that won't leave two more victims, one vegetal, one animal.

"Isn't there anything I can do to make the owl go away?"

"You can cut down the tree where it nests. I have a tree service guy's card in my truck. You want it?"

"I couldn't do that. My father would go nuts. My mother buried all the placentas from her pregnancies there. She said the tree was sacred. She used to talk to it from her rocking chair on the porch, like it could answer her. 'My tree of wise counsel', she called it. We scattered her ashes at the foot of it."

Her mother must have been a wise woman indeed with her companion tree and the birds she loved to feed.

"To tell you the truth, I wouldn't want to cut down such a majestic tree either. I'm afraid I can't do much for you, Daphnée. There is no magic formula to drive away horned owls and keep them away. And nothing says it actually nests here. But you know what? I've got a feeling it won't come back. It probably set up shop in that tree because no-one was living here and everything was quiet. You told me you normally only come in summer. If I have one piece of advice, it's this: make noise when you go out, exaggerate your steps, announce your presence when you're outside."

"Announce my presence? Like how?"

"Talk at the top of your voice, sing, whistle. The animals will hear you ahead of time. When we surprise them, that's when they react badly. Here's my card. Stay in touch."

"Thanks."

"Before I go, I'd like to ask you a question. But it has to stay between you and me."

"What is it?"

"Grondin & Brothers, at the end of the road. Do you know the family that has the farm?"

"Not really. We're not much for being neighbours, and they work all the time."

"I see. Thanks."

"I should thank you, Raphaëlle."

"Remember to change your bandages regularly, alright?"

"Don't worry about me. But one thing . . . Maybe I shouldn't mention it, but there's a rumour. People say there's a giant pile of carcasses at the back of the Grondins' land, hidden under last year's manure. The smell bothers the neighbours. It can't only be dead cows, right? But maybe you shouldn't go there, those people don't like company."

"I did smell something on the way here. Thanks for the info, Daphnée. And take care of yourself, promise?"

I finish my report in the truck. In my logbook I register the date, time and a few details and half-truths. I am careful to omit the possibility of a nest so the tree will stay standing with the owl undisturbed. In the distance, I spot dark birds turning circles. Probably an animal crushed on the road, every scavenger's delight.

The sun is going down and I haven't eaten all day. I'll take a look at Grondin & Brothers tomorrow. Right now, I need to put something in my stomach, then talk over the investigation with Lionel. Daphnée watches me drive away from her house. She waves and points at the opportunists swooping down in spirals.

As excited as a child who has found the key to a treasure, she calls, "Just follow the vultures!"

14

Just Follow the Vultures

OCTOBER 5

Back at the cabin, Coyote is the only one expecting me. Lionel left without a note after papering the cabin walls with thumbtacked pages of Marco Grondin's legal history, all in chronological order. From the right of the stove, they run all the way to the front door. Twenty years of informers. Twenty years of carnage.

I take a long walk with my convalescing patient who is almost over her injuries.

Everywhere I look, poacher, you are in the autumn mists. I have lost – only temporarily, I hope – the carefree feeling I once had in the woods. How can I get rid of you? An anonymous phone call to the police? That won't work because I have the evidence, and it is not admissible any more. I could admit my errors of judgment to the Ministry and hope that other officers from our F.A.M.U. will succeed where I failed. But I would risk losing my job, not to mention the not very encouraging precedent Lionel told me about. Would the Grondin family be open to a subtle warning that their son should change the way he makes a living? That's a non-starter, especially since they're hard cases, according to Daphnée. Maybe some journalist would appreciate a scoop, but I am afraid of making more enemies without accomplishing anything in return. I'm the outsider, after all.

You're a big fish. It is going to be a long haul, a perilous hunt, a fishing expedition that will need a miracle catch. One of the biggest challenges of my career. I could take your picture and have it framed like a trophy. But I will not hang your portrait in my office. No, in the outhouse instead.

I go to bed early, my dog at my feet, lulled by the wood-stove's heat. No use thinking about tomorrow. Better get some rest. But sleep is a trap.

*

I am blindfolded. My hands are tied to the ceiling beam with snare wire. My clothes cut away in front as if a doctor had to perform an emergency operation. Calloused hands grab the bait of my body. The smell from the open container on the counter. The odour of suet. His greasy hands cover me with musky paste. I hear his laughter close by, and feel his breath. He comes into me as he whispers in my ear.

"It's snow-goose fat, sweet thing. I'm going to ream you out until I've had my fill, and when I've had all the fun I want, I'm going to take you out into the woods, to my traplines. There's nothing better than a female in heat to attract coyotes. You're finally going to meet those friendly little animals you love so much."

I feel the man's penis harden and pulse. The fat liquifies in the heat of our bodies and runs down my legs. Like a stuffed turkey, the smell of rancid fat and dead fowl. My arms are numb, pins and needles.

"You'll see, your coyotes are a lot meaner than me. You know, it didn't have to end this way. You could have let me go on trapping. You could have accepted the fur as my little present and kept your mouth shut. We could have had a back country romance. But you had to stick your nose and everything else into my business!"

I picture the smashed door of my trailer and the skin of the red coyote on my bed. I don't want to die today. I cling to life like the beam that keeps my arms extended. Move my fingers, get the circulation going again. Find a way out. There has to be some promise I can make to dissuade my rapist. Convince him to cut me down. I won't fight. I know how to play dead, it's part of the survival instinct. I also know how to jam my thumbnails into his eye sockets. I hear the sound of a zippered case opening.

A pair of rough hands dishonours my temple. I am afraid for its silk curtains. Finely sharpened blades at the bottom of my neck chop off my hair. My braid falls onto the floor. I picture my skull on the pile of bones, one more rape victim in the woods who will never be found.

Marie-Ange Robichaud turns into a crow. She is calling, loud and harsh.

> *caw-craw, caw-craw*
> run for safety, run for vengeance
> *caw-craw, caw-craw*
> save her, avenge her

Through the roof beams I see the crow, wings deployed, gliding, turning on itself like a weathervane. I follow its flight and it makes me dizzy. I can't feel my arms. Everything is upside down. I am being dragged. My skin lacerated by needles. I will die in the forest because no-one thought to follow the vultures.

*

I wake up with a start. My sheets are soaked with sweat. I think of Anouk and wonder if her journal has crept into my dreams. Anouk Baumstark, flesh and bone, alone in her cabin. Does she suffer from nightmares?

The coyotes are singing at the break of day. Dawn is vermilion and sparkling with dew. From close by, I hear growling and throat singing. My dog is scratching at the door. It takes all my persuasion to keep her from running to join the pack when I open up to sniff the fall air.

"Stay on the porch, Coyote. Stay."

The coast is far from clear, puppy. And you coyotes that are still alive, keep your distance, stay far away from here.

It is time to follow the birds of misfortune.

*

I stop where Respite Road dead-ends, at the edge of the fields, where rumours begin and the stink rises up, in the shadow of birds of prey turning high above. The vultures glide in circles on the north-east wind.

The Grondin & Brothers farm. I know it by reputation. A beef cattle factory that is no doubt disturbed from time to time, as many farms in forested regions are, by predators prowling along the electric fences. In search of rodents in the underground cities beneath the mountains of hot manure, coyotes and foxes approach the farms at night, not knowing that kids will use them for target practice. Some say it is self-defence while others admit it is sport. This nocturnal massacre has become as ordinary as a video game. Men playing God, using high-powered weaponry to shoot down famished creatures.

Technology has destroyed the once-noble relationship between men and animals. It is a completely one-sided contest, and Marco and his kind have the advantage. They kill everything that moves, with none of the intelligence that old-time trappers had.

Above my head, black vultures glide in slow spirals. Their ominous presence is the arrow that points to the desolation on the ground. I need to see the bodies I have searched for in the woods. Like a weeping mother who, to complete her mourning, must rock her baby before letting him go.

I lock my truck and start walking. Up ahead, I see the fence of the calf pen. Inside the last building, cold bright light shines on the cows chained to their milking stations. The stench poisons my lungs. A mix of mouldy hay, cow excrement, caustic cleaning products, sour milk and blood.

I move closer. The trap is tightening around your neck and you don't even feel it, Marco.

When the vultures turn circles above the fields, I know from experience that a foetus and placentas have been put through the mixer and spread with a helping of manure. Then farmers wonder why coyotes come prowling around their places. They hate the animals and consider them vermin. But they are the ones who have perverted their habits with agricultural practices that ignore the basic rules of hygiene. They abandon those rules, but bubonic plague and other epidemics do not.

Life has not prepared me for the shock. My coyotes are there. My poor coyotes . . .

My legs weaken. Disgust, distress, incomprehension, rage, like a wave. With time, the decomposing pile, the heap of carcasses, has grown like a pyramid. I can't tell how many hundreds of Canidae are lying here, stripped of their fur, tails cut off, skulls naked. From the summit of this pile of bones, a vulture with a bloody beak sizes me up. He's the king of the mountain.

I hear a noise and wheel around. An armed man shouts at me:

"You've got no business here!"

"Raphaëlle Robichaud, Wildlife Protection Officer, Chapais sector. I have the right to enter private property, just like the police. Lower your weapon!"

"I know what you're going to say."

"Lower your weapon, sir!"

The man obeys.

"I came to see what species of animals are abandoned here. I followed the vultures. As long as you tell me there aren't any black bears or lynx on that pile, I will have nothing to say in my report."

"When we get a bear, we eat it. And my wife makes a very good lynx stew. No, there's nothing but those damned coyotes."

I have to stop myself from asking why he doesn't eat coyotes, too.

"Our boys trap them," he goes on with a disgusted look. "They're a nuisance. We've got to protect our herds. If it was up to me, I'd cut down the whole forest behind us, and we'd finally be able to go about our business."

*

Sitting in the wet grass, I watch the Rivière-aux-Perles flow past, my chin on my palms. Coyote is playing along the river. From time to time she comes back and licks me. She knows how I feel. A black mood born of the demoralising conclusions of adulthood. Human stupidity is boundless. Cruelty to animals an everyday occurrence. As long as there are milk cows chained up, traps used to capture animals with no respect for life and fair play, heavy machinery that clear-cuts the forests, and outdated laws that give free rein to industry, there will be women like me who think that the only solution is to fight fire with fire. My morale couldn't be lower. As Anouk B. says in her journal, the woods are turning into a place of disenchantment and sorrow.

My stomach is growling. I can't remember if I ate today. I get up and look for a snack in the truck. The coyote skin on the back seat mocks me. I couldn't leave it rolled up in the box with the snares at Lionel's. I decided to make it mine. Its smell in the vehicle is a reminder to keep my eyes open at all times.

I never thought I would turn forty with a pistol in my belt, a can of pepper spray within reach and a dog at my feet, yet still be shaking with fear. I have seen too much death lately and not slept enough. I drink my vegetable juice and call Coyote. She lies down on the fur as I push back my seat and set my computer on my lap, the screen propped against the wheel. There is a hermit I must apologise to.

PART THREE

Vendetta

15

Anouk Baumstark

OCTOBER 5

The graphic matrix display on the municipality's website lets me follow the course of the rivers in Saint-Bruno and search for Anouk Baumstark's property. The programme contains the names and identification of every landowner. But it is still a challenge in a village with a thousand tax accounts and just as many woodlots, all of them bordered by rivers: the Manie, Wolf, Saint-Denis, Grand-Bras, Petit-Coude, Amouraska, Pearl, and that's not all of them. Some roads have not been indicated on the map since the last time the cadaster was reviewed. I memorise them, since in the back country a G.P.S. is just about useless. Maybe that was what sent those three men the wrong way, and made one of them cross the border and lose his way miles from the others.

In her diary, Anouk often mentions her river, though she never names it. I remember what she said: *a river that falls before flowing into the sea.* Could it be the Amouraska, which flows into the pools of Les Sept Chutes? What if it was right after the bend where it meets the Saint-Denis? She cannot be far from Lionel's cabin.

I dig further into her journal, looking for landmarks,

and come to a page decorated with seagulls and waves in blue ink.

This morning, a moose pushed its way through the tall grass by the river and swam across. Sometimes I wonder what the instinct is that urges us humans to migrate. I wish I knew why I always look north. North of what? North of people, closer to wolves, whales, stars, closer to everything that makes the rest of you afraid. I am a lot more afraid of people than of animals, especially when I see the crowd on a downtown Montreal street turning its eyes and compassion away from a homeless person in need of help. I am afraid of your indifference. Our nation is modern, but intolerably cold. I would rather stay here, on the banks of my river, endlessly singing. I walk through the woods thinking of everything I do not possess. But that I do not need. I am one with the back country landscape, wide awake on the edge of this river of pink pearls, bursting with the spawn of rainbow trout. Clear and clean to drink here. Deadly and brackish down river. Below, it stinks of liquid pig manure, the Amouraska.

There you are, Anouk Baumstark.

On Google Maps, I click on the satellite function, and even if the aerial photographs are out of date, I spot a small shiny roof near the banks of the Amouraska River. I compare it to the address on the graphic matrix display – your hideout.

I will give you your journal back. Though that means

disturbing your solitude and maybe your supper. I could mail it to you, anonymously or otherwise. But I am curious. Curious to see whether you really do have red hair like peat moss burned by the sun. Curious to watch you study the stranger who has come to knock on your door. And curious to discover how you will react when you understand that I read your diary, every page of it, some parts out loud, before I got around to finding you. I am a little sad; my reading is over. My communion with you was my evenings' guilty pleasure.

My headlights pick out the bottoms of the tree trunks, and the spot where a kilometre-long track leads to your forest refuge. Anouk Baumstark. The first drops of anticipation roll down my armpits. I take off my cap and run a hand through my hair. Touching my long braid reminds me of the nightmare. My hair on the ground, a symbol from a dream that augurs no good.

The cabin is pretty much a dump with its gutter falling off and a giant tree branch lying across the roof. The branch must have broken off the headless spruce tree standing nearby. If a car was not parked behind the cord of wood and smoke was not coming from the chimney, I would swear the place was abandoned. The clapboard is missing in spots, the curtains are pulled, and it is dark inside. I step out of the truck and close the door softly. Walk thirty metres or so, my eyes peeled, the bend in the river, the garden freshly turned over, potatoes covered with earth in bins on the front porch, chanterelles drying on screens on sawhorses, a surprised heron taking to the sky. On the rotting steps, a sheet of varnished plywood keeps me from falling through the old planks. I clear my throat. Through the curtains, I see a lit candle on the table.

Knock

Knock

Knock

A figure moves inside, then pushes back the length of fabric. A few strands of red hair capture the evening light. Her eyes size me up. Then the curtain stirs, I hear military steps, and two bolts are slipped. The door creaks open and a gust of wind blows dead leaves from the mat into the house. Her feet are shod in tightly laced boots. I take a deep breath and look into her face: Anouk Baumstark's questioning look. She grips her hunting rifle, as if waiting for me to say the password, the magic formula, or at least some nicely styled words of contrition. Her body language says she is irritated at being disturbed.

"Raphaëlle Robichaud, Wildlife Protection Officer."

She leans her weapon against the door frame and shakes my hand firmly.

"Anouk Baumstark."

She motions me to come inside and shows me the single chair at her table. She pulls up an old trunk covered with a wool blanket and sits down across from me, at some distance, her arms and legs crossed.

I breathe in the smell of spiced tea, cannabis and apple sauce.

"You could let your dog out so he can walk himself. That wouldn't bother me," she says, motioning to my truck.

"Thanks, but I'm keeping an eye on her. She's injured."

"What happened?"

"A long story. It has to do with poaching."

An ungracious nod of her head. Anouk Baumstark offers me tea, pushes aside an overflowing ashtray, then sweeps some crumbs onto the floor with the sleeve of her sweater. Her clothes are patched where they've worn through in places, but are spotlessly clean.

"Do you want to bring her inside? I lost my cat, so there's no problem."

I can't help myself. My eyes move towards the ceiling that could fall on us at any moment. I notice that the main beam is supported by an eccentric sort of structure. Two pieces of timber screwed together, resting on a concrete block. The woman can use her hands.

"I installed a temporary beam. Go ahead, go get your dog."

"That's nice of you, I think I will. She'll get to stretch her paws a little."

I go out to the truck and come back, wondering what I can say to justify my intrusion, and how to confess that I read her diary from the first page to the last. The imprint of her hand on mine, the contact of two palms, strangers to each other.

"She's a female?"

"Yes. Her name is Coyote."

"I can see why. I knew you were a little more than just dog!"

Anouk Baumstark kneels and pets Coyote. My dog accepts the affection and moves closer to her, leaning her head against her generous bosom. Wholly submissive and trusting this unknown hand. I smile. I have never seen her so eager to be petted. Even with Lionel, a friend she has seen every day lately, Coyote shies away, tail between her legs, then hides between my legs and the edge of the sofa. When he opens the door for her, she stays close to the wall and slips out, avoiding his hand that tries to win her trust.

"Is she over her injuries?"

"Yes. Practically not a scratch left."

As if she knew we were talking about her, Coyote sighs noisily, then lies down at Anouk Baumstark's feet, closes her eyes, and is soon in a dream of plump, running rabbits.

"Ms Baumstark, I'm going to get straight to the point."

"Call me Anouk. Can you remind me of your name again?"

"Raphaëlle."

I glance around the room. Anouk examines me with a frown, her face unforgiving.

I have never seen hair that red. Red as a fox, pumpkin colour with wheat tones, pulled up in a thick chignon like a crown on her head. A long, fine nose scattered with tiny freckles. A swanlike neck held tightly by the collar of a black wool sweater, holes at the elbows and the sleeves unravelling, opening onto a second layer, also black.

I can't find the words. I take her notebook from my pocket and hand it to her. Her face lights up. She grabs it and holds it to her breasts.

"You left it at the Saint-Pascal laundromat."

"That's what I figured. Thanks. But how did you know where I live?"

"Investigations are my thing. Actually, they're my profession."

She studies my uniform. I decided to put it on this morning, even though it's Saturday; maybe my officer's outfit could protect me from bad dreams. Anouk's eyes alight on the shield-shaped badge on my shoulder. She explores the details. The sky-blue background, khaki mountain and green prairie where a moose with an impressive set of antlers stands, the Wildlife Protection banner where a partridge perches and, below, a white salmon in a navy-blue lake. Wildlife Protection depends on the profits of the hunting and fishing industry. My badge translates my impostor status perfectly.

"To what do I owe the honour of your visit, Mademoiselle Wildlife Protection Officer? You could have mailed my journal to me."

"Forgive my indiscretion, Anouk. A lady in the village gave me your notebook by mistake. I paged through it to see if there was a name. Maybe I was hoping to find some information for an investigation I'm carrying out in the sector. My curiosity got the better of me. I couldn't stop myself. I read it from the first page to the last. I'm sorry, I know that isn't done, I hate it when people go through my things . . . I don't know what came over me. Your story fascinated me. I wanted to know more. Unhealthy curiosity. I wanted—"

"To see what I looked like?"

"Yes. Because I felt we had a lot of things in common."

"The main thing is that you brought my journal back."

I smile and stand up, ill at ease and ready to take my leave.

"Wait, Raphaëlle. I don't want to keep you during working hours, but I haven't talked to anyone in months. I think this is the longest conversation I've had all year. Do you want to stay, at least until you finish your tea?"

She puts her hand near mine. Her perfectly clean nails are cut very short. Her penetrating feline gaze is hypnotising.

I sit down again, surprised at how gracefully she has accepted my intrusion. When she speaks, there is no hesitation, and her eyes are fastened on mine.

"You see, there is something bothering me. You're probably the only person who might have an answer. Since I practically never leave this place, I've never met anyone I could talk about this with. Before, I used to be completely terrified of coyotes. I even pissed in a pot at night and emptied it out the next morning. I was sure they were watching me, and that one night, when I was out gathering wood or getting water from the river, the whole pack would go for my throat. But as time went by, I started appreciating their music and their company. Maybe they ate my cat, I don't know, but that's life in the woods. I've been living here two years now. I like to look for animal tracks, and follow their comings and goings. Then, all of a sudden, nothing. Silence. How come we don't hear them any more? Did they just leave?"

"You mean the coyotes?"

"Yes. They used to be here every night, a dozen, maybe fifteen, it's hard to say. They never missed a date, they gathered by the river when the sun started going down. They would drink. They would play games. I would hear them laughing in the dark."

Anouk opens a little drawer under the table and takes out her makings.

"Would it bother you if I smoked? It's time."

"Not at all. Forget about the uniform."

"Uniforms don't mean anything to me."

I straighten up on my chair. Anouk's ways are certainly direct. The woman doesn't censor herself when she talks any more than she does in her diary. She offers me more tea. Our cups touch. Mine is decorated with a Brittany landscape. Hers with a mosaic of diamond shapes, Moroccan-style. Souvenirs of past trips, perhaps. I sip my tea carefully. It is burning hot. I would love to pour out my bitterness and answer her without holding back. Why don't we hear coyotes in the back country any more? And why do my eyes mist over when I think of them?

"Raphaëlle, I don't want to make you feel bad. I've gotten out of the habit of talking to people. Sorry. I'm really sorry. Tact is not my strong point."

"No, that's not it. Believe it or not, I was thinking of the coyotes."

"Then I'm not the only one who likes their animals alive."

"If you only knew."

"Tell me, then. Where did they go?"

Anouk lights the joint she's rolled with the skill of a connoisseur, and offers me the honour of the first puff. It goes back and forth between us, and the buzz has me babbling like someone who has held back for too long. She listens avidly. Every time I come across a poacher, I tell her, I think of those trappers, in the far north or from the past, who inspire such respect in me, who show awareness and consideration. Trappers who love the woods and are concerned with its balance and the future of natural resources. Who pass on this art of survival – a double-edged privilege, like that of wielding a scalpel – to others deserving of knowledge. Who harvest with moderation so there will always be plenty for others.

I tell her of my recent past, my quiet life among the maples, my profession as a keeper of the woods, and how my dog got caught in a poacher's trap. I couldn't help but destroy his material, despite the official procedures I know by heart.

Trappers in all their glory buy powerful pickups, A.T.V.s, snowmobiles, burning gas for nothing. They buy their traps and snares at hunting and fishing outlets, their alcohol, cigarettes and snacks at ragged convenience stores in villages empty three seasons out of four. They rent vehicles, motel rooms, campgrounds. Build camps and cabins, acquire boats, trailers and motors. Spoil themselves with a generator, a new chainsaw, even a brush cutter. Go back to the village for more alcohol, and since a cold wave is coming, new waterproof clothes with matching camouflage boots. The wife and kids who had no choice but to follow will be parked in a shiny new trailer. They will go to the village grocery to fill the fridge. I won't even mention the expenditure on weaponry, legal and otherwise, and permits, the access rights for the camps, and all the rest. In a world where money talks, it is hard to convince the ministry of the real value of a lynx in its natural habitat or a century-old white pine when, from the other side of his desk, functionaries are deluging him with reports of the economic benefits and yearly conservation budgets that will offset his guilt at cancelling trapping quotas.

I stop myself before I go too far and say what happened next. The break-in at my trailer, the red coyote skin on my bed, the fake profile, the suspect's file wallpapering the cabin, and the chronology of the evidence. This morning I knew Anouk only on paper, and now she is listening to me describe how I have lost faith in my employer. But I cannot very well confide the instruments and intrigues of my vendetta.

"If I understand correctly, it's illegal to destroy a trapper's equipment, even on public land?"

"That's right."

"If you want to know what I think, you did it to save your dog. You can plead that. Trapping isn't legal if the season hasn't started."

"Sure. But the trapping industry takes precedence over the welfare of animals in this country. You don't have the right to get in the trapper's way. I could lose my job because I purposely vandalised his equipment."

"But he was poaching!" Anouk says, indignant.

"He could always deny it, or claim he caught something by accident. If I had been thinking, I would have documented the site instead of destroying it. But Coyote is my baby! When I saw how badly she was hurt, I flew into a rage, I didn't think, I wanted to wreck his stuff because I was afraid she'd go back there, attracted by the smell. I know huskies. They're intelligent, but if there's fresh meat around, they'll get caught in the same trap twice. It's the same for them with porcupines. Instinct makes them attack, even if every time they end up with a face full of quills."

"I guess that's what happened to my pack of coyotes. My property is enormous. I cut some trails through it and I stick to them. There could be traps around and I wouldn't know."

"That happens a lot. Trappers ask permission to set up their material on private property. But poachers just sneak in. They choose woodlots where hardly anyone ever goes. On Crown lands, they have free rein. They've been running the show for too long. They have high-tech military surveillance equipment, and that makes them feel entitled. You should have seen it, Anouk, the number of carcasses and traps. It wasn't pretty."

"Isn't there a limit to what they can kill?"

I agree with you completely, and my eyes say as much. If we settled for what we truly needed, a fur coat passed down from one generation to the next for those cold winter nights, instead of shelves loaded down with bedding in the latest fashionable colours that match the curtains and the rug, and that are replaced to wipe the slate clean when a love affair is over, maybe we would get back in touch with ourselves again, and stop filling the void in our lives with credit card shopping.

I cross my arms. Stare at the spiderwebs on the ceiling, then entrust Anouk with what troubles me most. The violent nightmares, the feeling of being tracked down, my skin crawling at the slightest sound, the doors I have started locking, the fear of just how far he will go.

"I think the poacher is hunting me now."

I close my eyes, breathe in and picture the nest I had to leave. My trailer where I felt at home, my clothesline in the wind, the rusty smell of maple leaves, my little bit of paradise lost. Then the boots and the mud on my rug by the door. And the coyote skin that maybe I should not have kept.

"I don't want to play the victim, but I've met enough deviant men to recognise evil in someone's eyes. I had horrible nightmares afterwards. I decided to leave and not run the risk of being right about the danger."

"Not very reassuring. I'm pretty stressed out too these days."

Anouk looks up at the ceiling, then points to the window with its extreme close-up of a tree branch.

"Normally I can see the river from that side."

"You're lucky the glass didn't shatter."

The top of the ancient spruce tree must be heavy, with its whole length leaning on the roof. I dig through my pockets. I have that tree-trimmer's card somewhere.

"There's no guarantee that the cabin won't collapse in the middle of the night. The roof was leaking already, but now I've had to move my bed out of the way."

Anouk gets to her feet. At the foot of the temporary beam, she lifts a bucket half filled with rainwater.

"Enough to flush my toilet, good and clean, like normal people!"

Triumphantly, she goes off to empty the water in the bathroom, then returns the bucket to its spot.

"I won't make it through the winter like this. And I don't want to redo the roof. I know when they open it up, they'll find out the whole thing is rotten. My salary as a freelance translator with no electricity three-quarters of the time is not going to pay for five hundred square feet of sheet metal."

"Where will you go?"

"No idea."

Anouk lights the joint that went out, then throws a log into the stove. The first stars shimmer. The light fades, but not our conversation.

"I moved in with a friend not far from here. My door was forced. It doesn't close any more."

"Thieves?"

"Not even. The poacher."

"How do you know it was him? Were you there?"

She passes the joint to me. I'm nervous and take too big a puff and start coughing, which makes her smile. Some things I prefer not to say, but when I think of her diary that I read so greedily, I open up to her. That's only fair.

"He set up a trail camera to spy on me, and get his fill of pictures. I don't know how long he was watching me take my outdoor shower."

Anouk pinches the bridge of her nose, as if she had a sudden, devastating migraine. Triggered by hatred, no doubt.

"I hope the place you're living in now is safer."

"It is. I'm staying with my friend Lionel, in his cabin. He looks like Santa Claus and he's as kind as they come. Used to be a game warden. It's good to have a father figure around. The poacher trapped my dog, he's taking coyotes out of season, he broke into my trailer, and he has tons of compromising pictures of me. That gives me the creeps.

I see him everywhere I look. That handsome bearded face, his green predator's eyes."

"You have a picture? Show me."

"I have the memory card from the trail camera, and I found him on Facebook. I even created a fake profile to see what else I could find out."

I pull out the photograph folded in four and hand it to her.

"I don't know him. But a guy who struts around with a dead animal hanging off his neck makes me want to puke. I don't want to live in the same world as him."

"That proud look is what disturbs me the most. Why is he so proud that he killed a red coyote? He must really hate animals. And you know what? He broke into my place to lay that fur on my bed."

"That sick pervert! If it was a human, he'd be accused of committing indignities to a body. Why can't you have him arrested?"

"I've got his file. There's no lack of evidence. He was found guilty, and more than once. But the penalties are just for show. The fines are a joke."

"I'd like to tell you to go to the police, but I don't think that's a good idea. You'd know why since you read my journal. I talked about my first arrest, and it wasn't the last. You heard those stories about Native women, and what happened to them in cop cars in Val d'Or."

"I have no intention of going to the police. They're not all rotten apples. I'm sure there are more than a few who work to protect us, but in my experience they don't want to be bothered as long as a crime hasn't been committed. The poacher would have to rape me first. I'm not from the area, and the police must know him. He's a guy from a local family, he grew up here. Who knows, they probably played football together, and had the same girlfriends, and went to the same parties. I'm the troublemaker. The girl who's worried about the planet."

"That makes two of us!"

"You'd be scandalised, Anouk, if I told you how much a coyote skin costs. A good one, thick and full, in one piece."

"How much?"

"Fifty bucks."

"That's crazy!"

"You want to know how they justify killing them? By saying there will be more game for the hunters."

"That's why I live this way. I can't tolerate that kind of a world. I'd rather stay with my poets and the mice."

Silence settles in. Another sip of cold tea, another puff on the joint. I look at Anouk Baumstark, the philosopher hermit who let me into her house and has been listening to every twist and turn of my long story. Coyote keeps vigil at the window, her eyes watching a groundhog. Anouk notices it, too, and follows its wanderings until it leaves her field of vision. She gets up to straighten some things on the table. Her pensive smile moves me. Her calm captivates me. A sense of wonder expressed by silence. Her confident posture. Her army boots, tightly laced, her red bangs perfectly straight. The dark colours of her simple clothing. Rigour in her appearance, and in her thought, too.

"At the end of high school, in Montreal, my desk was next to the windows, and I had a view of an empty lot full of groundhogs. I spent all day watching them. I gave them names and drew pictures of them instead of doing the teacher's assignments. I failed physics because I was fascinated by Nature. That's a good one! The teacher changed my desk. Seventh row, next to the kids with behavioural problems. I couldn't see the blackboard or the groundhogs. That's when I traded a caricature of the teacher for my first little bag of weed."

"I like your drawings a lot."

Anouk smiles. The curve of her eyelashes like hieroglyphs. She is more than just beautiful. Her intensity carries authority. She opens a drawer under the table and takes out a few sheets of paper and a black felt-tip pen.

I slip into contemplation as she draws. I listen to her pen strokes and the clicking of the woodstove. Night has fallen. I should be going, but it feels right to be here.

"For you."

Anouk

"It's beautiful. The Ministry of Transport should hire you to illustrate the signs for animal crossings."

"You're joking!"

"I've always wanted to put up big posters on the notice-boards in our parks, with a message for our users. *Thank you for respecting the reproduction period of coyotes, wolves and foxes. No trapping from October 25 to March 1.* With your permission, I'd use your picture."

"With pleasure. But I'll make you a better one."

"I'm just fantasising. My posters wouldn't stop poachers from running wild. The laws are out of date, that's the real problem."

"The police don't really care about poaching, and neither does the Ministry?"

"There are three of us to cover our entire Fur-Bearing Animal Management unit. If they wanted us to be effective, they'd hire more staff, and younger people."

"How big is the unit? All of Kamouraska?"

"Much bigger! Imagine, from La Pocatière eastwards to Le Bic, and southwards to the border with Maine and New Brunswick. We have to stick to the roads. Three officers, that's a joke for such an enormous territory. We rack up the miles, but hardly carry out any anti-poaching operations."

Anouk hands me back the folded photograph she was fiddling with.

"And the guy who's after you is somewhere out there?"

"He's near here. Around Saint-Bruno."

"I suppose if you added him on Facebook you know his name?"

I hesitate, and think of the expression on Mme Galipeau's face, fear and courage combined, when she spoke the name.

"Marco Grondin."

I pet Coyote and wait for Anouk's reaction. She is taking her time.

"Do you know him?"

"Yeah. Marco from Grondin & Brothers. I've heard the name in the village bar. And it wasn't complimentary. Not one bit! The guy is a bastard. I don't want to get mixed up in your business, but if I can help out, I will."

"Thanks, Anouk. Look, I'm going to head back home. Lionel gave me a curfew and he must be getting worried. That is, if he came back to the cabin."

"Will we meet again?"

"We will meet again."

Anouk holds my gaze. Her smile is warm, yet playful. Like she was trying hard not to kiss me, her face close to mine above the table, her fingers running over the oiled wood, a few millimetres from my moist hands.

If you dare, I'll let you. I'll let you do anything you want.

I straighten up. Me and my big mouth. I said too much again.

A handshake for goodbye would not be right after everything we shared. Anouk pulls me to her side and holds me, whispers in my ear to take good care. Her breasts against mine, the bones of her pelvis against my body, our cheeks touching. Her embrace awakens my senses. I search out her perfume in the air we are breathing together.

16

Beartrap

OCTOBER 6

I wake up at dawn on the sofa in the cabin. Back aching like I'm a hundred years old. The autumn humidity has bored into my bones. I went to bed too late again. My recent sleepless nights have me seeing double. I rub my eyes hard and drag myself over to Coyote's dish to fill it. A raw egg on top as a treat. I stretch, and every bone in my body cracks.

October is a mournful month that reminds me how we failed to build a country. Our revolution fell short. Hostage-taking and closets full of skeletons. The month when the leaves fall one by one, as if Nature were surrendering to the War Measures, and admitting her vulnerability to the cold. I am getting older, too. But I will not fall like a dead leaf before its time.

Yesterday, on the way to return Anouk B.'s diary, I never imagined she would ask me to spend the evening, and that we would use those hours to remake the world.

Still no sign of Lionel. He must be carrying out his own investigation in the field, or spiffing up his moose blinds.

The only thing that has changed in his cabin is a new object right in the middle of the table. I didn't notice it yesterday. I returned late and a little too stoned to have driven the dark kilometres from Anouk's cabin to my new base camp.

The shiny metal apparatus on the table captures my attention completely. It is burrowing its way into my brain.

Then I see the other things that have changed here. The pages hanging on the walls have been returned to the file, which Lionel placed in the bag I use for work. He has read and analysed everything, and does not need to write up a report. The conclusion is there on the table, in plain sight.

An antique piece of equipment that Lionel unearthed to relay his message. A trap that offers no second chance.

On the kitchen counter, where he usually leaves his pipe and his keys, a piece of paper with a note addressed to me. I recognise the author from his rough penmanship.

Good morning, my girl.
A warning (from Einstein) to you:
"The world will not be destroyed by those who do evil,
but by those who watch them without doing anything."
See you soon, L.

Sunday. Daybreak is taking its time. I decide to go down to the village laundromat. Maybe I will run into the woman in the housecoat who never answers her phone.

The Admiral Motel is as grubby as ever. The hunting widows are playing cribbage, cigarettes hanging from their lips. I spot the dinosaur I was looking for – a phone booth. I dial the number, reckoning this time I might get an answer, calling from a local exchange, the 492. What do you know? It worked.

"Hello?"

"Hello. I hope you remember me. We talked in the parking lot in front of the laundromat last week. You found my notebook on the dryer. This number was inside. It's me, Raphaëlle Robichaud, Wildlife Protection."

"Oh, yes, I know who you are. Now listen carefully because I'm not going to say it twice."

"Please speak louder, I can hardly hear you."

"Now can you hear?"

"Yes, that's good. I'm listening."

"Five years ago, were you working in the area, Mademoiselle Protection Officer?"

"No. I was in forestry school. Why?"

"Then maybe you heard about it on the news. The young woman who disappeared, Liliane Corriveau, the one who rented a cabin near the Boy Scout camp on Otter Lake."

"I remember. At school we all thought it was strange that she would have gone out walking by herself and left her jacket and gloves in the cabin."

"According to rumours, the wild animals got her, but I don't believe it. And neither does my husband. Eaten by wild animals. I wouldn't be surprised if it was those criminals from Respite Road again that ate her."

"What do you mean, 'again'?"

"The Grondin brothers. Actually, the youngest of them. He assaulted our daughter at a party when she was in high school, ten years ago. She never pressed charges. She didn't want to be humiliated all over again by a courtroom of men. She went overseas to study. But she told us to be careful with that family. Especially Marco."

"I'm sorry about your daughter. But what makes you think they're responsible for the woman's disappearance?"

"The Grondins are all sick in the head. You should meet Marilou. She was good friends with my daughter at school. She went out with one of the guys from the farm. She fell into their clutches, too. They really worked her over, though the description isn't strong enough. They passed around pictures of her in class. You know the kind of pictures I'm talking about? The Boy Scout camp is where they go to do the things they want to hide, that's where they go to party with girls. And that's where they trap, those monsters, by the Three Lakes hunting camp. They went up there the weekend the student was there. My husband was working his woodlot. He saw them go by. They spent the night there. Did you ever see a picture of Liliane Corriveau?"

"No."

"A real beauty! Long black hair, like you. When I saw you at the laundromat, I thought of her right off. You look like her. Promise me you'll be careful, Mademoiselle. Very careful. You asked a lot of questions in the village. Everybody knows everybody else here. The walls have ears."

Click. End of conversation.

My hands are shaking with anger. I ball them into fists. Take a deep breath. Calm down, Raphaëlle. You need to go for a very long walk. A change of scene. Breathe in, breathe out. Do it again. Unclench your jaw.

Twenty seconds later, I am throwing my wet clothes on the back seat. No time to dry them. I have too much road ahead of me. Coyote is startled. I take off at top speed. Get out of this village with the hunting widows and the great outdoors shop. I head into the forest, imagining it in flames. Two birds with one stone. The fire would restore the ecosystem and fry my poacher. But I cannot intentionally destroy the habitat I have been working so hard to protect all these years. I have to find a better way.

But I don't have the inspiration.

I get out of the truck with one clear plan in mind. Get good and stoned. Time for my Sunday joint to calm my nerves and still my shaking hands. I feel like a piece of meat, the target for a smart, green-eyed criminal. I light up and inhale deeply, breathe out, then breathe in again. The smoke fills me and empties out the pain in my soul. It stifles my fear for a moment, but casts me back into it a second later to drown once and for all. My blood pressure drops. I stretch out on the sofa bed, my head spinning.

The pictures that come to me are hard to take. Clear-cut zones, the trees bled dry, the broken doorknob of my trailer, the beavers staring at me from their traps. The young moose I saw last week, shot full of holes and tied to a hood. I get up to vomit in the sink. Nothing comes out. My face is wet with sweat. I pour the pitcher of cold water over my head and cry every tear in my body.

It is therapy of a kind. I get a hold of my thoughts again. Coyote comes and licks my fingers.

"I love you, you know that? You're my first child. You're a test to see how responsible I am. I'm not just going to protect coyotes like you. I'm going to protect their habitat, too. That's a promise."

I think of the tree beside Daphnée's cabin. Her mother called it her wise counsellor. All answers are in Nature. I know what to do. I will go see Tall Pine. Commune with the woods. Maybe Anouk can be persuaded to leave her shack.

I need to escape and feel at home again in the forest, even if the place is crawling with poachers, bears and other dangers. If I do not have the magic notebook to calm me down, its author can surely help.

I get my supplies together as I wait for Lionel, who has to come out of the woods sooner or later. I find my walking shoes, hunting rifle and two orange safety vests. It is noon. My goal is ambitious. Walk the twenty kilometres to Tall Pine by nightfall. My birthday pilgrimage, slightly belated. A hike to get some perspective, anything to stop thinking about Gargamel.

*

Lionel says the timing is all wrong, but he respects my need to visit the old tree. I need to get ready for what might happen next. Everything is settled. Coyote will stay here. I changed my bandages for the last time; the wounds have given way to fresh pink skin. My old friend will pretend to be my father and call the office Monday morning. Mademsoiselle Robichaud has stomach flu. Now I just have to convince Anouk to join me. If my escapade does not interest her, I will go alone, an option that displeases Lionel. He grumbles into his beard all the way down the road, but he knows that if he came with me, we would end up talking about the monster in the woods the whole time.

I spot Anouk in front of her cabin, carrying an armful of long spruce branches towards her firepit near the river. She smiles and waves. The tree that was besieging her roof has been turned into a series of logs aligned perpendicularly across her road, keeping vehicles out. Lionel parks on the far side.

After the introductions, we pitch in to help move the remaining branches. I tell her about my plan.

"You should have let me know right away! I'll get a few things together."

Anouk has never met Tall Pine, but she is as excited as a little kid. Throwing a few items into a backpack, she bursts into song. "Oh, Tannenbaum, Oh, Tannenbaum, how lovely are thy branches . . ."

17

On the Way to Tall Pine

OCTOBER 6

Lionel and his logorrhoea of concern. No way to savour the silence that should have accompanied my birthday pilgrimage to Mont-Carmel. In the pick-up, Lionel is so exercised he has my ears burning. With all the art he has at his disposal, he sets out the catastrophic scenarios that will likely befall us. He conjures up the three lost men who were discovered too late, Gargamel who is still on the prowl, fishers and their needle-sharp teeth, and other evil creatures. I say nothing. I smile in anticipation as we head for Tall Pine.

We turn left on Route 287. This time, no forestry trucks, no clouds of yellow dust. Just a thirty-kilometre-long homily from Protective Papa. He is clearly afraid for his two protégées who are going off to play in the deep woods – too deep for his taste. Everyone is more fearful since the incident with the fishermen. Especially Lionel, now that he knows the identity of the pack of brothers who rule the back country. And whose happy hunting grounds are about to be shut down.

I block off that part of my thoughts. Gargamel, get out of my mind.

Finally we reach the Monk line, that part of the old Quebec City–Moncton rail link. A piss break at the old Bretagne station. Nowadays, the abandoned track is one of the main entry points into the Chapais sector, part of the unincorporated Picard territory. We eat our lunch in silence on the squared-off benches by the East Lake chapel. I don't care for places of Christian worship because they remind me of the masses I was forced to attend until I turned sixteen, but I inspect one of the plaques by the stations of the cross. There, I learn about the Indigenous presence here. This body of water that I have always thought of as East Lake is really called Kijemquispam. According to Lionel, in the Mi'kmaq language, *kijemquispam* means "the lake lying to the east". I promise you, Kijemquispam, that in the future when I speak to you, I will use your correct name. We should restore the Native toponymy that has been lost.

Anouk gazes hungrily at the landscape, taking in the air that smells of larch trees, lending an ear to the birds, listening with closed eyes. Her communion with the woods is sensorial, and sensual. I like to watch her be. I like the idea that she will sharpen my own senses just by being near. The rebellion written in her diary is contagious, and in the same way, she is breathing peace into me with her feeling of wonder.

We move on. Again, Lionel reminds us of the plan, the meeting place and hour of our return. We reach the beaver dam. He cuts the motor and pushes us out of his truck.

"Better hurry if you want to get there before nightfall."

Then he gets out and hugs each of us, as if we were

his two daughters at an airport, heading for some war-torn country. Of course, we'll be extra careful. Yes, we'll leave at dawn to be back at the dam at noon. The guns, the headlamps, the canteens. We have it all, Papa Wolf, don't worry yourself about us.

Now I am walking side by side with a red-headed fox down a trail as old as the world. Others who have come this way have flattened the ground, forming a path through the ferns that grow waist high. The young vegetation is vigorous. The saplings are scarcely higher than the brush, which means the last clear cut dates back several years. The forest was massacred here, but what is worse is knowing this recent period of peace is just a brief respite before another heavy tribute must be paid. The chainsaws will return as soon as the trees reach a profitable height. The table has been set. The access roads are laid out, the lower branches of the trees lopped off. No-one is keeping an eye on this great forest. It is too far from the villages for anyone to care if it is brought low.

"A teddy bear!"

Anouk points out a stuffed bear with neither eyes nor nose hanging from a tree. Once there were as many as fifty teddy bears nailed to the trunks. The border of someone's hunting grounds? The animals make me think of a children's cemetery. Maybe we are crossing sacred Mi'kmaq or Malecite lands. During the winter, perhaps the bears guide snowmobilers on their way towards the border. Further on, cairns fulfil the same function. The trail narrows. The sun is getting lower.

A lookout provides a view of the Appalachian Mountains on the American side. A vast wilderness. What pleasure to see nothing but trees all the way to the horizon. The border is only two kilometres away. A handmade sign points out the last stretch of trail to Tall Pine.

Anouk smiles at me, her cheeks red from exertion, her eyes shining with wonder. We are almost there. The light casts a halo over the wet branches crisscrossed by spiderwebs that catch dew, pine needles and insects paralysed by the cold. It is the season of slowing and rationing supplies. The forest is peaceful; its inhabitants have settled into their nests. Quietly, darkness descends. I pray my life will soon return to a more serene path. The silence of the woods is my alternative medicine: the feeling of being at the far edge of the world.

Every year, I travel to Tall Pine for my birthday. This path is my Camino de Compostela in the Canadian wilderness. On my first trips, Lionel guided me, passing on the torch of caring for the back country. A person needs to come and greet the tree, see how he is doing, like an old friend. I will introduce him to Anouk, the new pilgrim who will carry him in her heart. Maybe one day this forest will be given protected status. Until then we can only dream.

As we move further away from the road and its vehicles, and deeper into the forest standing proud, I trust my spirit will grow clearer, and the fog of nightmares dissipate. Anouk's beauty and the loveliness of the forest fill my thoughts. My companion walks in silence, as if she, too, needs to sort things out. Maybe she is thinking of her smashed roof, or what happened to her cat, or what she will do come winter. The act I am preparing to commit – that is what preoccupies me. I step up the pace, hoping to leave my plan and its premeditation behind.

"Raphaëlle, wait for me."

I stop at the foot of the steepest downward slope of our journey. Ahead of us, we have a kilometre or two of muddy track amid trunks festooned with moss. The ferns are almost as tall as we are, like a Jurassic jungle.

The sound of splashing water, the stream singing at our feet, is Morrison Creek. It flows not towards the Saint Lawrence, but into the United States. A different watershed where I fill my canteen and take a long, refreshing drink. Anouk gets down on all fours and puts her mouth to the stream. Laughs. Another mouthful. Like a happy vixen who recognises a spring venerated by generations from its taste alone.

Anouk catches up with me, and skips happily when she spots the giant moose tracks in the mud. Maybe our antlered friends are making this autumn pilgrimage with us. It makes sense to head for the mountains at the first sound of gunfire, when the leaves turn red from frost – time to run for your life!

The line that cuts through the forest marks the border. Another thirty metres and Tall Pine rises up before us. His Majesty, most serene green giant with open arms. His enormous roots spread out beneath the carpet of orange needles. We have come to see what is likely the oldest white pine in the former colony of New France. Sullied by graffiti of a heart almost as broad.

I love you Michelle

At least the vandal had the intelligence to remain anonymous. Rumours say his beloved's ashes are scattered here.

Tall Pine's roots are black in spots. Under the needles, the remains of campfires of so-called nature-lovers who did not bother to pick up their trash. Melted bottlenecks, burnt cans and cigarette butts. I have brought bags to pick up as much of it as I can and carry it out tomorrow, as I do every year.

Leave no trace, they say. I go further than that. I try to leave the place in better condition than I found it in. My pack gets heavy along the way, but my heart grows lighter. I have done my part.

"Oh, Raphaëlle, thank you thank you thank you, dear friend! I'm so happy to be here! I saw the big tree in Mégantic, but I didn't know there was one in Kamouraska. It's incredible!"

"You have to see Tall Pine. It's how we protect him. If you want to defend the territory, you have to live on it, and occupy it."

"How old is he, do you think?"

"Somewhere between two hundred and fifty and six hundred and fifty years old. The woods here were clear-cut more than once. Tall Pine is the last survivor of the original forest. He was used as a landmark when the U.S. border was being laid down in 1908. It's exactly nineteen metres from here, straight ahead."

Oh, sage with your elephant feet that mark the border, last witness of precolonial times, you grumble in the wind, you make the earth vibrate and welcome us with honours.

I close my eyes to savour the moment, and feel the caress of the north-easter. A snowflake tumbles through the air, dances with light, then a fine shower of crystals falls upon us. The sheer lightness moves me. The first snow, so delicate, moistens the tip of my nose red with cold. Winter is never far, and always patient. By now, my trailer with its staved-in door must be heaven for the ground squirrels that love chewing up mattresses.

I take off my cap and go to the tree, climb onto a root, and open my arms to embrace his trunk. Spread my legs and press my breasts and forehead against his bark. I hug the white pine. Hello there, old friend, I missed you.

Anouk does the same. She smiles my way. My heart is at rest. Finally, I can breathe.

Our fingers touch. I think of the number of people it would take to encircle Tall Pine's trunk. Three or four. Our fingers explore together. They sign a peace treaty on the bark as the forest sings its lullaby. Silence falls upon us like enchantment. Anouk draws me in. Like embers, her dark pupils burn. I try to understand what she sees in me, and whether she can read the thoughts I try to hide.

"You're beautiful, Raphaëlle."

She comes closer, takes my bare hands, and brings them to her mouth to warm them with her breath. A little shy at her touch, I look down at the pale maple leaves on the ground. Her hands stay with mine, and my fingers stay close to her lips. Snowflakes melt as they land on the ground. I struggle to find the words.

"I have a surprise for you, Anouk."

With my eyes, I show her Tall Pine's boughs, his great arms open wide. Above, on a U-shaped branch, behind the countless tufts of needles, two beams support the shelter.

"Raphaëlle, you're kidding me!"

"Not one bit. Tonight, you and me are going to sleep in a five-billion-star hotel."

18

Honeymoon

OCTOBER 6

"Got your harness?"

"Yes."

"Let's go, Anouk, better climb up before it gets too dark. Even if the footholds are shiny, we'll need time to settle in."

The treehouse sits far from prying eyes, hidden behind the needles, between the stately branches of the old pine. Lovers have carved their names, hearts and dates in the bark. Footholds have been screwed into the trunk in places where there are no branches. I climb to the first one and throw my leg over it. I take out the rope, unroll it, clip on my harness buckle and let the rope fall to the ground. Anouk ties on and tells me she is ready. I pull myself up carefully, my hands sweaty. I reach the platform. My friend joins me, no problem, she's a regular monkey. We sit side by side, looking over the edge. The sun is melting on the horizon, the colour of a blood orange.

"You're brave, Anouk, living year round in a cabin with no running water or electricity. I know how hard that life is. And during the winter, in the cold, all by yourself."

"It's not as bad as living in a trailer!"

"Sure, but I spend winter in the Gaspé. The trailer is

just for my job here. But I'm telling you, those October nights . . ."

"The humidity is the worst."

"It doesn't help being surrounded by trees, always in the shade."

"Living in a rundown cabin is a lot easier than living in society. I swear, Raphaëlle. And I've got running water: it's called the river. My solar panel gives me all it can. I don't ask for anything more. It's true, the tree trunk lying on the roof was a challenge. I'm not sure the place will be safe once the water seeps in and ice builds up, and with the weight of the snow – *crunch*, no more Anouk!"

"Don't you ever feel lonely? I mean, being all alone?"

"Sure, the way everybody feels, now and then. But you get used to the quiet. At the beginning, when I felt too alone, I went to the bar in the village. But I always came home in worse shape than when I started out. So I decided to just hunker down. When the loneliness gets me, I turn on the radio or write in my journal. I smoke a joint and converse with myself."

"I'd go to the bar with you sometime. When we've solved our little problem."

"Love to. When you're alone and you get the blues, what do you do?"

"I'm not really that alone. I've got my dog now, and I have Lionel."

"He really seems to like you."

"He showed me the path to this place."

The treehouse with its pointed roof looks as if it stepped

right out of a fairy tale. Fifteen metres up, the place is invisible to anyone not in on the secret. There is a reason why our great pine survived the clear cuts. His twisted shape would not have produced perfectly straight boards, which is what the industry demands. Maybe fate put him right on the line that separates two countries. From one generation to the next, he has been watching over the leafy desert, surviving the forestry barons, adding on rings, slowly turning into a mastodon. The tree-cutters let him live. Now he is the last surviving witness, spanning two very large pieces of real estate, though the border has been redrawn since the early days. People are glad now that they preserved the tree; his strong arms accepted a human nest in its embrace. A feline shelter, too. The mattress of needles that lines the floor from wall to wall is covered with fur and gives off the characteristic smell of lynx.

I unroll a rug on the bed of pine needles and stretch out. Anouk unlaces her boots and massages her feet. I do the same and we both put on dry socks.

"Good thing we had a pee before we climbed up here," she jokes.

"It was all thought out ahead of time. Especially since we're borrowing the lynx's penthouse!"

It is good to laugh. Good to have a friend.

I take a beeswax candle from my bag, place it in a little brass bowl lined with enamel, and light it. The flame fills our shelter with warm orange light. Anouk's hair glistens.

"Now you really do look like a fox."

"And you look like an owl! All you need is a big pair of glasses."

Free, light-hearted laughter. We are living in a dream. Anouk is all lightness, a long way from the embittered hermit I imagined.

"If you only knew, Raphaëlle. It wasn't easy being this colour. The only red-haired girl in the playground, the only one with freckles, not just on her nose, but everywhere else, the only one with a strange German accent. I had my share of insults and getting slapped around. I hated school for the longest time. I loved being in class, but when recess came around, it was hell. I would ask the teachers if they wanted me to sweep up or clean the blackboard so I wouldn't have to go outside. Like a fox, my red hair got me into a lot of trouble. Not to mention the guys who figured that red-haired girls were easy."

"I'm sorry you had to go through that, Anouk. I had the same problem because I was a tomboy. I liked to race with boys, and wear work boots, and feel the mud drying and cracking on my face. I liked climbing trees. I wanted to be in the Boy Scouts and camp out in the woods. I ran distances to get in shape, and made cross-country paths for myself, and never played hopscotch or skipped rope. They sent me to Girl Scouts anyway. The girls wouldn't have me because I was too boyish. I stopped paying attention and lived in my own world. They threw things at me, they insulted me. *Half-breed, feather girl, you should have been a boy.* The usual thing."

"You're part Native?"

"My great-grandmother. I'll show you a picture. I keep it in the truck and take it out when I need it. I look like her. The brown almond eyes, the jet-black hair. The genes jumped two generations, I guess."

"You're a Métis princess. You're beautiful."

"So are you, Anouk."

Side by side on the rug, in our warm socks, Anouk and I watch the dying day through the window that has no pane and is as narrow as a peephole. The details stay with me. Anouk tickling me with her fingertips as we put our arms around Tall Pine's trunk. Her warm hands that said *I won't let you go*. Her eyes, sweet but penetrating. Her kindness from our very first meeting, even if she wrote in her diary that she didn't want to see anyone. Then she adopted me right off. Our friendship was so spontaneous. When I talked about taking this hike, she jumped at the chance as if she had been dreaming of it forever.

But when I look down at the emptiness below, I feel it pulling me. Putting my anxieties on hold by coming here is a temporary solution. I can concentrate on the beauty of the landscape, the perfume of pine needles and the lynx musk, listen to the wind and the sighing of the branches, and feel my new friend's warmth, but the outside world nags at me. My bitterness builds up. Anger takes over from fear; either that, or it's feeding on it. Tears of injustice well up. I was just trying to do the right thing, and for that I was harried from my home and I could lose my job. I am guilty of vandalism, obstructing justice and, worse, hungering for revenge. I have fed the evil wolf within me. I try to control it, but the violence wants to break out.

"Anouk, did you ever want to take revenge against the men who hurt you?"

"Do I really feel like talking about that?"

She sighs. Her eyes stare at some faraway place.

"Sorry to bring up bad memories."

A heavy silence. I wait. The wind carries the sounds of nocturnal animals and the rustling of dry leaves. A wind that has turned cold.

"I learned something about vengeance. It doesn't heal you," Anouk tells me. "I was depressed for a long time when I was a teenager. The first man who assaulted me, the cop, was part of the problem. After what happened, I didn't think that talking to anyone would help. I never thought of calling him out for what he did – he, and the others. I kept it all inside me. Like a rock that nothing could move. Writing about what happened helped me get some distance. On paper, the teenager called Anouk Baumstark could help neutralise my past."

"And you never went too far?"

"Once I put a stinky fish in someone's locker on a Friday afternoon. The guy was rotten, too. I wanted his locker to smell like death."

She was telling me serious things, secret things, but I couldn't keep from laughing. That encouraged her.

"On Monday morning, the whole corridor stank like hell. I almost went too far a couple years ago. That's why I came here to live. You know, start all over again. Lessen the chances of running into guys I haven't forgiven. Distance myself from the irritants."

"Forgive? You can do that?"

"We'll talk about it in a few years. Maybe when you finally face your poacher, you'll feel pity instead of anger. You can decide to be stronger than what happened to you."

"Easy for you to say."

"I've been through it before, Raphaëlle."

"Maybe. But I've lost my peace of mind. Someone is tracking me. And it's not just me. It's the forest, too, the animals, the coyotes he's killing by the fistful. The village girls suffering in silence. I'm not going to let life just take its course."

"Give yourself time."

"You think it's the responsible thing to do just to stay out of danger? You saved your skin and that's all that matters? Meanwhile, the guys who assaulted you, who you didn't accuse, are assaulting other victims, and those victims probably won't get over what happened to them as well as you did. Ever hear of solidarity?"

"Ouch! Hit the target!"

She moves away, her shoulders bent. She wraps her arms around her legs and puts her forehead on her knees.

"The system is corrupt, Raphaëlle. You know it as well as I do. We both know the police aren't always on the side of justice. If you decide to talk, you set yourself up for a giant load of shit. And when the dust settles, the guy won't necessarily be behind bars."

"That's where we're different. I can't just hunker down

in my little shelter when I know for a fact that Marco Grondin is poaching coyotes, and assaulting women, and intimidating anyone who tries to stop him. I can't turn my back on that."

"What's that noise?"

Something is moving on the ground below. Twigs snap and a flight of crows swoops past our treehouse, cawing as they move among the branches.

caw-craw caw-craw
caw-craw caw-craw

My nightmare returns with their voices. The rape scene, Marco dragging me outside to be coyote bait. My skin crawls. I don't believe in premonitory dreams, but I remember the crow and the look in Marie-Ange's eyes. The bird's grating cry a message. *Caw-craw*, run for safety, *caw-craw*, run for vengeance. *Caw-craw*, save her, *caw-craw*, avenge her. Which one is it? Or both? My head spins, I close my eyes, I feel the tears stinging my eyes. I'm fragile, and ashamed to be fragile. Fuck those self-defence classes where they insist that first you have to be attacked before you can meet violence with violence and have the right to defend yourself. Fuck that idea. The poacher won't stop talking in my head. I answer him: Your time is coming.

Anouk points and I see a family of raccoons below. A flash of fur caps and the sound of a blade cutting through innocent flesh. I close my eyes and breathe in the cool air. Return to myself. I replace the bloody images by gazing at the ceiling planks and imagining forms and shapes in the wood, the way we do when we look at clouds. The small face of a lynx, coyote tracks, a crow, an egg, an owl's eye . . .

Anouk touches my arm.

"Are you lost in space, or just ignoring me?"

I smile the best I can.

"Too much in my thoughts. Sorry for what I said. I didn't mean to preach."

I rub my temples, small circles, and try to remain in the present.

"Are you alright?"

"Not really. I'm thinking about some bad stuff. And I'm ashamed. Ashamed of being afraid, ashamed of not knowing what to do."

"Shh. You'll be fine."

She comes closer and pushes a few stray hairs behind my ears. She smooths out my braid. Her tenderness moves me. I try to resist the emotion and keep my cool, but my chin is trembling and tears pour down my cheeks. I want to hide in a cave and bury my face in my dog's coat, but this woman is here now, with me, looking at me without judgment. She takes me in her arms. I sob and she shelters me against her body and rocks me, then begins to sing whispered words I can hardly hear. They are in a language I don't know.

> *Kommt ein Vogel geflogen,*
> *setzt sich nieder auf mein' Fuß,*
> *hat ein' Zettel im Schnabel,*
> *von der Mutter ein' Gruß.*

She lets me go and wipes my cheeks with her sleeve. Her eyes study me. I smile.

"I feel better, Anouk. Thanks to you. What were you singing?"

"A German lullaby. A bird carrying a love letter."

"It's beautiful. It worked on me."

I pull away. I don't know how close to her I want to be. I decide to move away just a little. Anouk warms her hands between her thighs.

"You're right, Raphaëlle. You're right."

"About what?"

"I've always kept my head in the sand. I don't confront, I hide. I'm not as strong as you are. Your fear is legitimate. Your anger and violence are too. You have the strength of your principles. You're going to find the solution. And if I can help you, I will. That's what I'm trying to say – let me help you."

"Stop, you're going to make me cry again. I'm sick of crying."

This time, laughter comes instead of tears. Her look is intense, her eyes linger on me. Her eyes move to my mouth, my teeth, my braid. I blush. Suddenly I can't look her in the eye.

"Sorry, I don't want to make you uncomfortable."

"I'm not uncomfortable. It's just that . . ."

"You don't have to explain."

"Please, listen. I read your journal, so I know your preferences. I mean, your orientation. I don't know if I should interpret your affection as . . . Look, I'm going to stop talking right now, I'm making a mess of things!"

"You silly girl! Of course, Raphaëlle, I like women. Men, too, sometimes. But mostly women. For me, talking about sexual orientation is as boring as talking about housework. So feel right at home with me."

She laughs. Her teeth are like gems. Her laughter is a flowing stream. My cheeks are burning. I am bogged down in the most awkward mish-mash of words. I touch her thigh. She looks up, suddenly quiet.

"I like women too, Anouk."

The vixen brings her face, full of smiles, close to mine. She would purr if she could. I wonder if her whole body is a constellation of freckles the way her nose is. She kisses my cheek, strokes my hair, loosens my braid, separates my blankets, then puts them back again. Her touch soothes me, even as childhood images return to taunt me. I hated my black hair. Why wasn't I blond like my brothers and sisters with their blue eyes? Why was I so different from my family?

I have had to come to this sad conclusion. My whole life, in the girls and women I have known, I've been seeking a best friend, a jewel to be my sister-in-arms. But I was never able to form a lasting bond with any of them, or remain close to my old girlfriends. And now, before me, I have someone exceptional. A free, strong, independent woman of flesh and bone, a woman who lives on her own in the woods, who is in charge of her life, and who is pulling on my braid so I will kiss her mouth. Part of me leaps at the idea of uniting my body with hers. Vessels ripe with sap sail through my body, I become graceful, my heart is filled with the thrill of heat.

It must be one or two o'clock in the morning. Time flies as we kiss. One story calls for another, and in the silences between them we hear a twig snapping or leaves rustling. We are deep in the woods, deep enough to receive a distinguished visitor we admire from our perch with its bed of needles. An elegant crescent moon watches over the souls of the sleeping forest. The stars step forward one by one like sparkling snowflakes travelling across the heavens.

I think of my life before I came to Kamouraska. Standing in my stocking feet on my balcony, I searched for the stars, and answers, too. The town of Rimouski where I lived was too busy for me. I turned asocial. I retreated into my apartment. I painted the walls green and put the furniture I didn't need out in the street to make more room for plants. I spent my pay on interior design. An indoor fountain to cover the sounds of the cars outside, and vases to accommodate the extra greenery. The result was soothing, but I was becoming more and more isolated. I kept the sepia photograph of Marie-Ange on the fridge door – that look of hers fascinated me even then. A prisoner of a time when women had so little choice. I preferred poverty under the stars to fortune in the metropolis. The job of Wildlife Protection Officer came out of nowhere and seemed to promise a future. I would live in the woods. Far from the Gaspé, but not too far; I could always return there for the winter. In my element, I would have a better chance to meet people.

In the woods, I learned to recognise the song of the night birds, and call to the great horned owl, the only one that appreciates conversation and will answer. The other owls just hoot once or twice, and are too high-pitched for my ears. Their calls cut though the quiet and give me the shivers.

The hours pass, and Anouk and I, curled up together like spoons in a drawer, tell each other about our lives. She describes her toughest winter cooped up in a cabin, and her dream of being a novelist and living from her writing. I go on about my worship of the goddess of the hunt whom I call upon when everything becomes too much, and my hopes of joining an eco-village or a self-sufficient community, the boycott of my toxic family, and my horror of dismembered Halloween decorations. Our last Christmas gifts to ourselves. She, getting drunk in a bar. Me, a coyote dog.

"When you can't take it any more, Anouk, what do you do?"

"I escape. I disappear. A change of scene. But I think I've just about had it. My cabin is a wreck, but the land is still there. I live by a river. That's success."

"I come here once a year to think about my life."

Anouk pulls away and stretches out on the bed of branches, her hands behind her head. Suddenly I am shy. Should I nestle up closer to her or stay on my side? When it gets cold enough, we'll have an excuse to come together, this time a little less sisterly.

"Anouk?"

"Yes?"

"Do you ever feel like going somewhere new? I mean,

for you, is it going to be your forest and your cabin and Kamouraska forever?"

She sighs.

"Yes and no. I've always liked heading out and starting over from scratch somewhere. But during the winter, I'd rather stay in one place and keep the fires burning, as long as I have enough good books. But now my roof is a mess, so everything's changed."

"And there's no-one to empty the cistern when you're not there."

"It's impossible. A leak through a smashed-in roof? The place won't make it through the winter. What about you? Are you going to leave the trailer when the cold moves in?"

"That's the plan. I was thinking about insulating part of the sugar shack. Lionel would help out. I'd be more comfortable in the fall that way, and I'd be able to keep my stuff dry when I go away. Every year, I put the project off because I'm always in a hurry to get back to the Gaspé. But I'll have to give up on that idea. Since the voyeur broke down my door and left that damned coyote fur on my bed, I'm afraid of ending up like that poor animal. I'm ready to share my life with the beasts of the forest, but that man . . . I won't have peace of mind as long as he's out there. Imagine, one night I forget to lock the door, and he happens to be hanging around, stoned. Maybe I'm imagining things."

"I'm afraid your instincts are right."

"You think so?"

"I promised myself I wouldn't repeat it because it's

gossip. I don't know Marco Grondin personally, but I know his reputation. At the bar, they told me to watch out for him. The barmaid said to me, word for word, 'Stay away, the Grondins are big trouble.' Then Marilou showed me her scars."

"Marilou?"

"It's her barmaid name. Or maybe it's her real one."

"I think it is her real name. She went out with one of the Grondin brothers. One of my sources said that a girl named Marilou got worked over. And not just that. Marco raped one of her friends who left the area and never pressed charges. The rumours say that the weekend the girl disappeared in 2013, Marco and his brothers were up at their woodlot near the Boy Scout camp."

"Liliane Corriveau, that student who was never found?"

"Right. My source said I look a lot like her."

"You're probably his next target, Raphaëlle. I'm serious."

"So it's not just me being paranoid?"

"The camera, the trap, the break-in at your trailer, the fur on your bed – he's a pervert. What's to keep him from doing what he did to the others if he never got caught?"

"That's what I think, too. But I won't let him have his way. Nature is on my side. I just have to give her a hand."

"I don't follow."

"I'm going to beat him at his own game, then lie low until everything blows over."

"Until everything blows over? I don't understand."

"Don't judge me."

"I won't, I promise."

"You won't talk?"

"I won't talk."

I tell her about the antique sitting with pride of place on Lionel's table. A trap with sharp teeth, made by a real blacksmith, fitted out with a long rusty chain and a ring to keep it in place so the animal cannot crawl back to its lair to die. The metal fangs bite into flesh with the strength of a vice. A handmade, efficient trap, but illegal, because it wounds the animal without killing it immediately.

"I've found plenty of them in the woods. This one is ancient. It must be a souvenir from Lionel's job, and he decided to keep it in his cabin. We didn't really talk about it. Part of the reason I came here was to reconcile myself to the idea that I'd have to use it."

Anouk listens, her eyes round and astonished. I wonder if my violence repels her. I feel like a monster, but a monster who has thought things over. I need to play my cards in the right order. The Wildlife Protection Officer with the beartrap in the forest of enchantment.

Avenge the coyotes, lynx, bears, martens, raccoons, minks, foxes, muskrats, fishers. Avenge the battered and raped women afraid to go out in the light of day. I refuse to live in fear. This game of intimidating victims has gone on too long. Marco Grondin is a perverted predator who kills for pleasure. He can't be cured. Neither women nor animals will know peace as long as he is on the loose.

"Two wrongs don't make a right," Anouk says softly, shaking her head and pulling at the hem of her sweater.

"True. But there's an insane predator in our woods. What do we do about it?"

I picture the vultures turning silent circles above the skeletons behind his farm.

"You want to teach him a lesson. I can understand that."

I don't look up to see whether she is serious. She hesitates, waiting for me to answer before incriminating herself.

"You want to set a trap for him," she adds, "but what if he never steps in it?"

"Tracking people in the woods is my job. I'll position it so the terrain will give him no choice but to put his foot in the wrong spot."

"What makes you think he'll be able to free himself? You want to put him out of commission, you're trying to injure him, but are you ready to live with the idea that things might go wrong? If he, or one of his brothers, or a trail camera captures the scene?"

"I'll be careful."

"Let's say it does work. You set the trap, he walks into it, he gets hurt without knowing you're the one who did it. What will keep him from going back to trapping once he gets better? You want to hurt him, but that won't solve anything. It's stupid to take the risk! You're putting yourself in danger, too, and for what?"

"Anouk, listen. You don't free yourself so easily from a beartrap like this one. I'd be surprised—"

"You want to kill him?"

Kill. That word. She put her finger on it. The nail in the coffin. Kill to protect. Like the mother bear that will attack anything that endangers her young. Kill out of self-defence. The vision of the Grim Reaper delighted to get to work, the Three Fates holding the thread of human life, Atropos the Inflexible who cuts it off. Suddenly I'm cold. My teeth are chattering. Anouk wraps her scarf around my shoulders and rubs my back. My blood starts flowing again. Her touch makes my worst fantasies disappear.

"What are you thinking about?"

"It's crazy, Anouk. I hardly know you. But I'm telling you things that are really my business, and in the process I'm making you part of my plan. I'm turning you into an accomplice to an act that could put us both in prison for life."

"Premeditation, conspiracy, aggravated assault or involuntary manslaughter. That sounds pretty close to life."

I gaze at my friend, so calm despite the gravity of her words.

"But, as you say, if he can't free himself and it takes people a long time to find him, it will be difficult to prove how it happened."

I have no answer. I will have to get used to those words, and that idea. And the fear that goes with it.

"Do you trust Lionel?"

"Blindly. He's my cosmic father."

"Is your place in the Gaspé in good shape?"

I nod, thinking of the high-quality outdoor equipment I have accumulated over the years, the endless cords of wood, and the easy sleep I enjoy there. The time it will take to recover. Coyote and I, far away and safe.

"I'll make a deal with you, Raphaëlle. I don't want to

touch anything. Nothing! Not the trap, not anything else. Do what you have to do with Lionel. But you can count on me afterwards."

"And your silence."

"And my silence."

Solidarity, in Nature, is stronger than the instinct to destroy.

Anouk tells me everything she's heard about Marco. She is an outsider in the region, but she's stopped in often enough at the bar to earn Marilou's trust. Anouk describes the alcohol-soaked night she spent chatting with Marilou. The story of the new flame who replaced her in Marco's bed. A certain Chantal who got punched in the head so hard she is practically deaf now. No accusations there either. Marilou figures the Grondin name counts for a lot, they have loads of money and everyone knows it. Their cousin is the mayor of one of the villages, and their brother-in-law has an important job with the cops, and the other brother is in the forest industry. You get the picture. All the pieces on the chessboard point to the delinquent kid who grew up never being punished for his cruelty to animals, and then to schoolgirls and local women. Marilou drained the last of her pint, gathering her courage to show Anouk the knife scars in her flesh that he put there to mark his territory. And destroy her beauty. He signed his name in her skin the way he branded his livestock. A big M hacked into the heart of her cleavage.

Concentrate, Raphaëlle. Weigh your words. That bad habit of pulling on my sleeves. Quick, check and see that she didn't spot the scars on my forearms. It doesn't look like it. She watches me. Her eyes are serious. No, resolved. Waiting for me to tell her the solution I have in mind. The answer that, until now, was my ultimate fantasy and a burden I couldn't share.

She slides closer to me. "You know the expression 'Danger in delay'?"

"I've heard it, but I'm not sure what it means."

"Not taking action can be dangerous, too."

I picture my great-grandmother's haunted eyes. If only I had known the woman who passed on my looks to me. Would you have given me your blessing? Does the balance of Nature have primacy over the White world's justice? I imagine your response. *It certainly does.*

I shrug, sit up straight and think about the question. Cross-legged on the edge of the bed of branches, we contemplate the horizon. The moon has risen above the sleeping forest. Anouk takes a jar of apple sauce from her backpack, serves herself a spoonful, then hands the utensil to me, sharing it naturally. I thank her with my eyes. Her long lashes lower. I savour the fruit with closed eyes. When I look up again, I feel the strength of her gaze. Her mouth is almost purple. The colour of plums.

She takes my hands and looks me in the eye. Our cold fingers warm.

Fire sparkles in her face. Criminal intent seals our communion. It is beautiful, but the hatred behind it is painful. It consumes you the way a sunset burns the eye when it is too enchanting to turn away from.

She holds me close. Our thighs and shoulders touch. We have grown used to the darkness. We hear a sound from below, careful steps on the fine crust of snow. This time I am not afraid. From the window, I spot antlers and hooves between the bare trees. A rare creature I have been lucky enough to see twice in my life, both times here.

"Look, Anouk. A white stag. I was hoping it would come."

It is like the one of Arthurian legend, or the one that appeared to Saint Eustace. There is no need to worship a divinity to admire the animal's mythological beauty, and be moved by it. Its antlers are mossy and massive, and its coat is grey. It shines like silver fleece in the moonlight.

Sudden sadness comes over me as I gaze upon this living legend that Lionel first told me about. The beautiful animal must hide in the deepest part of the forest and hope that humans who see it will not be believed by others of their kind. Hunting and fishing stories are often exaggerations, aren't they? If the fact of its existence gets out, my friend the white stag might end up at the taxidermist's and decorate a mantlepiece. Why do people have such a need to possess beauty? Why not leave it in peace in the hope of meeting it again one day? A thought for the red coyote skin on the back seat of my truck, its colour so close to Anouk's hair. The absolute conviction that the right thing to do, when it comes to the delicate balance of this planet, is to protect the most vulnerable. Run for your life when the tyrant comes too close to your trailer. And then, later, strike back.

My peace of mind was broken by the poacher, and

now the hour of my vendetta has come. A counter-attack to help Nature recover her balance, though at the risk of my ending up in a maximum-security prison and losing everything. My freedom, the years of my prime, my mental health – and my dog. My Coyote.

I concentrate on my breathing. It is the only way to fight that suffocating feeling. Enclosed spaces horrify me. Anouk's voice brings me back to this place, where the white stag walks fearlessly beneath our hiding place. The peace of that animal. I am not alone. I will not be trapped. Anouk, Lionel and I will make common cause.

"Sorry, lost in my thoughts again."

"I thought you just wanted to take me into the deep woods for a walk. Then you end up introducing me to the oldest tree I've ever seen. Thank you. I am completely undone. The giant pine, this shelter, the five billion stars, the owls singing with us, an albino deer, the crescent moon and your company . . ."

"I'm happy you came. I was about to lose my mind. Then I told you everything, and you understood."

"Let's not talk about it any more."

"I'll just say, for the sake of being careful, that we won't name the poacher."

"Of course not."

"Lionel and I call him Gargamel."

"Fine. Now let's go in a different direction. It was your birthday a few days ago. I have a little something for you."

Anouk takes a bottle from her pack.

"Maple whiskey. Let me propose a toast."

She lifts the open bottle and puts on her serious voice. Her accomplice's voice.

"To the coyotes!"

"To the coyotes!"

She hands me the stuff. *Coureuse des bois*, it's called. I take a generous sip that sends warmth down my throat and through my chest, smoothing out my rough edges. Under the spell of the silver stag below, we pass the bottle and work our way through it as the predawn sky whitens. We watch the sun push through the branches of Tall Pine, then sleep an hour or so, nestled close together. Warmed by whiskey and friendship.

Lying close beside her, I cannot tell which shiver is cold and fatigue and which is desire.

19

The Clauses of the Pact

OCTOBER 7

I awaken to caresses and whispers. I recognise that shiver – it is pleasure.

"Did you sleep a little?"

"A regular honeymoon."

Her smile is as dazzling as the sun that has slipped into our hideout to shine on her wonderfully unruly hair. Just like that, she kisses my mouth. Her lips taste like maple whiskey and our teeth knock together. We are that hungry for each other.

"Come on, we have to get going. We don't want to make Lionel wait."

The return to reality is always a shock.

On the ground, we wrap our arms as far as we can around Tall Pine to say goodbye. Then we piss between the roots, on opposite sides of the giant trunk.

My fantasy is that one day I will come and live here, right on the border, by Morrison Creek, and drink its water before anyone else does, with no-one around for miles. A wild and pure place, far from Man. Anouk laughs at the idea, happy that we share so many ambitions. She could live anywhere as long as there is silence, forest and a horizon without neighbours.

"And a roof that doesn't leak!"

I feel vulnerable this morning. Overwhelmed by the prospect that, when I return, a madman is waiting for me, and I will have to neutralise him. I am nervous. I jump at the slightest sound and walk quickly along the path, my breathing compressed.

We talk in low voices. The conversation goes from the medicinal plants we see along the way to playground nicknames from grade school. I am glad my friend is with me. Without her, I would have thought about Gargamel, and what the prison for women looks like, and the beartrap waiting on the table. We move towards our meeting point with Lionel, sharing everything, apples and silence, and above all indignation.

"Did you know, Anouk, that there's a black market for the gall bladders of bears? In Asia, they're worth a fortune. Aphrodisiac qualities, apparently."

"Like shark fins. Bear gall bladders. What will they do when there are no more virile animals left to give up their bodies to sorcerers' apprentices?"

"Aphrodisiacs, my ass! Infertility, low libido, depression – I'm sure that pollution and stress cause those things. And there's no superfood or miracle cure to fix it."

"Living in the woods is the best antidote!"

"You took the words right out of my mouth."

We reach the part of the trail with the teddy bears. Adrenaline washes away anxiety, and determination speeds my step. The suction sound of my boots in the mud makes me think of the marshes where amphibians live. They can freeze, then come back to life. Would I be able to survive those conditions?

We come to the first beaver dam.

"Raphaëlle, when we get back, things are going to happen fast. But a pact is a pact, right? You won't make a run for your place in the Gaspé without saying goodbye?"

"I can't promise anything. The main thing for me is to not get anyone else in trouble."

"Don't forget. To protect Nature, you have to stay alive. Alive, and not behind bars."

"They won't catch me, don't you worry. And they won't find me either. It'll look like an unfortunate trapping accident. They happen all the time. The public knows that in the woods search parties don't always find what they're looking for right away. Remember the three fishermen who disappeared at the beginning of the month? Days and days went by before they were found. And some are never found, like poor Liliane Corriveau."

We have only a kilometre or two to go. Questions are buzzing around in my head like a beehive gone mad. When a corpse is found in no man's land, what jurisdiction does it belong to? Who would suffer if the poacher disappeared? I mean, outside of a few half-dead animals patiently waiting in traps in the forest. They will perish from exhaustion, or suffocate, or chew off a leg and go to die further on, hidden in the ferns, this night or the next. I wonder if there is some way to find them and approach them. What words or sounds would convince them to let me come close enough to free them? I think of the lynx at the Biodome again.

I picture it in its glass cage with children banging on it, disappointed not to see it, determined to wake it up. Biodome lynx, if you only knew that the province of Quebec just gave the green light for the destruction of your species without bothering to take an inventory of your numbers. There are plenty of those animals, the government officials assure us from high in their offices, sitting on their chairs on wheels steered by the lobbies.

If you don't do it, you, the experts and top-level Ministry bureaucrats, who else will fight for the animals suffering in traps, the fur-bearing species large and small? I have seen institutionalised violence from close up. Not like the government elites who close their eyes, as they did with the missing and murdered Native women.

Lionel spots us and begins waving his arms, as if we were returning alive from the front. The man with the glowing smile clasps us to his chest.

"I was so worried about you girls!" he says. "I couldn't wait to see you come out of the woods. I can't tell you the kind of thoughts I had."

He stops and looks straight at Anouk.

"She knows. I told her everything."

"Is that so? Fine, let's go, girls."

Anouk and I nestle happily in his embrace, pressed against his Santa Claus belly and his rough jacket that smells of tobacco and pine. He strokes our hair the way I stroked the coyote's red fur, feeling the sadness and defeat of those souls that have known the violence of men but can be restored again with an embrace like this one, and with acts of true goodness. My gratitude is so strong my crow's feet fill with mist.

The atmosphere changes in the pick-up. Lionel has taken it into his head to get involved. He is old, and this is man's business.

"Man's business? You're kidding me, Papa Wolf!"

"I couldn't stand it if something happened to you, Raphaëlle. That guy is dangerous. You two have your whole lives ahead of you. Don't mess things up by getting the cops after you."

"The police are not going to be anywhere I am."

"My girl, they are definitely going to get involved."

"O.K., you're right. But I'll be far away, and there won't be any proof."

"At least let me explain my plan."

Lionel has been following our target the last few days, and he tells us what he has discovered. From the addresses in the files, and the comings and goings of vehicles, he knows that Marco Grondin still lives on the family farm on Respite Road. No sign of his brothers. They don't seem to come to the village very often. At exactly 6 p.m., he gets onto his A.T.V. and heads up to the hunting camp. He traps on his own, using the last hours of daylight to walk his lines, and returns with heavy burlap bags before sundown. He works in his garage a few more hours, cutting up the animals and oiling his traps, most likely. Sometimes he spends the night there.

Lionel explains for Anouk's benefit, since I know all about this, that there are three moose blinds near his cabin.

The first two, close to the road, have been abandoned. The third, deeper in the woods, is oriented so the hunter can watch over the clearing. Yesterday evening, Lionel took up position there with a pair of good binoculars and saw our man crossing the clearing from east to west.

Sitting in front, I turn the rear-view mirror so I can watch Anouk. She is biting her nails and glancing nervously out of the window.

"Anouk," Lionel says, "look in the bag at your feet, there are sandwiches for you."

"Thanks, but I'm not hungry."

My stomach is growling. I'm starving, but I won't satisfy my hunger just yet, though it isn't easy.

"Gargamel takes the same path every evening?" I ask Lionel.

"Yes. It's the one you can see from the blind. It cuts sideways from the road to the spot where your dog got caught in the traps."

"How is she doing?"

"Fine. She doesn't trust me yet, but she's going to be a good dog, and faithful to you alone. That's what counts. Let me tell you something, Raphaëlle."

"I know what you're going to say, and the answer is no."

"I know exactly where to put the thing. He does his run every evening. I saw him with my own eyes yesterday, and I compared the footprints. The same four-leaf clover pattern, the same size 12. I checked it with my tape measure. It's him, no doubt about it. Why don't you two take a little trip to the Gaspé for a few days?"

"Yeah? Because you decided everything all by yourself?"
I am boiling over with anger.

"You need an alibi."

"Pull over and park."

"Raphaëlle . . ."

"I said *park*!"

Lionel was not expecting my reaction. Anouk draws back. I get out, slam the door and walk around the truck to face Lionel, who barely has time to roll down his window. I have to be standing to tell him what I need to say.

"Listen up. Marco Grondin is my catch. It was my dog he trapped, my trailer he broke into, my privacy he violated, pictures of me naked that he jerks off to, so I'm the one who's going to hunt him down! I'll restore the balance of my life."

My rage takes him aback. I might have a point, he admits. Anouk is gnawing on her nails so hard the blood starts to flow. She is staying out of it. My hands are shaking. I get back into the vehicle, in the front. The windows are wide open but there is not enough air. The truck is sizzling with electricity. No-one says a word. They are waiting for the next step, the *how* of it. Despite my emotions, things are coming together in my head.

"Lionel, I am going to set the beartrap. If you want to help, find a way for me to get the hell out afterwards. That's all I ask."

My decision does not meet with their approval, and I know it. Lionel thought I would accept his offer. He would be the one who might have to sacrifice his freedom.

"You'll need to do things just right, my girl. I would never forgive myself if something happened to you."

Anouk unfastens her seatbelt and holds me from behind, with the passenger seat between us. She says nothing, but I know this kind of talk disturbs her.

"Count on me, Raphaëlle," she says softly.

"Not a word to anyone, girls."

Lionel starts the engine again. We drive to the cabin in silence. I use the time to think. Before making my move, I will need to go to the office on Monday and put the Marco Grondin file back in its spot, then clear the recent history from my computer and destroy the memory card. I note down each crucial step in chronological order so I will not leave a trail.

There must be nothing that could incriminate me or make people doubt that it was a straightforward accident in the woods.

My old friend reassures me. He will take me to the exact spot where I will set the trap. My fantasy about a personal vendetta is slowly turning into a conspiracy. When the job is done, I will disappear for a while. Lionel will go on living in his cabin. He will go moose-hunting as planned, and get in touch with me once the dust has settled. I will claim I am pregnant to justify my sudden departure. My employer, the Ministry, will be overrun with work during hunting season, and I will earn a black mark on my record. That makes no difference to me. Everything I do must fit together flawlessly – that's what matters. And that no-one can point a finger at Lionel or Anouk. Or me either.

"I'll need a ride to my Gaspé place."

Anouk volunteers. While I am at the office on Monday, the two of them will go to get her car from the cabin. They will pull off the green tarp covered with pine needles, and methodically pack up everything I will need for a long stay in the Gaspé. Anouk offers me canned goods and cannabis. All three of us swear on the head of Tall Pine that we will never betray one another. Our crime will be our hearts' desperate cry for the animals and the unavenged women.

When I think about the trap I am going to set, I realise it is a good thing that there are so few officers for such a vast territory. If I had socialised even the slightest with my colleagues, they would have learned about my troubles with Marco Grondin. My sudden departure coupled with the disappearance of the poacher I was tracking would have seemed more than coincidence. The word *abortion* makes people ill at ease; it is the perfect reason to quit. Like pleading pre-menstrual syndrome, a feminine taboo that inspires silence, blushing and compassionate nods: *of course, but I'd rather not hear the details, came back when you're better*. I will be one in a long line of fallen women. My parents would die of shame.

*

We shook hands on the clauses of our pact and zipped up our lips. Anouk, Lionel, Coyote and I are spending our last evening at the cabin. Lionel tends the woodstove in silence. Coyote rubs against my calves. She licks my hands, the sign she wants to be petted. She is altogether better. I am proud of her, as if I was the one who brought her into the world. She has put aside her wild instincts when calm hands come near, and offers affection. Anouk takes out her sewing kit to make repairs. Her open journal on the table teases me. I took a quick glance when I went to put a log on the fire, and spotted my name.

She knows I am interested, and hands me the book.

"Why not? You read the rest of it."

I want to read because I am afraid. Afraid she is eager to get back to her solitude. Afraid of her judgment. That she fears my violence. I have resolved to avenge Nature, even at the risk of awakening disapproval, even disgust. My tears well up again.

"You alright, Raphaëlle?"

"Will you always want to be my friend, even after-wards?"

"Don't worry. We'll be here for you."

Lionel clears his throat and brings me a blanket, then drapes it gently over my legs. I lower my eyes and start to read as Anouk concentrates on her sewing.

The fire crackles before me. I am not a hermit any more. Human warmth has entered my life. I enjoy Raphaëlle's company, and her coyote's, and even Lionel's. Proof, maybe, that my social dysfunction is not complete, and that the hope of living with others is not so crazy after all. The context is disturbing, but I need to come out of my shell. In the forest isolation of the last two years, I did everything to stay away from crowds, and individuals too, human encounters that can be rich at times. Without alcohol in my blood, I saw no interest in opening myself up to anyone.

That is not completely true. There was Riopelle. He was probably behind the anonymous postcards and ounces of pot wrapped up in placemats from sushi joints with quotations from Quebec singers. "Roll us a big one, so when we smoke the spliff, we'll be unproductive and sovereign once more." They could have been coded messages. Was the sushi a reminder of Operation Black Whale? I keep the placemats that he sent through the mail in my glove compartment. When I have all the pieces of the puzzle, I'll take them out and try to make sense of them.

Maybe there is no secret message, just his deep appreciation.

I suspect you miss me, Rio. Keep on buttering me up with good pot, old flame. I am counting the months. Nine months since last winter and those two nights with you. Bloody luck! Despite taking no precautions, despite our shared desire to mingle our fluids without a thought for tomorrow, I have bled too much these last moons to be in the family way.

I should write to you, but I don't know where you are hiding out these days. I'd like to tell you about Tall Pine and how I met the beautiful Raphaëlle.

And how your cannabis is a miracle cure for my menstrual cramps.

°

I
have
my period
Red alert
Lunar cycle
On the rag
Lady business
Russians have come
Visit from Aunt Flo
Red Baron stopped by
That time of the month
Red Badge of Courage
Having the painters in
Riding the cotton pony
Mother Nature's gift
Crimson tide
Shark Week
Moon time
Menses
Yoni
OM
G
°

Anouk smiles at me from her end of the sofa. Tosses me the joint. I drop it and it lands on the rug. I struggle with the lighter that slips out of my hand every time I flick it. I hate having sweaty palms. Finally. A big puff. I breathe out, my eyes on the fire and Anouk's hands. She is making some kind of object, an assemblage of red thread and twigs.

I am moved by the way she opens herself up to me so completely in her writing. I think of our wet kisses in Tall Pine's arms. I am beginning to fall for this woman I will have to leave tomorrow. After having, after having, after having . . . I can't put it into words.

"Hey, girls, this is no time to burn down the place," Lionel jokes.

He gets to his feet and picks up a book from the kitchen shelf. Runs his palm over its cover.

"For you. Your birthday present. With everything going on, I forgot all about it."

The book is weighty, and its black cover is rough. No title on it, nor on the back. I open it. I like the sound of its old pages, dry and crumbling.

THE WITCHES' ANTHOLOGY

On the cover page, I recognise the cramped writing I know so well.

For my girl, on her 40th birthday.

"Thanks, Lionel."

I turn the page and read out loud. "Witchcraft, a form

of traditional magic that uses supernatural forces to exert influence over Man and the course of life."

"That's just what we need!"

Anouk stands up and hands me the strange object she has been busy with for the last hour. A doll made of twigs knotted together with red thread, a T shape within an X.

"I've seen something like this before."

I twirl the doll in circles.

"I've made lots of them. I hang them in the trees, and above the graves I dig for the birds that break their necks by flying into my window. Little men and little women. Forest spirits."

"I don't remember seeing one in your cabin."

"I copied the shape, actually. It comes from "The Blair Witch Project". You remember that horror film with the cannibal witch in the woods? Around her house, there are all these twig dolls hanging in the trees. It's really scary. You just know that someone with a twisted mind lives there, and that you must never stray onto their territory because it's full of graves. And the answers to everything you want to know."

Anouk lifts the blanket and snuggles up next to me.

"We should absolutely start reading *The Witches' Anthology* right away," she tells me, "to learn how to cast a foolproof spell on the poacher."

"See if there's a section about spells."

Anouk is so eager and enthusiastic I wonder if she really does believe in the power of magic formulae. I like the idea of possessing a secret that will take me closer to the realm of the invisible, but I doubt it would be very useful in my quarrel with my evil neighbour.

The fire fills the cabin with warmth. Lionel produces a bottle of wine, pours three glasses, then goes back to tending the fire. The pile of logs by the stove is low, and he goes out to split more wood. He opens the door and Coyote follows, her tail in the air. He smiles and looks back at me. Yes, my dog has finally lowered her guard. The two of them go outside. When we are alone, Anouk leans over and kisses my neck.

The hours pass, the bottle is empty, and we turn the pages of the *Anthology*, inspired by the recipes of midwives and the discoveries of wise women dancing under the full moon.

Coyote yawns, her mouth wide open.

I look over to Lionel, my old friend. I can feel his love; I feel the same. He supports me in the act I am about to commit, and understands my need. He takes care of me, and that gives me strength. His desire to do good on this earth and help his neighbour send a message: not all human beings are rotten. And the rotten ones can always be composted. After they rot, new life will spring up. It is the same with selective tree-cutting. Some species, when eliminated, will allow others to survive.

"I wonder what would grow on a poacher's corpse," Anouk says, turning the pages.

A strange remark. She points to a chapter heading decorated with brambles. *Poisons.*

"Clumps of spotted water hemlock and ordinary

hemlock, a bouquet of immortelles, poison ivy and fly agaric, for starters!"

Rampant, poisonous flora with no known antidote, though it grows all around.

Lionel bars the door, something he never does, but given the circumstances . . . He runs his hand over my forehead and blows out the candle.

"Time to get some shut-eye, girls."

We prepare ourselves for the ceremony of sleep. Lionel settles into his rocking chair beneath his wool blanket. Coyote chooses the rug by the door and I take the futon. Anouk tends the fire, holding her twig doll. No-one, not even my dog, closes their eyes.

*

"Raphaëlle," she whispers, "you sleeping?"

"No."

Her eyes burning, she throws the doll into the flames and watches as it is consumed. Something in me is made more peaceful by her act, the humanoid figure in the stove. The evil spell has been cast.

I relax and dream a moment or two of utopia, a free Quebec where we might do things differently, where fur would stay on the backs of animals. The snow would mirror the red of foxes, the black of mink, the indescribable rusty grey of coyotes. My deepest wish is that one day humans will not have to destroy life to live, nor harvest the skin of other animals to fill their pockets, nor dominate to feel strong. I make that wish for myself, too.

I open my eyes one last time before drifting into my last night of innocence. I see Anouk and her ruffled reddish coat glowing in the firelight, her long, peach-coloured fingers clasped as if in prayer as she listens to Lionel whispering and scribbling hard on a sheet of paper. They are talking of the long road ahead. I hear the word "Gaspé" several times. Then the days and weeks of fatigue overtake me.

20

The Amethyst

OCTOBER 8

I am the mother wolf separated from her young, pacing her cage. The cell is made of bars and rock walls. I wear out my fangs on the iron and sharpen my claws on the stone. The mural painted on the back of the pen makes it look as if I am in the open forest. They watch my every move. I wait for the moment to pour out my fury on these voyeurs. This is not where I should be, contained, rationed, in the shadows, anticipating my time to kill. Immobility is killing me. *Tick tock tick tock tick tock tick tock*. I can't stand it. I need to spring and return to the forest without end on the other side of these walls. The guard brings me a pail of bones. Maybe he thinks a full belly will make me forget I'm in a cage with my little ones on the outside, howling and howling until I go mad mad mad with rage. Even if they are dead, I hear them calling still.

Tick tock tick tock.

The clock tells me it's four twenty-two.

Lionel is leaning on the fridge door in his denim overalls, his cap down to his eyebrows. I sit up and start braiding my hair, rubber band between my teeth. He hands me a burning cup of coffee. I try to dismiss my nightmare and the picture of the heap of coyotes behind the Grondin farm. No, I need to confront that image and move forward, step by step, towards the stink of those headless bodies with the vultures circling above. Turning in silence, soaring on winds and strips of flesh. Tearing apart and returning the bodies to the earth. Death is inevitable; it is a way out in itself.

I set down the coffee cup that is burning my hand. Concentric circles move across the liquid. My hand is shaking. I thrust my fists into my pockets and head for the door, Coyote on my heels.

"Take the time to have breakfast," Lionel tells me. "I'm going to run the vacuum and wipe down your truck with a rag. Here, this is the list Anouk and I wrote up last night, with everything we said and some new things added. Read it and destroy it. And leave your cellphone on the table."

Anouk comes and holds me from behind, then secures my braid with the rubber band I left on the table. I feel her breasts against my shoulder blades. She digs her teeth into my neck, and I remember my dream of the caged wolf. Anouk won't let go. The weight of her teeth and the warmth of her breath make me feverish, and I feel nauseous. I pull away with no explanation, and when I look down, my vision is blurry. A migraine. I sit at the table. Lionel pushes a steaming dish in my direction.

"Eat!"

I do as I'm told, then drink a glass of water, and I don't care if it runs down over my sweater. I start to recover my senses. Anouk understands my need for space and what this act means to me. And the freedom I will feel once it is over. She takes the sheet of paper from Lionel and helps me go through the list in the chronological order I rehearsed ten times last night with my spiritual father.

Then she stands up, crumples my two copies of Marco Grondin's photograph into a ball, and throws them into the fire. They disappear completely.

Our eyes fall on the coyote skin that Lionel rolled up and put on my pile of survival stuff by the door. There is too much. Much too much, but I don't protest. They take care of the bags, and I'll do the hard work.

Anouk sees me glaring at the heap of equipment.

"It's because I'm coming with you, Raphaëlle. I'm going to drive you to the Gaspé, and when we get there, we'll see if we can live together. Until Lionel gets in touch, once the dust settles. Say you agree. It's important for me."

"It's a relief for me. I haven't slept in two weeks. I can't imagine driving all that way alone. Then getting there, sweeping the chimney, priming the pump . . ."

"One thing at a time, darling."

Lionel gathers up my plate that I scarcely touched and hands us thermos bottles full of coffee. He points to the table and our conspiracy list. It is the final step of my vendetta, the last nail in Marco's coffin.

"Take it from the top one last time. And give me the memory card, I'll destroy it right now."

1. *Drive to the office, respecting the speed limits.*
2. *When you get to the parking lot, don't forget the cardboard box on the seat to collect your personal belongings.*
3. *Lock the truck and go to the office without attracting attention.*
4. *Put Gargamel's file back where it belongs.*
5. *Clear all history that has anything to do with this case.*
6. *Put your Glock in its holster, then in the drawer with the lock. Add your uniforms and lock the drawer.*
7. *Open Word and write your resignation letter with the date and the name of your superior. "This letter is to inform you of my decision to resign from my post as Wildlife Protection Officer, effective immediately."*
8. *Print, sign, then put the letter in an envelope with the key to the drawer.*
9. *Empty your desk.*
10. *Try to meet a colleague and mention that you are quitting.*

"It's alright if you seem upset. Your reason for quitting will be more credible."

"Great. I need to look pretty much destroyed. I'm pregnant and there's nowhere to go but back to my family. Heartbreak, abortion, boo hoo hoo. I shouldn't have to act too much to look completely messed up."

"Go on, now."

"Alright. Next . . ."

11. *Go outside with your box, envelope and truck keys. Walk to the Post Office.*

12. *Send a registered letter to the Lower Saint Lawrence Wildlife Protection Agency. The envelope should contain your resignation letter, key to the drawer and keys to your truck.*

13. *Walk to the Sainte-Anne Saint-Onésime road. I'll be waiting for you by the train tracks.*

"In the parking lot by the old station?"

"Yes. I'll be a little ways back from the road."

14. *In the meantime, Anouk will have had time to pick up her car, fill the tank and load her bags and yours.*

Anouk lifts her right hand to her forehead and maintains a military salute a little too long for Lionel's liking.

"Good. After that . . ."

15. *I'll drive you to you-know-where. You will take off your boots. You will wear my old shoes. You'll go to the spot I show you, you'll do what we said, and you'll come back the same way.*

16. *Then we'll go to the car. Anouk and Coyote will be waiting with everything both of you will need to take off and stay gone for a long time.*

17. *I'll burn the shoes and go back to the spot to see if we've caught the big fish. I'll get rid of any prints and the instrument, and bury it somewhere I alone will*

225

know. While I'm at it, I'll disarm the traps and snares in the area.

I close my eyes and take a deep breath. The forest free of all those traps.

18. *Absolutely no contact from then on. You leave your cellphones behind.*
19. *Now, we burn this paper.*

"Raphaëlle, Anouk, girls, listen to me, both of you. When you're in the car and everything has been taken care of, drive, but don't get stopped because you're driving too fast. Drive like tourists all the way to your destination. I'll take care of the rest. Stay in the woods and don't talk to anybody until you hear from me. I'll write what you need to know."

*

After just one kilometre on the road, I am having trouble following Lionel's advice. Obey the speed limit. I need music to relax, but I can't stand the radio. On the steering wheel, I tap out the rhythm of a Chopin nocturne that Grandma loved so much. Then my thoughts start to run wild.

I think of the ambush mechanism, the rifle that poachers and clandestine cannabis producers attach to a tree. The gun goes off when an animal, a civilian or a Wildlife

Protection Officer trips the brass wire attached to the trigger. I think of those men who would rather kill than end up behind bars. Not so different from me, really. They know, as I do, how difficult it is to find someone, dead or alive, on the vast Crown lands. And rifle shots are nothing unusual during hunting season.

I spare a thought for officer Gérard Martineau who came face to face with two twelve-gauge shotguns loaded with buckshot, the heavy-grade ammunition used for hunting big game. He had been tracking a poacher and a moose outside of Forestville.

A thought for those names carved in stone, in memory of the officers who died in the line of duty.

I reach the office, park and begin to carry out the first items on my list with complete self-possession. Do I have the murderer's cold blood in my veins? A sudden thought occurs to me. I am afraid of catching an animal or a hiker by accident. That thought is like a fault line, and doubt takes root there. Should I go back and wait, hidden in the pines, and keep watch? Lionel and Anouk are waiting for me. I can't reach them on the phone. The die is cast. Focus, girl.

The stone around my neck reminds me of what my body feels in the present moment. Between my breasts, I am wearing Anouk's lucky charm amethyst on its long silver chain. She unhooked it from her neck and put it around mine. I had never received jewellery as a gift, and hadn't even noticed the pendant she wore beneath her layers of clothing.

I warm the amethyst in the palm of my hand and kiss it.

"Bring me luck."

I dream of truce.

*

The door of the Ministry of Forests, Wildlife and Parks closes behind me. I must have been convincing in my role as a woman in crisis, but I remember nothing of it. I move forward, concentrating on the cold mist stinging my face. My clothes are damp. I am trembling with exhaustion or anticipation or both, I hardly slept at all, tormented by nightmares of beartraps snapping their jaws shut. I conjure up the skinned, beheaded coyotes. The memory of vultures turning in the sky. *Fill your mind with gore, that way you'll find the strength to deal out death*. But my armour is weakening, I can feel it. I am giving in to my woman's vulnerability, afraid I have fallen for a fox on the American border. A thought for the silver doyen of the forest. My lovely stag with the whitest coat in the Appalachians, will you survive the year? I cling to your lucky charm, Anouk, and your kisses in the arms of Tall Pine, your cheeks dotted with freckles, our noses reddened by the early morning cold, but finding a way in the darkness. I move forward, lugging my big cardboard box, absurdly empty. Every step rattles my small collection of red pens, as red as the blood of poached animals, along with green ones that stand for the sap of felled trees. In that same box, the random objects of my life at work. The desktop cactus as repulsive as I might become in Anouk's eyes because of what I am about to do. A wool hat that smells of wood smoke and is full of holes from embers, a lighter, an enormous clay pot brought back from California, and the photograph of Marie-Ange and her husband. The look in her eyes takes on new meaning. *I will stand my ground and retaliate.*

*

I step out of the post office. I did what I had to, and now I am an ordinary civilian. I just have to make it to the railway track and hope my ride will be waiting. I'm hot, I'm sweating and I stink of fear.

Lionel opens the door and we head for the back country. I unlace my boots and put on man's shoes too big for me, hide my braid under my bulky coat, and put on my old hat. The beartrap is waiting patiently in a plastic bag. Lionel hands me gloves. Parks the pick-up. His reassuring words are meaningless. I get out and move forward. Soon I will be there. The spot you will pass by when your time comes. Where you will place your foot.

My only certainty is an amethyst hanging around my neck. The pendant moves from one breast to the other, slipping over my sweaty skin like a pendulum marking time and the rhythm of my steps. I hear gunshots.

Fire in the northern forest. It is raining lead and smoking cartridges on the back country's carpet of dry needles. Armistices exist on paper only.

I am sure the animals feel it coming in the stars, the deadly period, the strategic window in the calendar of Man when they must lie lower, freeze more thoroughly, fear the heaps of apples in the forest, the blocks of salt, the calf carcasses. Bait lures the most famished, snares surprise the young who trust the trails too much. But the veterans know, this time of year, that it is better to choke back your hunger than satisfy it. Sniff out the fresh boot prints. Pick out the shapes of hunters too impatient to sit still. Keep far away from the blinds that spit fire and bring low the biggest moose, the sleeping grouse and everything else that moves in the foliage. Run for your life.

Only the wolves and coyotes used to protest with their nightly song. A call as old as the hills, a symphony.

Poaching cut their music short.

I praised their howling. It reminds us that this territory is theirs, their hunting grounds, their space beneath the moon. Then I stopped hearing you, coyotes, singing in the night. Follow me, brothers and sisters, we will sound the call of the mountains that stretch all the way to winter, we will sow fear with our assembled voices, dog and wolf together, so our rivals and our prey freeze between a rock and a hard place. Lie low, you who think yourselves sly. From the forest skirt to the taiga, we lay down the law.

A loon betrays its distant lake. The water is smooth and glassy like a mirror. The guardian of sleep issues its plaintive call. Its blood-red eye spots me and cautions me to stay far from the places where the wild ones have left their skins behind.

My feet move towards them of their own volition, step by step along the poacher's trapline. They are calling me, eager to be found.

All those that fly, bound and leap along banks, ponds and marshes. *Rich dressed pelts*, the explorers said of their skins scented with bark smoke. The warm down of water fowl, fur trophies ornamenting lovers' beds and garments. Queens of salt and fresh water, my wild ones, you shall be avenged.

PART FOUR

The Devouring

21

Eye for an Eye

OCTOBER 8

I am transgressing society's sense of propriety and violating the Criminal Code, but I am more afraid of poachers taking the last great mammals than I am of life in a prison cell. Sometimes, history teaches us, disobedience and rebellion lead to progress.

I have lived life behind bars ever since I started working here. Trying to do a job with a skeleton staff, registering animals whose heads were used for post-mortem target practice, and writing up reports about acts I consider ordinary butchery, except that they bring in piles of cash.

The main thing is not to impede the workings of the regional economy, I was told countless times. Sorry, but you're off target, Monsieur le Ministre. You have a romantic image of the forest full of game, and you have hung that picture on your office wall. The reality on the ground is something else. We are witnessing mass destruction. The vast, magnificent wilderness that charms the imaginations of foreigners and city-dwellers when they think of Canada will soon be a thing of the past.

I cannot participate in this masquerade with a clear

conscience. As a woman, I will not tolerate the violence that haunts our villages.

And I can't go on ignoring the carcasses and the remains of your prey. Did the victims of your carnage feel that their end was near? Do you feel that yours is coming, too?

Vultures have been turning circles in my head since I discovered the horror of my decapitated coyotes. Rage has been boiling in me for years. I have choked it back again and again, but now it is overflowing. Turn a blind eye to everything I know about you, the hundreds of corpses heaped up behind your family farm, the warnings of one woman and the whispered confessions of another, your irreverence towards Nature who offered you her generous bounty – I won't do that any more.

The beartrap in my hand is the descendant of the well-maintained traps of the past, which hung on the walls of the hunting camps back when this country was a colony. The trap was a promise: the children would always have something to eat. I never thought one day I would use one on a man. Eye for an eye, tooth for a tooth.

I still find these outlawed traps in the woods. The government decided that trapping methods must limit the pain inflicted on the animal to the level acceptable in the food industry. An odd standard. I wonder which animal suffers more. The cow separated from her calf the day after its birth or the coyote slowly strangled by a snare in the night, its muzzle turned into exploded flesh? Which mutilation is worse, the chick with its beak sanded down on a wheel or the beaver caught in a leg-hold trap that, to save its life, chews off the limb? Those images keep me awake at night.

I set the beartrap, then place it between two bulging roots on the trapline that Gargamel will walk later in the day. The mechanism's teeth are camouflaged under dead leaves and pinecones. It is waiting to snap shut pitilessly. The evening light will make it invisible, I hope.

Have patience, toothed trap, the big game is approaching.

Further along the trail, I hang an object to attract the predator's attention. He should be looking up when he absent-mindedly sets his foot in the exact wrong spot. I attach an owl's wing to a young cedar. Well-known bait that trappers use. The one I am after will think that someone is encroaching on his territory, picking off the lynx. Objects that twirl in the wind are irresistible to felines, and that includes this wing with its white plumage accented by a subtle orange tone. Bright colours, even in the evening, will throw off Marco's concentration.

A person needs a lever to open up a beartrap. Maybe you'll manage to do that. You know the killing mechanisms better than I do. But you will be seriously injured. Enough to attract the fauna with long canines. You will push deeper into the forest, trying to save your skin.

Make sure he never gets out, fur-bearing friends.

Maybe my footprints will be discovered, but the shoes will have long since melted in Lionel's firepit. No tyre tracks since my good friend took the precaution of staying on the asphalt when he dropped me off. And a pick-up parked around here at the start of hunting season is nothing unusual.

Now I just have to get back to the road without running into you.

You have a long history of violence. The hundreds of minor infractions, dated and numbered, accompanied by photographs of your poaching spots. A list of all the pet dogs and cats with collars found in traps or used as bait. The distances, as the crow flies, between your traps and the houses where people live. The names of the landowners who did not give you permission to trap on their property. The written declarations during a conversation between Wildlife Protection Officers and a woman who owns a woodlot in Saint-Bruno who will not accuse you, even if her identity is protected. She is terrorised. The word *terrorised* is underlined twice. The list of laws and regulations that were not respected. A description of dangerous and non-biodegradable garbage left in the forest. Reports meticulously filled out. Conclusions based on reliable information. The work is worthy of a monk in a monastery, but Gargamel has continued his business with impunity up until this day, while our hands are tied by a legal system that serves the industry. And then there are the women, too. The ones I heard about, and the ones I didn't.

I would have liked to hear you make excuses to a judge, but I had better stop here. I will not be another Jane Doe rotting in the back country.

My lucky star, Marie-Ange Robichaud, and you, Sirius, the Dog Star, and the Great Manitou, and all the goddesses of the hunt and the vestals, the spirits of the forest, the sacrificed animals – may you grant me my wish. I have set a trap for a poacher and he must not escape it.

My amethyst burning in my hand, my prayer spoken, I retrace my steps. On the way, as I did before my final exam in forestry school, I recite the trapper's code of ethics for the hundredth time to forget the instrument of death I left behind. I move forward, and do not falter, to reach Lionel's pick-up without coming across the Devil in person.

1.   *Obtain permission from landowners before trapping on their land.*
2.   *Do not set traps in areas where farm animals might be caught.*
3.   *Check traps at least once a day, preferably in the early morning.*
4.   *Record trap locations accurately.*
5.   *Identify all traps with waterproof name and address tags.*
6.   *Use as much of the animal as possible before disposing of the remains.*
7.   *Dispose of animal carcasses properly so as not to offend others.*
8.   *Make an effort to trap in areas with a surplus of animals.*
9.   *Promptly report the presence of diseased animals to wildlife authorities.*
10. *Support and help train new trappers.*
11. *Know and follow all trapping regulations.*
12. *Support enforcement of all regulations.*
13. *Dispatch trapped fur-bearers in a humane manner.*

*

Through the leafless branches, I catch sight of Lionel's truck. I jump inside. The motor is purring. We drive to the post-boxes on Sugarmill Road. My lovely fox is waiting for us at the wheel of her old jalopy with Coyote on the back seat. She starts barking happily when I approach.

My goodbye to Lionel is brief but painful. Neither of us speaks. The old sea wolf holds me close. For one last time, I breathe in his benevolent father smell.

Two taps on the fender, and it's time to head off. Drive and drive and drive, to the far edge of the landscape, eastward, towards the hope that all will be well.

22

Tooth for a Tooth

OCTOBER 8

The forest echoes with an endless curse, a poacher's primal scream. His heel has been crushed in the jaws of the beart-trap. The effect is so devastating that even the most primitive of men would lose consciousness.

The survival instinct puts an end to the coma a few hours later. The sun is low. The inhabitants of the forest begin to stir, excited by the ferrous odour.

Despite the blood that spurts out with every attempt to loosen the jaws, and his fingers that slip on the metal vice, the man is able to jam a branch between the teeth of the trap. The wooden lever cracks, but does not break. He manages to free his boot. His knowledge of traps made of triggers and springs pays off. Manipulating these instruments every day has given this experienced killer great strength and dexterity in his fingers. Once the mechanism is opened, Marco Grondin picks himself up and moves into the forest, towards his pick-up parked a kilometre further on. He is limping and his sight is clouded by adrenaline. A kilometre is a long, long way when you are in that kind of pain.

He does not take off his boot to attend to his wounds or

see how bad the injury is. He knows that the tightly-laced leather is holding his foot together and that there is no time to lose. Blood is pouring through the openings in the boot. Pain surges inside him with every step, and the sock around his perforated flesh is soaked with warm fluid. His life energy is flowing out of the holes in his body.

Ears are listening. The forest is attentive to the sound of wet suction from a foot limping along its Via Dolorosa. That is the first indication. Laboured breathing. Snapping twigs. No rhythm to the steps.

Appetites sharpened, the witnesses hold their breath.

The forest is dense and thick with branches. No-one ventures here, especially not in the marshy places where alders reign and scavengers abound.

The man jumps awkwardly from mound to stump with swamp water up to his calves. He has almost reached dry land, but he stumbles the first time in the cold mud, and drops to all fours. He makes his way over trunks and crosses a clearing where raspberries and thistles grow. The ditch that borders the road is within sight. He thinks he is out of the woods, but he falls a second time, then hears a buzzing sound. The air is vibrating around him. Something tickling him all over his body, a bad omen. He is horrified to find himself inside a cloud of stinging insects that did not appreciate being awakened.

In the ground is a nest asleep around its queen. Disturbed by the wounded man's awkward foot, hundreds of wasps swarm him, stinging him, opening up holes in his skin, showing no mercy. He wants to run, but his leg is paralysed.

He struggles, but they are everywhere, aggressive, in his sleeves, the collar of his sweater, his ears and nostrils. His heart is beating too fast. He is panicked and dizzy. He falls to his knees. The wasps zigzag in all directions, fly up and descend upon him. The swelling in his face is more dangerous than the bites on his body, and he almost forgets about his foot.

Everything goes black.

The impact makes a wet sound. The man hits the side of his head against a rock. He loses consciousness again, his face unrecognisable and swollen against the wet earth and the random gravestone.

Yes, the trap did bite. And the wasps' venom paralysed. The sun went down. Fate is writing the last chapter. Slowly, the creatures of the forest move closer, curious about this offer of meat.

The stars begin to glow in the grey sky. The man awakes because someone has touched him. Once, then again. He opens his eyes and sits up. An enormous animal is at his feet, her eyes on his. She displays no ill intent or intrigue, only the obvious truth of her queenly dominance in the food chain.

Powerful jaws find the injured foot and sniff at it.

To his horror, Marco understands that a large she-bear is licking the pool of blood in which he has fainted. Too weak to drag himself away from the animal, not even a few metres, the man tries to get to his feet by leaning on tree roots, but they break under his weight. The trees will not get involved. Even they will not help you.

The bear raises her head and breathes noisily. She recognises the man by his unnaturally strong smell of pine, and of rancid grease from the traps, of beaver oil and of the fluids from his victims that scent his jacket. The bear picks up something else, too, a sulphurous odour. The acrid musk of a man who is sweating freely, drowning in fear. Bile rising into his mouth. Helpless tears of pain.

At the scene of the crime, the carpet of moss has been ripped away. The track of a body painfully dragging itself along. All around, the prints of an adult female bear. The owl's wing has stopped waving in the wind. Blood everywhere, the cold ground turned over, and the uncertain fate of a man lying a hundred feet from the road.

Between the tops of the naked trees, the North Star shines, almost blinding in its whiteness. The Big Dipper points out the way to all who will look.

Marco has to lift his swollen eyelids with his fingers to see. But complete darkness is more comforting than a glimpse of what is crouching in the darkness, patiently keeping watch.

The she-bear is in attendance. Sitting, waiting, all the time in the world. The poacher suddenly remembers the trap, the vice around his heel, its teeth digging into his flesh, his warm, coagulating blood, the pain that caught him unawares and will not leave. A few metres away, his boot, torn apart. He doesn't remember taking it off.

The bear stands up, seeing that he is awake. She stretches from her watchful posture and lumbers over to his body. He panics. He tries to escape, dragging himself away from the trees.

Marco is only a few steps from the road, and his pick-up and first aid kit, but his body refuses to carry him. Numb, swollen everywhere, covered with painful welts. The wasps have flown off, but he hears them buzzing in his ears, and feels the pulse of each of his hundreds of stings. He does not know if the sound of an A.T.V. coming towards him is a hallucination. Or if it is moving away. In the silence that follows, the bear's breath is very near.

Mama Bear moves over to the boot, sniffs it and swats it away, then pushes her nose against the man's bloody foot. He screams and starts throwing rocks as hard as he can. Still too alive, she judges, he might hurt her. Patience is the greatest wisdom in the woods. Better to devour an exhausted prey than risk a fight. She pads off to her lair and lies down with her three cubs. Let the meat hang a while more.

23

Kilometres

OCTOBER 8

I lost track of how many rest stops disappeared in our rear-view mirror, and how many kilometres we racked up as if we had the cops on our tail. My fox has a heavy foot, and I am grateful. My eyes say farewell to the places that have been my landmarks over the years. Goodbye monadnocks, so long islands, good evening beach with the mineral spring and the eel-fishing setup. At Trois-Pistoles, we take the King's Road that follows the river to our destination, still far off. Route 132 shows us the coast. Saint-Fabien, Rimouski, Mont-Joli, Métis-sur-Mer. The Charlevoix mountains disappear on the far side. The estuary opens onto the gulf, the wind is more insistent, the cold more penetrating. The sun is going down over high tide. The seagulls ride out the waves. Salty air comes in through the windows we leave ajar. The familiar smell of algae and the feeling of peace move me. My eyes fill with tears that I don't wipe away.

"Where exactly are we going, Raphaëlle?"

The question is a legitimate one. Here she is, having decided to come with me without knowing where we are going or how our exile will end. Lionel must have had a hand in that. He must have told her about the paradise waiting for us, since he came with me there once before.

What is he doing right now? Did he do what he intended and drive the roads in search of a pick-up with a cold hood, walking distance from the trapline? Did he return to the spot to see if our ambush caught the poacher and remove the murderous object from his foot? Is he at the cabin, boiling the trap in the big kettle he uses for cooking corn? Or digging a hole six feet deep at the far end of his land for the weapon? Marco Grondin will not have that chance. His body will not know the peace of burial. Anyone looking for him will have to follow the vultures.

My head is spinning. I am in no shape to drive. I settle for glancing nervously in the side-view mirror to see if we are being followed. That occupation absorbs me; I am unable to concentrate on anything else. I think of our destination. The peninsula, the turn-off, the secondary roads, the colourful signs, the last curve, the entrance to the yard. The quiet place where I spent my girlhood vacations on the beach. Cling to those living memories, and escape the darkness.

I am just old enough to walk. I am wearing a white cap decorated with pretend precious stones. Blue jean shorts and a turquoise pail. It is summer, the tide is out, the beach is rich with treasures and trash. I have not learned the adage according to which one person's garbage is another's gold, but I am picking it up through experience. I fill my little pail with bits of ceramic. I have so many pieces that the plastic handle bends with the weight. Later, I leave my loot near the pier and kiss my knees as I watch the waves break against the dyke. I am a little lighthouse against the horizon. I breathe in the salty happiness; even then I know that the sea and the moon regulate my moods. I have acquired a pearl of wisdom. I am happy to be here with my river, my pier, my beach. And a pail full of treasures to show Grandma, who fell asleep on a chaise longue under her blanket with the pink seashells on it. Or maybe she is meditating. Hard to tell with her dark glasses. I have a sudden, rebellious idea: what if I asked my mother to abandon me? I could move here with my grandmother. Spend my life in L'Anse. But I am six years old and I like my school, I even have a boyfriend my age who gives me kisses at recess. Marie, my teacher, is nice. She defends me when the older kids push me around. How do you get to be friends with the big kids? I'll ask Grandma. One thing's for sure, I've never been as happy as I am here and now. When she sees me, Grandma purrs and opens her arms. She has a great idea: let's go back to the house and have some apple crumble. Then try to glue together my pieces of broken ceramic.

Anouk glances at me and puts her right hand on my thigh. She caresses me gently as she drives. I emerge from childhood and remember her question.

"We're going to L'Anse-Pleureuse, to a lake there. I'll guide you once we get close. I inherited some land from my family. My grandmother's house burned down a long time ago, but the camp in the woods behind it is great, you'll see."

"In any case, darling, we have enough supplies for the whole winter. I put all my canned goods in the trunk."

"And I've got dog food for two months. After, we'll see. Maybe we could trade some of your good pot for meat for Coyote."

Anouk watches the road with a smile. She seems strangely euphoric, imagining what the camp will look like. I don't think she will be disappointed.

We drive eastwards for several more hours, rocked by the sounds of her favourite albums. The inside of the car is smoky from the half-joints we light every hour to ease our tense shoulders, sharpen our concentration and help us philosophise about good and evil and trapping. Coyote is sleeping like a log, knocked out by the smoke.

We officially enter the Gaspé, sprinkled with a dusting of silvery snow. As bright as the hope for a new beginning.

Lionel placed the sepia photograph of my ancestors' wedding behind the sun visor, exactly where I kept it in my Ministry truck, with Marie-Ange's face peering out. This time, it is on the passenger side. I salute my great-grandmother. I am returning to my roots. Yawning, Anouk asks me to put on some music to keep her awake.

I open wide my window and go through the bag at my feet. Anouk nods happily. I have chosen one of her favourites. Soon, the three Acadian voices of the Hay Babies launch into a tune she knows by heart, and sings along with.

> *J'connais un grizzly bear qui dort pas l'hiver*
> *Qui rôde dans mon coin des bois[5]*

We stop in a parking lot in front of a wharf to sleep an hour or two before getting back on the road. We curl up in the foetal position, facing each other. A contortionist in the passenger seat, I examine Anouk's wool socks. She wiggles her toes against the heater vents.

I don't know how much time we spent by the wharf, nor why my tears flowed so freely, nor how long Anouk spent caressing my cheek and forehead and hair.

She shivers. A tiny earthquake that says it all. The fire within, the adrenaline of flight, the latent desire between us. Or is it stress, fear and fatigue? Her face is pale. Her eyes, circled by dark skin. But God, she is beautiful, my freckled girl, her hair tied in a feral knot, wind-blown and silky like a fox tail, her fine nose and her mouth that cannot lie. Her hands soothe me. Her mouth keeps me from hyper-ventilating. Her fingers run free.

Peace – a spirit, a spark. Passing fancy or mission in life? They should leave us women in peace, with the coyotes and the woods. I always fear the worst when the present moment is beautiful.

"I'm hot, Raphaëlle. I'm going to take off a layer if that's alright with you."

"Can I help?"

Four hands pull off her cotton top, revealing shoulders scattered with freckles and a few darker beauty marks. I take off my turtleneck. I could use a shower, my skin bears the scent of crime, my armpits are sour and the hair there has never been so long. But I stop caring when she kisses my neck and collarbones. She leaves my bra on, but caresses me everywhere else with gentle desire. I am like a lake stirred by the wind. Skin to skin, I hold my fox close like a childhood companion from the past. I cling to her and kiss her, there is no holding back, she is my reality now, the only thing keeping me from the void, a matter of life and death.

"The white pine, Raphaëlle. That's it! The first time I saw you, that's what struck me. After you left there was this smell of pine in the cabin."

"I thought I stank like fish!"

Anouk laughs uproariously and puts her tongue in my mouth. I pull away. My head is spinning. It felt so right a moment ago. My head is flooded with images. The smashed door of my trailer, the man who must be bleeding out by now, the search party that will soon be organised, the headless coyotes, the barking dogs of the canine squad, the sea breaking over the jetty that protects the wharf, the scream of chainsaws cutting through the forest, moving ever closer to Tall Pine; Sophie, my ex, yelling at me, furious because I'm packing my things; my parents praying at the table; my brothers and sisters who are strangers to me; my unclean hands.

"Give me a second, Anouk, please."

"I'm sorry, I'm going too fast. You turn me on, it's crazy, I've been dreaming about this for days. And now I'm all over you and not even asking how you feel."

"No, no, it's good. I want it, too, but it's just been so long. I want it, but not now, not here."

My accomplice turns the key and starts the motor. We eat up the kilometres and stick to our plan. I hope everything will go well, and that the hours will bring us closer to the Gaspé, *mon amour*, and a new night. We will discover each other safe from the authorities' prying eyes. In a better position than this one.

"Sleep now, Raphaëlle. You'll drive later on."

"I'll stay awake with you. That's the co-pilot's golden rule."

I pull the amethyst from under my shirt and give it a kiss. Anouk smiles. She knows I need a break from my torment. She tells me the story of the purple stone. It was a gift she gave herself, and now it is mine. In her old life in Montreal, her boss asked if she was ready to apply herself, increase her output and translate a certain number of words per day. Guaranteed, paid work. No more waiting around for contracts like the other freelancers. Before deciding, she went to a bar near the park where all the demonstrations start out from. The idea was to have a couple and think it over. One glass of wine followed the next. The intoxication of financial stability was within reach, but she also understood that as long as she stayed with that boss, she would have her freedom – but economic freedom only. The money she would earn from her language skills would allow her to do what she wanted, but she would have to spend her days in front of a screen. She paid her bill and went into a jeweller's on Saint Denis Street to buy something to celebrate her decision. The clerk had just the thing. She pointed to the amethyst, the symbol of strength and wisdom, a drop of stone on a silver thread, purple like the Northern Lights reflected on the snow. At the corner of Mount Royal and Saint Denis, standing on the crowded sidewalk, Anouk stopped stock-still. She heard Roméo Bouchard's voice, an echo of his book that she was reading, as if his stentorian tone was issuing from the last page she read.

The servitude of consumerism carries with it the servitude of work and that of the mind.[6]

Those wise words put an end to my friend's careerism. She went back to the office, running with sweat. The heat wave, matched by the stress of her resolution, ended this way.

"No, thanks, Boss. I'm changing my life. No more concrete, no more scheduling that ignores my menstrual cycle. I'm heading for the woods. I want the unexpected. I'm in the mood for madness, low points and great joy, the wonderment that flows from the unpredictable – it could even be chaos. I am going to find myself a cabin and write my own words, and embrace silence."

She tells me, laughing, that she had never spoken that much at work. Of course, it had to be her goodbye.

24

The Night Shift

OCTOBER 9

The wind gives me energy. The endless sea breaks on the beach. We could have driven straight to our destination, but this spot is our last chance to contemplate the river before heading inland. Anouk was happy when I suggested we camp facing the waves. The road had worn her out.

I watch her preparing the ground in the shelter of a great rock. She is splendid despite her fatigue. Her red hair falls free onto her shoulders, and her grey wool sweater is loose around her breasts. We are parked in a nameless rest stop. Sitting upright by a tall clump of sea oats, the wind ruffling her fur, Coyote plays supervisor. She leaps up and sprints to the shore, digs up frightened crabs, strong-smelling fish skeletons, orphan sandals and other lost objects.

I have my chores, too. I go through the trunk and take out everything we will need to sleep together warmly, in the horizontal position at last.

We perform each task patiently. We unroll the tent's waterproof fabric, gather driftwood, assemble and level the stones for the firepit where we will place the grill, stretch out the blankets in the tent, including one for the dog in front of the opening, which we will use to wipe our feet before entering. We prepare a teepee of wood, and after gauging the wind, add some bigger rocks on the side the gusts come from. We fill the teapot and kettle, then take out the canned food that we will eat with a spoon.

I watch Anouk's supple hands tying the ropes that keep the tent steady. Her hair falls in her face and that doesn't seem to bother her. Now she is digging a spot for the fire in the sand with her bare hands. All jobs make her happy. The preparations for our camp are like the rhythm of an age-old dance. At times she looks my way and I feel our together-ness. Setting up camp is a pleasure. In no time, we have a roof above our head, millions of stars to keep us company, and a fire to celebrate the well-tempered choreography of two nomad women who can make and break camp without a fuss.

A V-shaped flight of Canada geese salutes us. We sit cross-legged on the beach. The birds are migrating; the ground has started to freeze in the north. Winter is at our door.

"What do you think they are saying?" Anouk wonders aloud.

"Bundle up, it's going to get cold!"

"Ah, your sense of humour is back, Raphaëlle. A good sign."

The flames waver in the wind, and smoke blows in our faces. My eyes sting. I think of the twig doll flaming in the stove, the old shoes melting, the trap, the man whose disappearance might have been reported by now, Lionel pretending to have gone moose-hunting as he does every autumn, but this time with an eye on my predator among the shadows of the Underworld. I wish Lionel his yearly moose. I have seen how he does it, speaking to the animal, finger on the trigger, walking towards it, laying his hand on its still-warm flank. Then, kneeling, thanking the splendid, healthy animal for its sacrifice. Once the carcass has been bled and emptied, the quarters of meat are wrapped in cloth. Later, Lionel will return the bones to the place where the shimmering beast fell and offer them to those that are hungry. An act of gratitude.

*

I refuse to cut it short, even if Anouk is tired of her hair curling up in rat tails on her neck. Gently, I untangle the tangle, and while I am at it I massage her head and neck and shoulders. She sighs and relaxes. I smile inside when I realise that she and I, acolytes of the need for action and accomplished exile, are bound not only by the ideal of a virgin forest, the affection for old-growth trees, and a certain form of misanthropy, but also by a deep desire to eat one another alive. I am so absorbed by the thought of sleeping in a tent with this enchanting woman that I almost forget what put us here.

I loosen her long curls, then braid them delicately, whispering, with each crossed strand, the intentions that come to mind. The braid of three wishes, a game from childhood. You whisper a wish into your girlfriend's ear for every strand you braid until the work is done. Back then my best girlfriend and I built cabins out of kitchen chairs and flowered bedsheets. Clothes pegs were the key to our structure. Once our shelter was just right, we would slip inside and read our favourite stories, draw bracelets of leaves and barbed wire on each other's bodies, and practise opening our mouths and moving our tongues to master the French kiss.

I tie Anouk's braid and kiss her neck. Bite, but just a little. My breath on her shoulders – she shivers. The down on her skin stands straight. I will wait for the darkness of the tent to be naked. I have scars I am not ready to explain.

Anouk opens a bottle of wine. Hands me a glass filled to the brim, the way no-one would pour.

"Thank you. Will you forgive me if I go bottoms up instead of sipping?"

"Be my guest. *Santé*, Raphaëlle."

"To yours!"

Red wine. Flash of a pool of blood in the woods and the trail of broken plants leading to a body. The hallucination of the dirt on my hands. Blood crusted beneath my nails. I shake off the picture.

Anouk comes to me on the sand. She all but sits on me, pushes a strand of my hair behind my ear and arranges my bangs as if I were a doll. Just by touching my body, she knows she can still my anxious nature and cast out the ghosts.

Coyote is lying on the blanket in front of the tent. Anouk has unrolled the reddish fur of the poached animal. My dog has adopted the skin. She presses her nose into it as she watches the heaving ocean, studying the waves of the rising tide. Then she drifts off to sleep, rocked by the sea.

I take another mouthful. Anouk watches me empty my glass in silence. The wine slides down my throat and warms me. I hardly taste it at all; I am that thirsty to be washed from within. Then I go to the sea to forget the distant forest where Marco Grondin might be dying.

I take off my boots and every piece of clothing as Anouk watches hungrily. I throw myself into the water, letting the cold run through me and take me from all sides. When I emerge, I am reborn.

Anouk wraps herself around me and presses her burning skin to my shivering body. Then she closes the tent door behind us. The refuge of her body accepts my tears.

Inside, timid moonlight filters through the screened flap. Starlight is like hope in the dark sky. Our bodies come together, uncertain in the dark, but with no hesitation. I am eager to feel her and throw aside the wounds of time. I will warm my soul in the very best way. Sink my teeth into life, and this body opening before me. Grief and cynicism will turn into daring. I bathe in Anouk's peach-coloured skin, seek out her orange tuft, my mouth full of promises. Our hair mingles on pillows made of our rolled fleece jackets. The moving quest for each other, our impatient desire. In this place, the worst danger is that the tide will claim the clothes we left on the sand.

I hear echoes of the sea, the whipping wind working at the tent's double roof, and the tinkling of Coyote's collar as she dreams. I give in to Anouk's fluid hands. On the beach she undressed me with her eyes. *Show me, I want to see everything*, her hunger said.

She covers me to keep me warm. She wears her goodness like an aura. Nearly invisible, she moves slowly towards me, in me, her tongue and fingers like the waves on the shore, the same rhythm, advancing and pulling back, her hands daring and then daring more, like the tide pulling back, only to rush forward. Her fine agile fingers find my fur. Her palm marries my mound of bone and discovers the warm opening into pleasure. She slips her fingers along my most tender parts, whispering beautiful words in my ear. I lift my body to hers, I open wide as a book and search out her mouth with my tongue. She lets me do everything. The fire is lit; my body stiffens. My lips open and I want to cry out so loud the birds will awaken in the topmost branches and the rorquals will hear my song. I thrust my fingers into her hair, bite her shoulder hard, seek shelter in pleasure. Her finger finds my point of no return. You don't know what's waiting for you, vixen, in our winter quarters. My muffled cry turns into laughter flowing from the heart, vibrating in my throat. I grab your hand that is still at work, I hold it tight with all my might. Stop. You understand and smile, delighted. Your glittering eyes like twin fires. You lick your fingers like the animal you are, and gaze at me.

"Your turn."

In our cocoon of warmth, between your slender legs, one by one, kiss by kiss, I discover the path set down by the treasure map that leads to happiness, a fox's rich cave, a lair where I breathe in your wild scent. Your bush is dense and silky like moss reddened by the autumn where the dew alights, a picture for my contemplation.

I listen to the sea and tie my comings and goings to its waves, and Anouk's hands guide me. Her rhythm is languorous, putting off pleasure, making me wait, but not too long, yes, there, as her fire lifts her hips from the ground.

I feel her heat rising and the tension in her limbs. Right now, so close to savage pleasure, I can forgive my act. I am doing good for the woman who has awakened my taste for life, the irresistible thirst, the same struggle Nature undertakes.

Anouk points her toes and stiffens her legs. I don't know if I should continue or slow down. She scratches at my shoulders, a message I can't mistake. My tongue enters her, my lips wrap around her, I take her into my mouth and my reward is a sigh. She is almost there, a little more and she will lift her body and her limbs will tremble beneath me. She opens her mouth wide, throws her head back, and praises the moon, the ocean, infinity.

Pleeeeeeease!

The call of an animal, the pulse of ecstasy. I come out from under the blankets and kiss my fox. She tastes her musky sap on my tongue. We laugh when Coyote answers her cry. Laugh again, echoing her.

I am happy in the arms of this woman, touched by her sweetness and serenity. I caress her, I curl up against her, I feel her in the darkness. It is a new emotion, as if lightning has ignited the carpet of dry needles inside me and sparked in my heart an affection that can heal everything, but that has the power to destroy.

Anouk, *you*.

My forest fire love.

25

L'Anse Pleureuse

OCTOBER 10

I hear the crow, *caw-craw, caw-craw*. I want to look, but my body will not obey. Like a forest spirit, I am everywhere. I see and perceive every presence. Marie-Ange, guide me down the muddy path to the brambles that tear at the flesh and the footprints of that man.

The great horned owl hoots its ode to darkness. Gophers head for their holes. A raccoon family walks in single file. They have caught the scent of blood. As they pass, their paws melt the fine layer of snow. The bare ground reveals their path. Lifelines that cross, run parallel, then turn away.

I know your fear.

The pack approaches. A first call guides the animals towards this wooded section that smells of cow, putrid slabs of meat, this forest edge that carnivores visit only if they have to. The smell of death attracts them. Beyond the nauseating effluvia of sickened calves abandoned here, their noses sniff out new flesh. It is you, at the end of your rope.

The pheromones of the eviscerated red coyote still cling to your clothes. The mother's smell of milk and blood hangs in the air and the pack howls for death, moves closer in search of the warm belly and wet nipples of its nursing queen. The voices mingle as the howling reaches its final chord. The coyotes sing a happy song. They have come to the right spot.

Hurry up, pack, it's that way. You discovered the trampled grass of the guilty party who stinks of the murdered members of your kind. The killer's body in his cemetery of domestic animals.

They won't be afraid of you any more. They will express their mourning with their fangs, they will devour your clothing soaked with the scent of the female you took from them.

Their shapes will dance in concentric circles, they will leap and cross and form a barrier of dark moving fur. When coyotes keep watch, they do not reveal their intentions. They tighten their ranks and encircle their prey, which will not escape them.

Their laughter is vengeful. They are salivating, there is foam at their mouths from the long run from the horizon to this clearing. The moon is shining too brightly, like a lamp made to dazzle and blind.

With a thought, I cover the sky with grey silk. I call down twig dolls, crows, snakes and eels. We crawl towards you with our venom.

The coyotes have stopped howling. Their warm breath forms hellish scrolls. Their fangs glow in the darkness. There are even more of them now.

Your eyelashes flicker. Your eyes open, but there is a veil between you and the world. Your eyes close. Heavy, terribly heavy. A death rattle. Your life is draining away.

Time to set the table.

Her Majesty has appeared, fresh as a daisy. Well rested, she arrives at the banquet while her cubs sleep safely in their lair. A breach opens up in the circle of coyotes, and the large bear lumbers forward, head high, towards the feast that the night shift has prepared for her. Let the celebrations begin! The devouring will take time. All the guests will be sated. Choice cuts for everyone. Even the vultures have been invited.

*

Startled awake. Just in time to escape the feast scene. I sit up, shake my head, rub my eyes. Anouk is snoring gently by my side. I listen to the murmur of the sea, then pick out the sound of Coyote's collar. She must be playing on the shore. I am not afraid for her any more, and that is a blessing.

I squat down and look for my clothes in the dark, then wrap myself in a sheet. The waters of the gulf are calm. I walk through piles of algae. Fight off the sudden image of a bed of oozing leeches and biting salamanders. The sun rises, heralded by a cloud of crows.

Coyote gallops straight at me. Together, we walk towards the dawn, our feet and paws licked by the waves. I wash my hands and face in seawater. I breathe in deeply, completely, for the first time in a long while. My rib cage fills and empties, and the salty air gives me a foretaste of freedom.

*

"Raphaëlle?"

Anouk sticks her face out of the tent opening. I wrap the sheet tighter and go to lie beside her, ignoring the sand on my skin. Coyote gnaws on a piece of driftwood.

The walls of the tent vibrate in the wind. I like cabins and rooms without curtains, and windows that open onto woods without neighbours.

"Are you ever going to build your bunker? Sorry, your *boon-ker*."

Anouk laughs. A different kind of pillow talk: she describes her father's genius that was so close to folly. Everything that separated and united them, including the German he taught her whenever he could.

Heavy rain begins beating down on our shelter. Thunder rolls. Time to pack up. We stash the camping gear on Anouk's cardboard boxes that contain our preserves for the winter. They are efficiently stacked, with labels that make my mouth water, even if, once again, we will not have time for breakfast, and have to depend on coffee and adrenaline for fuel.

> *Wild strawberry jam with chia and vanilla*
> *Yellow beets with thyme honey*
> *Cinnamon apple sauce*
> *Caramelised onions with maple syrup*
> *Summer squash soup with nutmeg*
> *Cream of potatoes, coconut milk and cumin*
> *Rhubarb and lemon jam*
> *Lacto-fermented carrots*

Pickles, dill and mustard
Daffodil capers
Garlic flower pesto
Spruce honey

"What's this?

I pick up a glass jar with no label.

"Chai spices. Star anise, fennel, cloves, cinnamon, nutmeg and, a special bonus, astragalus flower. They're all plants that warm the body and stimulate circulation. I macerate them in gin and mix them with black tea and maple syrup. It's a winter drink. Usually I leave it over low heat on the woodstove, and every time I throw in a log, I take a sip or two. The stuff saved me from freezing in my cardboard cabin last year."

"You won't be as cold this winter, Anouk. There will be two of us. We'll alternate wood detail during the night. We'll help each other out."

I think back to our first kisses in Tall Pine's shelter. The taste of maple whiskey on her lips as soft as the skin of a plum. Her mouth, a sweet dish. Savour slowly on a bed of pine branches and lynx fur. To be in the same bed with this woman, a caress away, is a state of wonder like the first time a wild animal comes near and lets you touch it. The opening act of trust.

> *For you I am a fox*
> *like a hundred thousand other foxes.*
> *But if you tame me,*

and we come to need each other,
for me you will be unique in this world.
For you I will be unique in this world.[7]

Soon we will be at my place in L'Anse-Pleureuse. On the Robichaud land I inherited because no-one in the younger generation of the family wanted to live so far away. Far from what? Distance is relative to needs. And mine are satisfied in the forest. I find all I need in the Gaspé, the great Mi'kmaq peninsula. *Gespe'gewa'gi*, the last lands. I will listen to their people. I will find my roots in the heart of the Gaspé. *Gespe'gewa'gi*, the cradle of my great-grand-mother. Her line.

*

The view of the bay on the way to my place is inspirational. The forest of pointy spruce, golden birch and blood-red maples. Finally, the sign, the flashing light and the familiar track that leads to the hunting camp on the far side of the lake.

We move down the steep flank of the pine forest where we will spend the winter. My cabin, a palace for mice, appears in a clearing. Water has flowed down the inside of the windows, and puddles have pushed up the linoleum. The smell of creosote hangs in the air. Anouk laughs out loud. She feels at home here. This place is as small and rustic as her cabin by the Amouraska River, with the same smell of humidity. We will burn it off with a few good arm-fuls of firewood.

Coyote finds a new game killing and eating the mice that have taken over. Soon they will be fleeing the sinking ship.

The barn is the high point here. It is filled with an incredible quantity of hand-sawn logs, old tools, antiques that have been half cleaned or dismantled, and construction cast-offs stacked along the walls. Everything for repairs. With nails and with hope. The concrete floor is stable and the frame solid. I intend to live out my old age here. Renovate the barn and add a big loft and keep the ground floor for the cords of wood and a workshop. I lean against a beam and smile.

"You look happy to be home."

"There's nothing left for me in Kamouraska. Except for Lionel and Tall Pine, of course."

"We won't get in each other's way here. There's enough room for separate bedrooms."

Anouk gives me a mischievous look. I will have to make peace with what she said. Did she come to the Gaspé to be with me, or because of her circumstances? Dark ideas quickly take over. If she really believes what she wrote in her journal, she is more than comfortable with solitude. My need to leave came at a convenient time, with her roof damaged by a fallen tree – is that why she's here?

"Raphaëlle, what are you thinking about now? You shut yourself up in silence when you're unhappy about something. There's a black cloud hanging over your head."

I turn my back and walk to the window. Anouk follows, keeping her distance. We stare at the lake, as smooth as a mirror.

269

How does a hermit see living together and being part of a couple? That is a slippery slope. I do not broach the question. The window is fogging over. I close my eyes and feel Anouk's presence close by. Seconds pass, then minutes. I have not answered her. I hear her footsteps, the sound of the barn door and whistling.

I open my eyes and see Coyote running along the edge of the lake to catch up with her. She has her hands in her pockets, and she is walking towards the forest. Then I see the heart drawn on the foggy window, for me.

My confidence returns. I use the time alone to get busy. I air the place, gather up what I need, and push the snow off the cords of wood.

"We're going to have a fine winter," Anouk promises, coming back from her walk with my dog.

She brushes off her shoulders. The snow falls to the floor but doesn't melt. Soon the room will be warm and our things put away. I do not remember where I put the mop, and I lost a mitten along the way. I search everywhere, then forget what I am looking for. I drop into a chair by the door.

"Do you think you'll like it here?"

My throat is tight. I am afraid of her answer, afraid she will leave. Or worse, that she will spend the winter with me, and as soon as the warm weather returns, go back to her land. Fix up her cabin. A thousand projects, all without me.

"What kind of question is that? We have a solid roof and a good woodstove. And plenty of wood to go with it, and my provisions."

Anouk studies my frozen expression, my lack of reaction,

my eyes that will not meet hers. Her answer is not the one I was hoping for.

"Alright. Let's get the stove going and our things inside. Time to prepare for winter. In the Gaspé, when the cold sets in, it doesn't let up. Here, grab this box, we'll move the preserves into the barn."

Every time I move back here, it takes forever to unload the car, every square inch filled with blankets, woollens, snowshoes, and provisions.

"Does the fridge work?"

Anouk points to the refrigerator. It is not plugged in.

"It should."

"I'll wash it before I turn it on."

Water from melted snow is boiling on the stove. Slowly we are burning off the dampness in our house. Our provisions will stay dry. Anouk finds a pot, adds cider vinegar and hot water. I notice her nails, the red cuticles, bitten down.

Bruised. Battered. Broken.

Don't go there again.

Anouk scrubs every inch of the old fridge. She knows how to occupy her mind. I know how to let mine go off track. I had better not get too heavy and exhaust her compassion. I don't want to be a weight, only a source of joy. If that's possible, at least for a while. Nothing really ever lasts.

"All done!"

Anouk performs a short victory dance, rag in hand. I plug in the refrigerator and it begins to hum.

"We could add to our supplies with a trip to the general store."

"Not just yet. Let's wait a few days before showing ourselves in the village."

For our first supper at the camp, we feed each other with tenderness and warmed preserves. The heat from the stove mists over the two windows that look out onto the lake. From time to time, a trout jumps. The circles on the water reach the three ducks meditating on the surface.

Coyote is sitting on the shore, her ears upright. All the patience in the world. She will be happy here. She will gain weight. During the cold season, I will slow down and live. My daily ambition will be a walk in the forest without my watch, in the company of the beautiful Anouk Baumstark and my dog, her injuries behind her. We will fill our pockets with medicinal plants to make tea, and mushrooms to identify. The passing crows will caw, and we will answer. Then return to our warm place to read *The Witches' Anthology*. Sip Anouk's spicy potion. Be in love.

26

The Canine Squad

OCTOBER 10

There are vultures circling in the sky. These flying shadows are a common sight above back country animal pens. Nothing surprising about the black-headed birds patiently gliding above the farms and along the roads during hunting season. The moose that have bled to death in the forests, the heavy sacks of organs left in ditches, the heads of young males with insufficient antlers, and the bony paws left on the ground are banquets for these clouds of scavengers.

On the poaching line, dead calves are a common sight. They attract hungry fur-bearing animals, and the scavengers arrive after them. Nothing will be lost. Everyone will get a good feed, and they will scrap over the remains. The clean-up crew will erase all traces of the butchery. Only the bones will remain, and they will return to the earth and disappear beneath the seasons of fallen pine needles, maple keys and wet leaves.

In the woods, with the falling snow and the passing years, the bodies are swallowed and digested.

*

There is a farm vehicle missing. It belongs to the youngest son who has not been seen for three days. The Grondin family had a bad feeling, and this morning they went to the provincial police to report the disappearance of one of their clan. At first they thought he might have fallen asleep in the attic of the barn with a lady friend, or left to check his traplines the day before. But there was no sign of him in the garage, despite his captures that were hanging, ready to be cut up, waiting for him in a buzzing of flies and the stare of empty eye sockets. The last time they saw him? "I figured he was going to his woodlot, up by Saint-Bruno."

The canine squad is deployed near the Scout camp, where Marco's truck is discovered, parked by a culvert leading to the new logging road. His footprints on the muddy shoulder have had time to dry, and the leaves torn from the branches over the previous windy nights mask the windshield. The unlocked doors open onto a complete mess. The officers prepare their dogs, letting them sniff Marco Grondin's scarf left on the front seat along with other items that belonged to him. The search is on. Everyone remembers the efforts expended weeks ago to find the lost fishermen.

One officer complains loudly. We put a man on the moon in 1969, but we still don't have a cellphone network here. His colleague examines the boot prints and broken ferns, dismissing the possibility of another accident in the woods, another endless search, another day freezing their balls in the back country.

The object of their search is not far away. But the

scavengers' concentric circles that point to the carnage are invisible behind the dense, straight ranks of spruce.

The dogs are in a frenzy, besides themselves as they rush from one trapping site to the next, unearthing carcasses, guided by the agents armed with objects that belong to the missing man. Less than a kilometre further on, after following Marco Grondin's perfectly visible boot tracks, the dogs insist on turning around. Angling off towards a clearing, they pull and pull on their leashes. They want to dig there, yes, right there, right now, behind that tall dead tree. Not six feet under, but only a few paw-strokes deep, they dig up first one pentagonal white plastic label, then another. Both display the same number.

In low voices, the agents conclude that the object is an I.D. ear tag from Quebec's Agro-Traceability system, and most likely it belonged to a sick calf that was brought here so its owner would not have to declare it. Easy to make it disappear fast in the form of bait for large carnivores – two birds with one stone. The delinquent farmer's negligence will betray him soon enough. It will be child's play to identify the place where the animal began its life.

The dogs go on digging furiously, their faces black with earth. Finally, a rounded form appears. The occiput of a skull. Narrow bones are visible through the fabric of a large canvas bag with handles.

The dogs are called off. The officers move in. One of them takes out tweezers and lifts a length of fabric. It falls apart on contact and reveals the contents. Human remains in the foetal position.

"Arms tied," the investigator whispers to his colleague, then orders his men to seal off the site and call in homicide.

"The I.D. unit is on its way," they inform the sergeant-detective.

The dogs are rewarded with vigorous affection. The sergeant-detective, kneeling by the body, examines the rounded orbital arch, the pointed chin, the occipital crest. Clearly the skull of a woman or a teenager. The hypothesis will be corroborated once the coroner has seen the shape of the pelvis. Judging by the absence of insects and the condition of the bones, the skeleton was buried several years ago. Maybe it is the Corriveau girl.

The empty eyes of the human skull stare at the men. Despite their discovery, they know their day is far from over.

*

"Close your eyes, Anouk."

I am guiding her along the stream that flows into the lake. The rushing water can't wait to reach its goal. I enjoy its power. The noisier the tumbling water, the deeper it cleanses my soul. The stream throws itself against the rocks in its path with no hesitation, nor the slightest regard for who is watching or the damage it may do. It launches itself mindlessly, obeying its own gravity, each drop of water finding the path towards its destiny.

"You can open them now."

"Oh! It's so beautiful!"

"When I was a kid, I would lie down in the stream, fully dressed. I liked to move the rocks around and make little pools and waterfalls for the fairies."

"We should build a dry sauna out of cedar right here. It would be great to get good and hot, then jump into the icy water – and start all over again."

"I'd love that. Come on, then, I'll show you the cedar grove."

In the natural cycle of a wilderness forest, different types of trees compete fiercely for light. Which pine cone or maple key will dig its way into the ground and sprout first? Which saplings will push their way out of the wet pine needles and leaves to emerge from the shade, then spend centuries growing? They will form the first windbreaks, gathering snow in mounds around their feet. That will be where animals naturally seek shelter from the storm and hostile eyes. The escarpment and the barrier it creates have protected this part of the forest from cutting, ever since the beginning. No horse would have been strong enough to pull the logs to the road. No stream was deep enough to float the wood out. Generations of venerable sages have grown here, slow-moving beasts and hermits in the heart of this ancient forest of white pine, cedar, black spruce and a few rare paper birches. Just enough of them so that, on our daily walks, we can gather small rolls of parchment that will turn our timid embers into a roaring fire.

In the rush of water, I hear a high, thin voice that reminds me of a lullaby.

My child is like the water, like the living water. She flows

like a stream, my darling daughter. Run, run, run, you'll
never catch her.

No, you won't catch me.

Here in the heart of the Gaspé, the path to my forest
home unfolds like a fauvist palette. The autumn colours
have fallen at our feet and been covered with a dusting of
white, the assurance that snow will erase our tracks, extin-
guish the fires and freeze the movement of things. Silence
in all directions, the calm feeling of knowing we are very
far from everything. It is dazzling to be anonymous again
and blend into the forest, far from every eye and every law.
I will be the living water no-one can catch.

"We're almost there!"

My yurt, built ten years ago. Its roof is still holding up.

One Christmas, my grandmother gave me a present: a
season ticket to a series of films and lectures at the Spect'Art
in Rimouski. "Les Grands Explorateurs", it was called.
Mongolia on horseback, the endless steppes in all directions, nomads living in brightly coloured yurts, the faces of
children with almond eyes, the wind that never stops blow-
ing. My Grandma saw how enthusiastic I was, and slipped
me a few thousand dollars on the sly so I could build a
yurt here. Easy to heat and portable, the round tent would
have to last until I earned the money to return for good
to the Gaspé. When that happened, I would need a real
house. The last few years, the yurt has been my winter
quarters where I go at the end of my autumn contracts
in the Chapais district. The family camp and the barn are
still my anchor, but when the winter cold settles in, I move

278

to this smaller space, which is easier to heat and less exposed to the winds.

The carpet of snow bears no human trace. No-one has been to the yurt since the first flakes of this early winter, which imposed its will in mid-October. Climate change, or a cyclical drop in temperature? The ground is already freezing and will stay frozen until May. The snow will climb from our ankles to our armpits.

We move past markers hanging from the trees at eye level, strips of fabric that blaze the trail. An alert person can't get lost here. Just follow the trees whose cambium has been gnawed away by the moose that, like me, use this path that was opened a dozen years ago.

Trusting and curious, Anouk lets me guide her along the path, her eyes wide, her senses awakened. She jumps when a partridge takes off, then smiles when we reach the clearing. Rays of sunlight find their way among the trunks as if through the columns of a chapel and cast a glow that inspires meditation. I step up my pace like a child who can't wait to get to her room, her sanctuary. Here, the trees serve as pillars, forming a palisade of wood.

It is not much further, just behind the young spruce whose pointed crowns cut the horizon into saw-toothed shapes. Sharp as arrows. Proud weapons of resistance.

Anouk is speechless. My hideaway would inspire envy in any woman who dreams of peace in the forest and a more perfect harmony with Nature. The shape of the dome follows the form of Mongolian yurts. The wooden door is squared off with an axe and finely sculpted. There are shapes, half-animal, half-human, men who are deer and women who are fish. A portrait of my chosen family that has evolved according to my jackknife and my friends. At the top, in the lintel, a design of foliage and worked lettering darkened by the years.

I step inside and breathe in the familiar smell of my lair. We go into my den as if we were entering the belly of the earth. Light filters in through the skylight. Coyote slips through the open door. She knows this is her place, too. Everything bears my scent.

Anouk runs her finger over the letters carved into the lintel.

Sauvagine

"Is that an old word, '*Sauvagine*'? I've never heard of it."

"It's a hunting term for wild birds that have a musky, fermented taste, or that smell gamey. And it refers to skins used in the fur trade, and the bodies of animals hunted for their fur. In other words, what's left over."

Anouk sighs.

"When I first came across the word in an old guide about how to fight poaching, I wanted to write an article. It was going to be an appeal from a rogue Wildlife Protection Officer in defence of wild animals. Instead, I carved the title of my project into my door so I would never forget that I felt like the *sauvagine* too, sometimes, stripped of my right to live freely. I was raised to be productive and serve the system, a good consumer keeping the capitalist cogs turning. All that time I spent in the field, trying to protect nature, ended when autumn was over. I'd go back to my yurt. I wonder if I'll ever have the time to write my treatise, or manifesto, or damned article, whatever it is, and make my voice heard."

"When you look at your door now, what do you think?"

"I avenged the *sauvagine*. There was danger in delay. Neither art nor justice would have triumphed over you-know-who."

"I was so afraid he would hurt you, Raphaëlle."

All it takes are those words for the flashbacks to return. Fur mingled with blood. I push them away.

"We should be hearing from Lionel pretty soon. Though part of me isn't ready for the news. I'm in no hurry to visit my P.O. box, if you want to know. I'd rather imagine Gargamel on the sidelines, like in a cartoon."

"What can we do not to think about him?"

"Make love. Smoke up. Invent nicknames for the stars."

"Doesn't it nag at you, not knowing whether he put his damned foot in the right spot?"

"Absolutely. All the time. But every time I think about it, I have to reprogramme myself. Redirect my imagination. I picture the animals that are so magnificent. Coyotes, foxes, lynx, bears, beaver, martens, muskrats, mink, ermines, all the species I love to observe. I picture them alive, in their dens with a new litter, playing to their heart's content, running through the back country in total freedom. If my trap sprung, those animals won't be caught this year, and

281

they'll have young. And the young will reproduce, then die a dignified death. Not a sudden death, like victims."

"Let's not talk about it. I'm sorry I brought it up. We have to stop torturing ourselves."

Anouk bites at her thumb, hard enough that it bleeds. Her cuticles are pulled away, her nails are short and broken. I feel bad for her, and guilty. But I won't let us go on hurting because of him.

"You know, Anouk, I didn't do what I did on a lark or an impulse. That man was a public danger. He had to be stopped. We can't be tormented by remorse if we agree that Nature is better off without him, right?"

"Let's not talk about it any more. We'll make a new reality."

"It's a promise, goddess. The subject is closed."

I reach for the lever and open the skylight in the centre of the dome. I want to evacuate the stagnant air before throwing on more wood. The roof's fabric has an opening for the stovepipe. The stove is an old cast-iron, potbelly model that must weigh a ton. I remember how we pulled it here on a sled, a metre at a time, huffing and puffing and sweating. Lionel, always more present than my own father, helped me tug it inside.

The fire has been laid. Coyote stays with us even if, as a rule, she does not tolerate the heat. Before she got caught in the poacher's trap, she was more playful. Now she walks with a heavier tread, as if the trap around her neck, the fear and her convalescence have left her weak and tentative.

"My dog hasn't been the same since the accident."

"I didn't know her before, but she'll adjust. She went through a lot, you know."

"It's as if she grew up too fast."

I lean against the school desk that holds paper for starting a fire, and shake out a little pot on the top. I have done it so often that rolling has become automatic. I lick the glue and roll the joint in expert fashion. Push the hair out of my face. Light the joint. Inhale slowly, savouring it, breathe on the lit end to keep it going, then share my vice with my new flame.

I open the stove door as Anouk lays the red coyote fur on the floor, then pats the spot next to her, an invitation. I blow smoke into the air as if it could make everything weighing on me that much lighter.

On the fur, in our round shelter, we return to the age when the Gaspé welcomed its first inhabitants. It is warm inside now. I pass the joint. She lights it again, eyes on the fire. The flames dance and hypnotise. Mary Jane is making her effect felt. The room is as smoky as a hookah salon.

"It's funny, Anouk, smoking with you reminds me of university. During the breaks, I would slip out of the building and roll a cigarette with Alice. It was the first time I felt attracted to a woman, outside of my best friend Marie in kindergarten. I didn't understand what was happening and how to deal with it. Alice was beautiful. She had style, a Parisian accent studded with Quebec swear words. Refined and vulgar at the same time. I knew she'd be a fireball in court, she'd run over everyone. She and I liked to talk as if we were in the courtroom, with 'highfalutin' language.

You know, 'My dear companion, would you grant me the pleasure of your company? Let us conspire together in the open air with a good spliff.'"

"Was the attraction reciprocal?"

"Maybe, a little. I managed to tell her what I felt just before I dropped out of law school."

"You did? I started in law, too, and gave up after one session! In the middle of pleading a simulated case, I burst into tears – out of pure embarrassment. I turned as red as a lobster. I ended up in legal translation instead. I was better with dictionaries than with sophistry."

"I know how you feel. The road to justice is paved with money – that's what disappointed me. I failed an exam that way. I was supposed to sue the guy with the money, not the guilty party. I didn't understand that. Afterwards, I didn't know what to do next. I had never stepped off the straight and narrow, and never failed at anything. I'd always followed the direction that was laid down in front of me like the arrows on the floor in airports. For a change of scene, I signed up to be a guide for whale-watching cruises in Tadoussac. The job made me sick. I never got my sea legs, and I hated chasing after whales!"

"You never saw Alice again?"

"My last night in town, at the goodbye party in my apartment, she was there. We drank a lot, and the last party-goers were putting on their jackets. We went into my room. I had my father's awesome old sound system, an amp and two speakers in wooden cases. The perfect machine for belching out sound."

"What were you listening to?"

"'Something' by the Beatles."

"Abbey Road."

"My favourite album. 'You're asking me will my love grow. . .'"

"You've got a nice voice. What about Alice? Is she still on your mind?"

"We spent hours, just kissing. I liked that because the pleasure went on for a long time, but I was afraid to go further. Afraid of being awkward. Later I thought that maybe I'd confused friendship and admiration with attraction. My C.D.s are so scratched they're practically unplayable, especially my favourites. They stick and jump and ruin the atmosphere and the rhythm. But not 'Abbey Road'. I kept it for special occasions. For kissing Alice. Or contemplating the horizon from a mountaintop and smoking my magic herb that makes beautiful moments sacred. Or crossing the Rockies by car, when you're on the Trans-Canada and you see that wall of rock coming closer, those stone goddesses forever coiffed with snow. Or finishing off a mushroom trip, lying on my mattress, contemplating the twinkling of the heavens in the ceiling. But most of all, most of all for kissing Alice who let me play with her white blouse. Loosen the straps in the middle. Her neck was covered with goose bumps. She smelled of lavender and cigarettes. That was her – sweet and rough at the same time. I never saw her again, but the smell of lavender, and sometimes tobacco, takes me back, along with that soundtrack. 'Something in the way she moves . . .'"

"You just kissed and nothing else?"

"I didn't feel she wanted it as much as I did. You know what I mean?"

"I do."

"I wanted Alice to hold me tight, I wanted her to make the moves. She let me do what I did and kept her hands to herself. I didn't want to push her. We were drunk, we fell asleep, each of us on the far side of the bed. The next morning, I took the ferry. I lost track of her. Years later I met Sophie. A real jewel, but so insecure and anxious that her jealousy made her impossible. I couldn't breathe with her around. I don't know why I'm telling you this."

"It's good if we can be open books. I'm interested in your past."

"You're the first lover I've ever brought here."

"Lover?"

"I'm not afraid of the word, Anouk. You turn me inside out. You do something to me . . ."

And you're helping me get through this nightmare.

"I was the hermit who couldn't stand people, but since you came to my cabin the first time, all I've wanted to do is hold you and forget everything else. I don't care where we are as long as I can get to know you better."

"That's something!"

"It sure is."

Anouk lifts up her sweater, then pulls her layers of woollens over her head. Then come her gaiters and her pants. Her nipples are altars the colour of summer fruit. The firelight plays over her tanned skin that I know only by taste, in the darkness. I linger at the tattoos that snake across her body and speak of her past. Small black stars at the nape of her neck, the vestiges of her punk teenage years. A pentacle between her breasts, the five-branched star, the symbol of sorcery. Her flame-red hair, the ink on her skin like amulets, her feline eyes – she is larger than life. The enchantment of her nudity and the glow of her beauty – she is as shameless as a cat. Everything about her pulls me in.

She nods in my direction.

My turn to be looked at. I close my eyes and pull off my protection, my carapace, and show her my marks, one by one. I do not have tattoos, but scars by the dozens. Most of them are on my forearms, but some are at the top of my thighs, pink parallel lines, lacerations of a prepubescent broken heart, the kind that hurts the most. The pain you inflict on yourself to make the emptiness inside more visible. The burning maple logs and my sharp sense of shame bring beads of sweat to my skin. I raise my eyes to hers. Truly naked, without weapons, I lie back on the coyote fur by the stove.

Anouk takes me in her arms, frees my braid from its rubber band, then sculpts my hair into a loose chignon. She pulls me closer, to her mouth, then I am beneath her and she is kissing my lips, my chin, my neck, between my breasts, nipping at me. She breathes in the scent of my ribs that lift to meet her. She reads what my pulse is saying, and kisses my navel, then below. Nothing inhibits her. This is truly the first time, this certainty that I can tell her everything, my worries, desires, tenderness, the way I feel vulnerable next to a body I want. She turns over and offers her thigh as a pillow. Her bush is the colour of wheat. Our kisses are greedy, but we are slow and attentive until I roar, and she roars, and our bodies sparkle like rubies. We are released. Anouk makes magic live within me. I want to give her back twice as much, pleasure carries us and we dive into each other, mouths and tongues, talons and beaks. Hold on to me, my sweetness, you are my territory, let me do everything for you, savour the pleasure that lies curled in my fur, a sigh of ecstasy between the petals of your flower, you, the beautiful beast of my most extravagant dreams. To hear you come and feel you quiver against me, then fall back against my body, your war cry, your salty sweat, your wild mass of hair, sources of joy. I touch you. Happiness is palpable.

In my ear, you say your first *I love you*.

27

My Pretty Girls

OCTOBER 17

Our bodies in repose in the timid morning light. After our
first embrace on the coyote fur, we pursued pleasure, licked
and rocked each other, then slept like babies. Days and
nights followed, and then came the morning of my deadline,
when I had to face reality. There would be no turning back.

Coyote is still sleeping by the door. She opens one eye at
the soft rustling of the sheets. I don't much feel like getting
up, but the choice is not mine.

Anouk gets out of bed first, pulls on her wool socks
and rain boots, then goes outside, well shod but quite naked.
She is off to gather twigs to rekindle the fire. I watch her
move, solid on her two feet, her limbs tense with the cold
and the effort.

We have all we need to survive here, and for a good
time to come. We could stay in this cabin for however long
it takes. All winter, until our provisions run out and the
torment outside ceases. That is, if Lionel has good news.

I say a silent prayer.

Her arms full of birch bark, beard moss and hirsute
spruce branches, Anouk squats down on her heels. Her rear
end forms a heart shape I cannot help but admire. I put on

her clothes and she puts on mine. A role play, an exchange of skin and scent. We share everything.

The fire crackles. My fox leads me outside by the paw, a jackknife in her hand. I am afraid she will slash her palm and ask me to seal our pact that way, the marriage of blood sisters and witches as in the movies.

With the door to the yurt closed, I contemplate the details of the sculpted wood lintel. The title of the article I will probably never write. The title from the heart that became a chapter of my shared life. Anouk drives the blade into the lintel. At the end of the inscription, she patiently carves an "s". The plural that speaks of our love affair in the woods.

Sauvagines

I kiss her, then start off on foot, heading for the end of the road where the postboxes stand. I must go by myself, the way I did when I set the mantrap. The possibilities buzz in my head. He died, he did not die, he is injured, Lionel is in deep shit, he did not recover the trap, my departure attracted suspicion considering the circumstances. Around and around in my mind until I pull the keyring from my pocket.

Every time I put my key into this damned postbox, it goes in backwards. I take it out, turn it around, try the lock again. I can never get it right. The lock is cursed. This time, the key goes straight in the first time. The little door opens onto a reason to rejoice. A letter is waiting for me.

Great Goddess above.

The envelope, heavy with humidity, has no return address. The cramped handwriting of my sea wolf. I tear it open. Shake out the lined paper folded in three. Hold my breath.

My pretty girls,

All is well. The hunt was successful. The big buck gave up the ghost. I can go back with an easy mind. I have done my duty. We have our moose.

The cabin is free and unlocked as usual, make yourselves at home if you want to come and spend some time here. But I suspect you are very comfortable where you are. Send word from time to time so I won't worry.

I have news from the back country. The body of Liliane Corriveau was found. I heard through the grapevine that it was a complicated business. The Canine Squad dug her up near some animal carcasses. The investigation will take some time. They found a lot of poaching sites. Then, a second body. This one belonged to a poacher, as it turned out. A guy named Marco Grondin who had an unfortunate accident or an unpleasant encounter with a bear. Hard to tell. But apparently there is a link between the two bodies. The girl had the same fatal injury to her head as the dozens of calves that were used as bait. The Grondin & Brothers farm must have tried to dispose of their sick calves by leaving them in the woods. Maybe the girl met the same fate. The principal suspect is in no shape to defend himself.

They talk about nothing else on the radio. The three men who disappeared, and now the girl's murder and the poaching that goes on in the sector. At least, thanks to the search, people have started picking up the equipment that has been lying around for years. But one thing pisses me off, and that's how the news was presented. The police talk about wild animals and the dangerous things that can happen to people in the woods. What they should do if they encounter a bear, for instance. I'm afraid the public will decide that animals are the real danger, they're the guilty parties, and not someone else.

In any case, enjoy the winter, my doves, my girls, and don't hesitate if you need anything.

Lionel

The Code of Wise Hunters

The blanket of snow has grown thick. Two months have passed. The yurt is the perfect place to give birth. Coyote brought a litter of seven puppies into the world. Two were stillborn and five survived. A dog's life! We gave them names inspired by the Big and Little Dipper. Since the beginning of time, star-gazers have made up hunting stories about what they see. A deer, pursued, running up into the sky. A trio of gazelles that turned themselves into a constellation to avoid being brought down.

"Did you know, my fox, that Zeus transformed his lover Callisto and her child Arcas into the constellation of the Great Bear to protect them against Hera's jealousy? Though, of course, not everyone agrees about what really happened."

"What's all this talk of jealousy? We're in the middle of the woods!"

"And besides, we got past that a long time ago. Remember, open books?"

Our puppies bear the names of stars. In a way, this litter has become, like the stars, a way of guiding our lives. Polaris, the whitest of the group. Alcor, the alpha male that must be tamed. Mizar, who intends on outshining Alcor. Delta, for her dark triangular patch of fur. And Muin, the Mi'kmaq name for the Big Dipper, the last and sturdiest of the group. The pack has forced us to go out hunting for meat. The puppies wolfed down the rabbits we caught in one sitting.

A thought for Lionel. We owe him our freedom. A thought for Tall Pine, the last back country survivor of his kind. A thought for the red coyotes we avenged. Even without their mother, they will recover. A thought for Liliane Corriveau's family, who can finally give her a proper burial and begin the long work of mourning.

A part of me is always returning to Kamouraska. We aspire to the wisdom of the First Nations, who teach that the Earth does not belong to us. But we can still turn to the great expanses of the forest, knowing there is refuge in my yurt in the Gaspé winter with Anouk. And we can camp on her land in the summer, along the Amouraska River, among the white spruce that goes on forever. We are more secure than if we had money in the bank. Poor, but rich. The forest is generous, and always new, offering us its fruits. Magical places, shared places, shelters for love and wildness.

In the past, I felt alone in the crowd, crowded into the city, my back against the wall. The chaos inside me was a big bang, a shock to my universe that pushed me away from other people. Now I understand why. I was not made for solitude, and neither was my lover. We were made to tend each other's fires, keeping an eye on the peaceful forest, in concert with the pack singing to the stars. Protecting the deer and the white cedar, taking litters of coyotes and their descendants under our wing.

To do this, we need, and will need, many, many allies.

Notes

1   Association des agents de protection de la faune du Québec (https://www.aapfq.com/memorial/).
2   Government of Canada search engine, Bryophytes.
3   Antoine Laurent de Lavoisier.
4   Sonny Bono, *Bang Bang (My Baby Shot Me Down)*, 1966.
5   Hay Babies, *La Bear Song*, Folio EP, 2012.
6   Roméo Bouchard, *Survivre à l'offensive des riches*, Montréal, Les Éditions Écosociété, 2016, p. 15.
7   Antoine de Saint-Exupéry, *The Little Prince*.

Acknowledgements

A thank-you to the real poacher who inspired this literary vendetta, a way of expressing the frustration of a woman who was powerless against your violence in our fragile forests.

Thank you, Myriam Caron Belzile, my cunning editor, who, with her usual energy, helped me veer off my beaten track. Thanks for standing by me during this novel. Thank you, David Homel, for your beautiful translation, and thank you Mountain Leopard Press for your trust and fierce enthusiasm for my work.

Thank you to all the wise hunters and trappers who keep their art alive, preserving the balance of Life in our north woods. You deserve our appreciation.

Thank you to my lucky star for having spared Sequoia, prisoner of three snares.